Books by Ann McMan

The Jericho Series
Jericho
Aftermath
Goldenrod
Covenant

The Evan Reed Series
Dust
Galileo

Hoosier Daddy
Backcast
Festival Nurse
Beowulf for Cretins
The Big Tow
Dead Letters from Paradise
The Black Bird of Chernobyl

Short Story Collections
Sidecar
Three Plus One

Anthologies
Soul Food

THE BLACK BIRD OF CHERNOBYL

ANN McMAN

Bywater
BOOKS

2024

Bywater Books

Print ISBN: 978-1-61294-287-2

Bywater Books First Edition: July 2024

Printed in the United States of America on acid-free paper.

Cover design: TreeHouse Studio

Bywater Books
PO Box 3671
Ann Arbor MI 48106-3671

www.bywaterbooks.com

This is a work of fiction. Except where indicated, names,
characters, places, and incidents are the product
of the author's imagination, or, in the case
of historical persons, are used fictitiously.

The lines from poems quoted in this novel
are in the public domain.
Auden, W.H., "Funeral Blues," 1936.
Dickinson, Emily, "#76," c. 1859.

*For Hambone, my furtive, constant companion
during a cold October in Vermont.*

"I'd rather be dead than sing 'Satisfaction' when I'm forty-five."

–Mick Jagger

Part I
Ghosts of the Present

Christmas Eve, just before midnight

No Rest for the Weary

Look around.

It doesn't take a rocket scientist to see that today's world is a simmering hellscape of equal parts disappointment, rage, and grievance—or what the locals, with practiced economy, would call a big ol' hot mess. Lilah'd never had a problem with this perspective. The macabre geography she inhabited was one she'd always been temperamentally suited to. It *worked* for her—and not just because she had all the outfits . . .

She'd never questioned her life or any of her choices because she'd never had reason to.

But she'd become aware that everything about the temple of her familiar had changed the night Dash dropped off a yellow blanket he'd just retrieved from the county morgue. It was an hour before midnight on Christmas Eve, and she'd drawn the short straw because their mortuary was the only one still open—as usual—and she'd made the colossal blunder of answering the phone. It was one of those rare Christmases when it snowed—the first time in more than a decade. Of course, that threw everything in Winston-Salem into panic mode. The entire city had been on lockdown since midday. Everything had ground to a halt. Public transportation, frenetic last-minute shopping trips, holiday parties—all shut down.

Well, every kind of activity but *this* one.

Death tended not to be bothered much by the weather.

Fifteen minutes later, she stood just inside the big bay doors at the back of the building, trying to dodge the swirling snow while Dash backed the county's nondescript black van into their receiving area. She thought about Dash as she waited for him to get out of the van. He was a wiry little guy of uncertain age who'd been ferrying bodies around for the county since the Dead Sea was just . . . sick. Standing there in the cold, Lilah thought back over how strange it was that in all the years she'd known him, they'd rarely had conversations in the daylight. That was largely because Dash delivered his dark passengers during the night shift.

Lilah's father always called him *DoorDash*—death's delivery man.

That was about right. But this modern-day Charon piloted a beat-to-shit Ford Transit Van that burned oil and belched black smoke like a steam shovel.

"What's the story with this one?" Lilah asked, idly—more to kill time than anything else while Dash transferred the body bag to one of their gurneys.

"Beats the hell outta me. Some urban camper who froze to death under the Miller Street overpass—poor bastard arrived dead, and stayed that way. No ID. Merry fucking Christmas." Dash handed her a clipboard. A chewed-up ballpoint pen attached by a frayed string swung crazily in the cold wind. "Gimme your Santa Hancock on this so I can get the hell outta here. This is my last drop-off."

Lilah signed the chain of custody ticket and handed the

clipboard back to him.

"Kind of sad."

Dash looked at her with his colorless eyes. "Holiday spirit gettin' to you, Stohler?"

"Of course not." Dash's suggestion irked her. "But even you have to admit there's an epic sadness attached to dying alone in the cold at Christmas."

"Yeah. Just like a goddamn Tolstoy novel." He tore off a copy of the receipt and handed it to her with a shrug. "Seems to me like we die alone no matter what damn day of the year it is." He shrugged. "Oh, well. Whoever the hell he *was*—now he *ain't*. That's it."

"That's it," she agreed.

Dash continued to stare at her with narrowed eyes. The snow had gained in intensity while they'd been standing there. The baggy cardigan she'd pulled on wasn't doing much to keep the wind out.

"You okay, Stohler?" He asked.

"Oh, yeah." Lilah nodded and waved him off. She wanted to get back inside. And she figured their latest John Doe had already spent enough time outside in the elements, too. "You get on out of here. You've got places to be."

"What about you?"

"What do you mean, what about me?"

"Don't you have someplace to be?" Dash asked. "I mean besides this damn cold-cut pantry?"

"I didn't," Lilah laid a hand on the black bag atop the gurney, "but it seems I just acquired a date for the evening."

Dash laughed. "You're a freak, Stohler. Anybody ever tell you that?"

"All. The. Time."

He gave her a little salute and climbed into the van. She stepped back to avoid the explosion of black smoke she knew was coming. She watched his taillights recede until they disappeared behind the snowy curtain of night.

Lilah punched the button to close the bay doors and stood there a moment, shivering and alone with her new companion.

Mom always said I went for the silent type . . .

"Come on, Mr. Doe." She kicked off the foot brake and pushed the gurney toward the freight entrance. "Let's get this party started."

Part II
Ghosts of the Past

Three Months Earlier

Let's Make a Deal

When Lilah's father told her he'd hired a community outreach liaison to "liven up the place," she didn't mince words. She told him he was nuts.

Okay. She might *actually* have said he was fucking crazy, but it was the same idea.

"Why the hell do we need to 'liaise' with anyone?" She demanded. "We've already got more work than we can handle. We're one of the busiest mortuaries in town. Our coolers could go condo."

"It's not *about* increasing business—and please remember that we're now calling ourselves a *funeral home*. It's more comprehensive and less off-putting to families." Abel Stohler's voice had that patronizing tone it sometimes got whenever he felt Lilah wasn't expressing proper reverence for the profession—which was always. "It's about improving our brand and becoming more responsive to the needs of the community."

There was no way Lilah was going to get into the whole "brand" conversation with him. *Again.* She opted for the safest route.

"In what ways are we *not* responsive?" She asked.

"Lilah?" Abel made an oblique gesture toward her framed Claude Clay, Undertaker, print from the comic strip, *Tumbleweeds*—the only thing that could loosely be described as artwork on display in her small office. "'You plug 'em, I plant 'em'" is hardly a welcoming sentiment to greet grieving families."

"I don't *greet* families in here." She warmed to the topic. "I do not greet them here *or* there. I do not greet them anywhere."

"Which is precisely why we need Sparkle."

Sparkle?

"What the hell is 'sparkle'? Some new kind of rose-scented disinfectant?"

"*No.* Sparkle is Sparkle Lee Sink. Our new liaison. She starts on Monday."

Lilah wasn't sure which part of his explanation she found more abhorrent: that he'd actually hired a *community outreach liaison*—whatever the hell that was—or that there actually *was* some unfortunate human being named "Sparkle."

"You cannot be serious."

"Do I not sound serious?" he asked in his most serious voice.

"You're right." Lilah demurred. "If what you're saying is true, you *don't* sound serious—you sound deranged."

"Lilah . . ."

"Dad . . ."

He leaned forward on the only other chair in her office. It was a cast-off, slat-backed Shaker model that groaned and complained more than their cranky business ops manager, Kay Stover, did on the last billing day of the month—which was saying a lot. The solitary chair served as an additional testament to the fact that Lilah never welcomed customers into the small space—or anywhere else in her life, for that matter.

"Look." Her father's tone had taken on that timbre it

10

only acceded to whenever he was finished with a debate and was wholly dug-in on whatever he'd already decided to do. "Christmas is only twelve weeks away. After that, I have exactly one more week before I formally retire and hand the reins of this business over to you. I want to do everything I can to ensure that it continues to run smoothly—and that you are spared from being bogged down in the aspects of daily operations that you've always found to be onerous."

"Onerous?" Lilah was impressed by his word choice. "Mom still forcing you into doing those Wordles every day to improve your vocabulary?"

"No. And Wordles are only *five* letters."

"Noted."

"Why are you being so prickly about this? You'll have next to no involvement with Sparkle. She'll interact primarily with Kay Stover, the service managers, and the guys."

The "guys" were the Freeman brothers—men who had come to work for the mortuary back during the days Lilah was busy spending her time devising new and creative ways to set off fire alarms at the reformatory—or, as her parents preferred to call it, Forsyth Country Day School. The brothers' given names were Geronimo and Hamlet—but everybody just called them Gee String and Hambone.

She had never asked why.

Here at Stohler's, Gee String and Hambone took care of . . . just about anything that needed doing. Lilah liked to think of them as specialized, in-house Swiss Army knives—Grim Reaper's Edition.

But liaising with people who still had a pulse?

To her, that functionality was plainly missing from their combined arsenal of tools.

"I'm sorry." She queried her father for clarification. "Did

you say this Sparkle person would be working with the Freeman brothers?"

Abel nodded. "Unless you're ready to set aside your long-standing disdain for other human life forms and begin participating in public relations activities."

"I'd sooner lace my cold brew with strychnine."

"I thought as much."

Lilah wasn't going to win this argument and she knew it. So, the better part of valor was to capitulate, and tell her father she wouldn't get in the way of his new outreach liaison. As long as this Sparkle person stayed above stairs, she'd continue to run underground operations just like she'd always done. And since her father was determined to stay involved as director emeritus for the next year, *he* could be the one to integrate his plucky little ambassador into their quirky Body Shop of Negative Outcomes.

"Okay," she said, with a smirk. "It's *your* funeral."

Opal Mae Denise Gilley Shoaf
March 29, 1927–October 22, 2023

Opal Shoaf, 96, died Sunday after the good
Lord had finished the last puzzle piece
of a life well lived. Opal was born to the
late Maxine Gilley and Therren Gilley. She
graduated from Mt. Tabor High School and
had a distinguished career as a stay-at-home
mom. She married her sweetheart, St. John
Shoaf, who said he was going to marry her
the first time he laid eyes on her while she was
waitressing at the Woolworth's in downtown
Winston-Salem. They stayed married for
almost 67 years.

Opal loved cooking for her family, friends,
and entire congregation. She was known for
creating too many special recipes to list, but
barbecue slaw, rivels, cherry yum yum, apple
cake, and banana pudding are just a sampling
of things people would line up for. But best
loved were her snickerdoodle cookies—
Opal would always bake those for church

fundraisers and other special occasions. In addition, she loved knitting for her family, collecting frog figurines, doing puzzles, creating masterpieces with colored pencils, telling stories, acting silly, and cross stitching and crocheting with the best of them. In retirement, she loved taking trips with Nancy and Udean's Christian Tours. She was sharp as a tack until she succumbed at the end.

Visitation will be on Wednesday, October 25th at 12 noon at Stohler's Funeral Home in Winston-Salem.

Posted by Stohler's Funeral Home, Winston-Salem, NC

Half Baked

"Well, if that don't beat all."

Lilah looked up from the coffeemaker to see Rita Kitty standing in the doorway of their tiny kitchen. The flamboyant hairdresser didn't wait to be asked to elaborate.

"I'm talkin' about that stick figure platinum blonde I have to do hair and makeup on." Rita Kitty opened the fridge and took out a Diet Dr. Pepper.

"I'm afraid I'll need a bit more to go on," Lilah prompted.

"You *know* who I mean. That Brittany what's-her-name. The big-boobed dental hygienist who run off with that married periodontist last year. The one who up and died after some damn-fool carrot cleanse."

"Oh." Recognition dawned. "Mrs. Dankwith. Yeah. She came in yesterday. As I recall, her family wanted her regular beautician to do her hair, but apparently, that salon doesn't coif corpses."

"That don't make no kind a sense." Rita Kitty shook her flame-red head with disgust. "Hell, most of them women are

15

already more dead than alive with all that Botox mess they're shot up with."

"Is that what you came in here all het up about?"

"No. It's just that this Brittany person is the third body this month I got who's just had one of them salt-peels. It's like some damn epidemic."

"You mean microdermabrasion? They say it's very popular these days."

"Yeah? Well, they look like they been left too long on the hot dog roller at Sheetz—all red and bubbly. Don't these women have something better to do with their damn money? How the hell am I supposed to cover that mess up?"

Lilah topped off her coffee and headed for the door. She was up to her eyeballs in paperwork. It had been a busy week—busier than usual for the period leading up to the holidays. Besides, she didn't want to tarry in the breakroom any longer than necessary.

She didn't want to risk running into Sparkle.

It was obvious their *liaison* had already been in there: the air was full of the cloying scent of cinnamon and whatever-in-the-hell else she'd whipped up and now had baking in the small oven. Probably more cookies. The whole place smelled like a freaking patisserie. Thank god the fumes from Sparkle's ubiquitous Eau de Martha Stewart confections didn't permeate the embalming suite downstairs.

The scent of fresh-baked snickerdoodles didn't tend to mesh well with formaldehyde.

"I don't know, Rita Kitty. All I can say is thank god you always figure something out."

"Well," Rita Kitty tsked, "it's gonna take the patience of Job and a butt-ton of Pure Canvas Primer. At this rate, I'll have to start buying that stuff in *bulk*. You'll have to clear it with Kay

Stover. I don't want her chewing my butt out for the extra cost."

"I'll take care of it."

Rita Kitty exited the kitchen, clutching her Diet Dr. Pepper. "See you downstairs."

"Is that Lilah I hear?" The soprano voice rang out from the corridor just beyond the breakroom.

Lilah closed her eyes and cursed her luck. *Sparkle.* Of course. Why the hell did she have to tarry, talking with Rita Kitty about damn salt peels?

"There you are." Sparkle entered the small kitchen with her trademark enthusiasm. "I've been looking all over for you."

"Why?" Lilah feigned interest. "You run out of rainbow sprinkles again?"

"Of course not," she quipped. "I buy those in bulk. I wanted to go over arrangements for the Crotty funeral. The family has asked for some special considerations."

Lilah was immediately suspicious. "What *kind* of special arrangements? And why would they have discussed those with you instead of Kay Stover or one of the funeral directors?"

Sparkle's model-perfect face took on the *here-we-go-again* countenance it tended to adopt whenever she knew she was gearing up for a fractious conversation with Lilah—which was nearly every time they talked.

"Honey—everyone in this county knows someone in the Crotty family. Half the schoolchildren in Winston-Salem sold candy bars to raise money to help little Maribelle, who was born with Rett Syndrome."

"What-*ever*. That's no reason for you to be discussing service arrangements." Lilah took in Sparkle's ensemble—which today was comprised of a form-fitting floral frock that, in her mind, resembled a 1960s church fellowship hall tablecloth. "And what the hell is up with this outfit? We've discussed your need to adopt more somber attire."

"*Somber?*" Sparkle held up a manicured finger. "This place is already one step away from becoming the next Wuthering Heights. It could stand to be a tad less funereal."

"You *are* aware of what we do here, right?"

"Contrary to the prevailing wisdom in this industry, a modest infusion of color lends warmth and conveys an open and welcoming environment."

"We can buy some throw pillows for the lobby."

"Your father engaged me precisely to add these attributes to the business."

"Don't remind me."

Sparkle tsked. "Why are you always so prickly?"

"Why are *you* always so plucky?

A timer dinged. Sparkle rushed over to the stove to don a pair of fat oven mitts and remove two trays of *some* kind of cookies.

"That's another thing we need to discuss." Lilah fanned the air in a lame attempt to diffuse the heady aroma of spices. "Could you please stop baking during business hours. It's intrusive."

"How in the world can a platter of hot cookies be intrusive?" Sparkle plucked one off the baking sheet with a napkin and held it out to Lilah. "Come on. Try it. You know you're dying to."

"Apropos of dying, I'd rather try *that* than one of these infernal confections."

"I don't believe you mean that." Sparkle waved the hot morsel back and forth beneath Lilah's nose. "Come on, grumpy. It's Opal Shoaf's recipe."

Lilah resisted the temptation to take the cookie and grind it into the photo of Jesus at Gethsemane someone had posted on the bulletin board beneath the "All employees must wash their hands before returning to work" placard her father had placed there about a decade ago.

"If memory serves, Mrs. Shoaf died of peritonitis. Correct?"

"Yes. But how is that relevant?"

"I suspect she ate too many of these. They reek of *noblesse oblige* and too much nutmeg. A fatal combination, in my view."

Sparkle finally took the hint and lowered the cookie. "Does everything with you have to be a contest of wills?"

"Let me think . . . Yes."

Sparkle sighed and returned the cookie to the baking pan. "At least the Shoafs will appreciate these."

"The Shoafs? You mean you're *serving* these?"

Sparkle nodded.

"Today?"

Another nod.

"At a service?"

"Of course. They requested them."

"Cookies? *At a viewing?* Since when do we serve confections during a visitation?"

"Since Kay Stover approved it."

"Kay . . ." Lilah couldn't finish her sentence. She held up a hand. "I need a moment."

Sparkle transferred all the hot cookies to a serving tray and covered them with a festive hand towel.

"You take all the time you need. I've got to hustle. The doors open in fifteen minutes. And I must say, Rita Kitty did an exceptional job on Mrs. Shoaf. She looks just like her photo in the church directory. I thought backcombing was a lost art. That woman is an artist." She picked up the tray. "Now if you'll excuse me, I've got to go make sure Hambone didn't 'fix' the punch

19

again. Last time, he spiked it with a pint of Old Grand-Dad—which, if you ask me, doesn't mix well at all with Crystal Light."

Lilah suddenly felt like she'd folded space and ended up in the middle of a Smurfs remake of *Little Shop of Horrors*.

"Ms. Sink?" Lilah waited until Sparkle turned around to face her. "We'll talk about all of *this* later. But if you *ever* call me 'honey' again, I'll rip out your intestines with an unsterilized trocar wand. Understood?"

Sparkle stared back at her with an unreadable expression, before quietly retreating from the kitchen.

Hambone sat rigidly on a straight-backed chair, fussing at a shiny spot on his scalp, searching for a nonexistent wisp of ginger-colored hair—one that had gone missing years ago. Lilah was used to this reflexive response whenever he got nervous, which wasn't all that often. But when she'd found him outside washing mud off one of the hearses and asked him to meet her in her office when he'd finished up, she noted how quickly his hand took up its fruitless quest.

"What I want to know is why in the living hell you've been helping Sink stage these damn covered dish events that are flimsily passing as funerals?"

"Well. Now that ain't nothin' to get all riled up about, Miss Lilah."

"Riled? I'm not riled."

"All due respect, Miss Lilah. You sure do look riled to me. And I've known you since you were just a little thing, followin' your daddy around and polishing the hubcaps on the hearses to earn your allowance."

Lilah forced herself to count to ten. Twice.

"Hambone? This is a mortuary—not the Betty Crocker test kitchens. We don't *serve* casseroles, congealed salads, cocktail weenies, or whatever-in-the-hell-else strikes the fancy of that Sparkle enigma. And we sure as hell don't spike the freaking punch with dime-store hooch. Understood?"

"Yes, ma'am. But that there punch thing—that wasn't me. I wanted to use some of the good stuff that Kay Stover keeps hidden in the bottom drawer of that old filing cabinet in the storage closet beneath the stairs. But Gee String? He allowed as how Kay got real mad at him the last time he borrowed some of her liquor to calm Wardell down after he cut himself with that Stryker saw. You remember that?" Hambone shook his head. "Poor fella like to never stop bleedin'."

"Hambone . . ."

"Don't know what we'd a done to keep him settled down until the EMTs got here. He was lucky Gee String found that finger and tossed it into the Big Gulp Wardell'd been drinkin'. Law, the saw flung that thing all the way across the room. We like to never found it. Ain't it amazin' how they can put them things right back on good as new? I swanny. It's just like them Snap-On Tools."

"Hambone . . ."

"So, I had to use some liquor out of one of them bottles Miss Rita Kitty uses to clean out her makeup brushes. She says that 80 proof kind works the best, so I borrowed some of that. Truth be told, I didn't think it tasted all that bad. But then, I never did much care for that Crystal Light iced tea."

"Hambone, please." Lilah held up a hand. "I sincerely don't care what kind of hooch you used to spike the tea. The point I'm trying to make here is that we're not in business to become

21

the next K&W Cafeteria. The only hot hors d'oeuvres I want to hear about you mingling with are the ones you rake out of the Franklin stove." She jerked her thumb toward the crematory building behind the funeral home. "Do we understand each other?"

"Yes, ma'am." Hambone quit searching for his phantom lock of red hair and dropped his hand to his lap. "Sure is a pity, though. That Miss Sparkle? She makes them grieving families feel real special. I heard as how people all over town are sayin' Stohler's is the best place in three counties to get a proper sendoff. She just makes everyone feel welcome." He shook his head. "Pretty little thing, too, with them green eyes. Looks just like her daddy."

"You let me worry about . . . *Sparkle*. You just stay out of the kitchen. Okay?"

Hambone got to his feet. "Yes, ma'am. Is that all you be needin' with me?"

"Why? You got a hot date or something?"

"Well. No, ma'am. But I did just hear the van pull in from that pickup out at Laurel Fork." He tsked. "A two-fer. Husband and wife. Married sixty-seven years. Went to bed last night and woke up together in Glory Land. If that don't beat all."

"It happens that way sometimes."

"Yes, ma'am. If you're lucky."

"Let's just hope they didn't share a lifelong passion for Calabash shrimp."

Hambone chuckled. "Now that *would* be a first, wouldn't it?"

"Let's just file it away as a bad idea, okay?"

Hambone nodded and left her office to go help unload the happy couple. As she watched him make his way down the narrow hallway that led to the back door, she marveled at how Sparkle had managed to charm him, and his dour brother, in such a short space of time. The Freeman brothers weren't easily duped or taken in, either. They were old school. Between the two of them, they'd forgotten more about this business than she'd learned in the past thirty years following her father around. They were an institution at Stohler's. And neither of them suffered fools.

She thought about Hambone's assessment of Sparkle's effect on their reputation.

It was a ridiculous supposition. No thinking person would choose a mortuary based on the quality of its . . . *comestibles.* And no matter how much credit Hambone wanted to give her, Sparkle Lee Sink wasn't some miraculous linchpin that would catapult Stohler's into the limelight as one of the area's premier mortuaries. Business was too competitive these days. Methods and techniques changed as rapidly as consumer expectations. Even death was a market-driven economy now, and nobody wanted to cleave to old world ideas and tired traditions. Folksy mores and outmoded methods were going right down the storm drains together—just like that old couple from Laurel Fork. Old things were passing away, and all things were becoming new. And no cutesy innovation from some enterprising sororitette with a cookie press could ever change that calculus.

No matter how green her damn eyes were—or how well that flowered dress clung to her curves.

"You got a second?"

Kay Stover lurched back from her computer screen and glared over at the dark figure leaning against her doorjamb.

"How many times do I have to tell you not to sneak up on

me like that?"

Kay was a small woman with untamed hair and shocking blue eyes. She'd been the business manager at Stohler's ever since Lilah's father had lured her away from the local Cadillac dealer where he'd bought his first fleet of hearses, way back in the early nineties. She was an institution at Stohler's. Hell. The woman would've been an institution wherever she chose to hang her green accounting visor.

"Like what?" Lilah dropped her voice to its lowest register and tried not to smile. The truth was, she delighted in scaring the bejesus out of Kay—which wasn't hard. The woman had always been wise to her—ever since the time she'd found twelve-year-old Lilah, stretched out inside one of their best solid mahogany caskets, reading a dogeared copy of *Rubyfruit Jungle.*

"Like the goddamn ghost of Lorraine Bracco." Kay pushed her black-rimmed bifocals further up her nose.

"Lorraine Bracco isn't dead, Kay."

Kay snatched up an ancient, self-inking PAID stamp and slammed it down on an invoice.

"Tell me something I *don't* know. Like why you think it's necessary to lurk around inside this damn crypt dressed like one of the four horsemen of the apocalypse."

Lilah entered Kay's office without being invited and dropped into a battered chair with ugly plaid upholstery and sagging springs. It creaked dangerously beneath her weight.

"Why don't you get a new chair in here?"

"Because I don't tend to get many visitors. And when they can't be avoided, I want to be sure they don't hang around too long."

"Point taken. I'll be brief."

Kay plucked her ubiquitous worry stone off her desk—

which didn't bode well for Lilah's prospects—and folded her arms with practiced impatience and waited.

Lilah imitated her gesture, and they sat staring at each other for the better part of ten seconds.

"So much for brevity." Kay yanked off her glasses and tossed them onto the desk. "You wanna quit getting on my last nerve and tell me what's on your mind so I can get back to work and make some progress on these past due invoices?"

"Sure. One word. Cookies."

"Cookies?"

"You heard me." Lilah waited.

"Never touch them. Loaded with saturated fat and too much sodium. Those things are like munchkin assassins, waiting to steal your soul."

"A commendable dietary stance, Kay. But not what I'm asking, and you know it."

Kay sighed. "I assume you're asking about the Shoaf funeral."

"That, and several others. All of them featuring a surprising array of delightful pâtisserie."

"I wouldn't go that far. Those snickerdoodles have too much nutmeg to suit me."

"While it's true that we could sit here for hours debating the finer points of baking with spices that are or are not included the autoimmune protocol, I'd rather discuss what led you to take leave of your senses and allow this eclectic enterprise to become part of our roster of bereavement services."

Kay looked for a moment like she was about to debate Lilah's assessment of her perceived lapse in judgment. But that didn't last long. She plucked an oversized ledger off a sagging credenza that was piled high with papers and flipped it open before dropping it down on the desk in front of Lilah.

"*This.*" She pointed to a column of numbers. "This is what led me to greenlight Sparkle's harebrained idea and create a budget line to underwrite her culinary whims. Look at these receipts. An eighteen percent increase in revenue. And all of it is rolling our way on the backs of those little two-inch morsels she bakes up each day in that sorry excuse for a kitchen you call an employee lounge."

Lilah was no whiz at accounting, but even she could recognize an impressive-looking row of numbers when she saw one—and all of them appeared to add up to a banner-looking quarter for Stohler's.

She looked at Kay. "Has Dad seen these numbers?"

"You're kidding, right? He calls me at least four times a day to see if our self-styled 'cookie-gate' is still trending."

"Just *great.* I'll never get rid of her now."

"Get *rid* of her?" Kay was incredulous. "Are you nuts? In my opinion, you need to keep right on riding Susie Homemaker's apron strings all the way to a colossal return on investment."

"Kay? You know I glaze over when you use business terminology."

"Need me to simplify it for you? Okay. Be. *Nice.* To. Her."

"Seriously? In what ways am I *not* nice to her?"

"Oh, for god's sake, Lilah. You think no one around here has seen that blonde Barbie doll you stabbed with about a hundred dissecting pins?"

Lilah feigned innocence. "I have no idea what you're talking about."

"Really? The one wearing only an apron with 'Sparkle' written across it in glitter? Bring anything to mind?"

"It was a slow night."

"Yeah? Well, it's been a slower couple of years. Our profits have been on the skids ever since Walmart started selling caskets at wholesale prices, and national conglomerates like FSI began gobbling up mom and pop operations like this one. We need a niche to stay vital. And that human bounce house named Sparkle Lee Sink might just have baked us right into one."

Lilah closed her eyes in mortification. This was a nightmare. And not one of the good kind she looked forward to.

Be nice to her? Be nice to that perfectly proportioned enigma named *Sparkle?*

There had to be some other way.

She gave Kay one of her best morose looks. "This isn't what I signed up for."

"Get used to it, Morticia." Kay tossed her worry stone down on the desk. "Death in this country is now a twenty-eight-billion dollar a year industry. And more and more of it is being carried out through e-commerce. You can't just hide out downstairs in that cave of yours, pumping dead bodies full of antifreeze. The times, they are a changin'." She opened a desk drawer and withdrew a letter. "Check this out." She passed the folded sheet of paper to Lilah. "Last week, I received this query from Salem Baking Company. They've been following the escalating popularity of social media posts about our innovative approach to aftercare. More specifically, they're focused on one of Sparkle's signature cookies: the ginger chew. They're interested in exploring the feasibility of adding these as a line of branded cookies called *Stohler's Eternally Delicious.* At first, I thought about tossing this into the shredder with the rest of the nonsense that crosses my desk every day. But then, I thought about it."

Lilah looked up at her from the letter. "And you realized that shredding it wasn't visceral enough? You wanted to dissolve it in glutaraldehyde? Back over it a few times with one of the

27

hearses? Have Gee String run it through the Franklin Stove?"

"No." Kay took the letter back from her. "I decided to follow up with them. They're coming here to meet with you and Sparkle on Friday."

"What?" Lilah shot up from the chair—which wasn't an easy feat since its springs were about as elastic as old Mrs. Shoaf's saggy jowls had been. "Are you insane? Why the hell would I want to meet with them about some infernal damn ginger chaws?"

"It's ginger *chews*. And if memory serves, you now *own* this joint. And your father insisted."

"He would. Nobody knows what a sadist that little man really is."

Kay actually laughed, which was a rarity. "I've heard Abel Stohler called a lot of things in the thirty-plus years I've worked here, but *sadist* is not among them."

"Oh, yeah? Don't be fooled by his gray flannel, insurance salesman vibe. The man can be a pit viper when it comes to devising innovative ways to torture me."

"Lilah. You said that same thing when he made you wear the wrist corsage Tommy Kinard bought you for your senior prom."

"Did you *see* that thing? It was the size of a casket spray. Besides—it didn't match my outfit."

"You were wearing mukluks and a pair of black Carhartt coveralls."

"So what?" Lilah shrugged. "I was coerced into going. I wanted to stay home and watch the *Halloween* marathon on SyFy."

"Well, don't get any ideas about bailing on *this* event. Wear whatever in the hell you want, but you're *definitely* showing up— and you're going to sit quietly and listen to what they have to say."

More than anything, Lilah wanted to flee—just like all the times she had beaten a hasty path of retreat after pulling the fire alarm at church. They only caught her about half the time. *Okay. Maybe two-thirds of the time.* But it had always been worth it—especially on those damn Moravian lovefeast days when the services lasted an eternity and ended with everyone sharing tepid coffee and sickly-sweet buns.

Now, here she was again: a prisoner of yet another sweet confection laced with too much damn nutmeg.

It was a goddamn conspiracy. But she knew it was pointless to resist.

"What time?" she asked Kay, who sat regarding her like the cat who ate the canary.

"High noon." Kay beamed at her. "They're taking you out to lunch."

Lunch? *Just kill me now.* Lilah turned to leave.

"I don't understand why you're so bent out of shape about her."

Lilah looked at Kay with confusion. "Her?"

"You know who I'm talking about. Your reaction to her lacks proportionality. I mean . . . isn't she your type?"

"My type? You're delusional. I don't *have* a type."

"Uh huh. You keep telling yourself that. And one last thing?" Kay called after her. "If I were you, I'd be thinking about buying a commercial-sized oven for that breakroom."

As Lilah headed for the stairs that led to her crypt, she wondered if they had any more boxes of dissecting pins stashed in that storage closet where Kay Stover kept the top-shelf hooch.

Opal Shoaf's sendoff was in full-throated swing.

At last count, more than 165 people had packed into the viewing room, forcing Hambone to roll back the accordion doors that linked the space to another parlor that, fortunately, was not in use that day. So many people had showed up that the parking lot and available on-street spaces were quickly filled, and Gee String started running a shuttle service to the mortuary from the downtown parking garage on Cherry Street.

Sparkle had to enlist the help of Rita Kitty to keep hot trays of snickerdoodle cookies coming from the tiny kitchen. They were going as fast as they could replenish them.

There were so many people milling about inside the funeral home they quickly ran out of chairs. Mourners were spread out all over the place. Some of the younger attendees even perched atop closed caskets in the sales room, munching on cookies and scrolling through messages on their cell phones.

Photographers from the local paper milled about snapping candid photos of smiling people holding up hands full of hot, fresh-baked cookies.

The din grew so loud that Lilah and Wardell heard its reverberation downstairs in the embalming suite.

Wardell raised his shielded eyes to the ceiling.

"What's going on up there? It sounds like a herd of cattle vacuuming."

Lilah looked up from the arterial tube she'd been inserting into the body of young Jerry Crotty, who'd died in a freak accident while racing his modified stock car on a popular track north of the city. She took off her mask and craned her neck toward the stairs that led to the main floor. There it was again. That telltale odor of cinnamon and nutmeg.

Cookies. More damn cookies.

She backed away from her table and began shucking off her gloves and gown.

"Will you finish up Mr. Crotty? I need to go upstairs and check this situation out."

"Sure thing, boss. And bring me some of them cookies. I missed lunch today."

Lilah scowled at him before heading for the stairs.

Once she reached the main floor, the hallway was so choked with people she had to elbow her way through to get close to the front reception room where the Shoaf visitation was taking place.

It took a while. She was sure this had to be a fire code violation. She'd never *seen* so many bodies in the place—and that included the aftermath of a tragic train derailment with forty-two fatalities.

"Excuse me. Pardon me. I'm sorry . . . would you mind letting me through? So sorry for your loss. Hello. Thank you for being here. I just need to sneak past you here. No, thank you—I don't care for cookies. Excuse me. Hi, I just need to scoot by you. No, I'm not related to Mrs. Shoaf. Yes, I have heard that I look like Mrs. Addams. Excuse me. Sorry to interrupt, but I need to get through here. Sorry. I didn't mean to step on your foot. Yes, I work here. Yes, sir, there are other bathrooms located up front near the main reception area. No, I don't have any extra toilet paper, but I'll find someone for you. Pardon me. Excuse me."

Jesus H. Christ. Would you people quit scarfing those damn cookies and let me the fuck through here?

It was when she'd finally advanced as far as the entrance to the selection room that she saw several teenagers inside, swilling cans of Monster energy drink and lounging about atop some of their highest-priced display models.

That was the last straw. Lilah exploded through the crowd separating her from the showroom packed with high-priced inventory with all the wrath of an angry God splitting the temple veil. She burst into the showroom like a dark vision of unholy retribution.

An unexpected occurrence for a room that reeked of Axe body wash.

"What the serious fuck do you all think you're doing in here?" she roared.

Five sets of terrified eyes landed on her—all bearing looks of shock and disbelief.

"What the shit *are* you?" One of the pimply-faced teens backed into a display case of cremation urns and sent half a dozen of them teetering before they went crashing into a personalized "Forever Remembered" Memorial Birdbath. Dyed blue water splashed out of its cracked bowl and spread like a tidal wave across the white satin and cream organza interior of a Titan Orion Series Orchid Steel Casket.

Three of the other teens discreetly slid off the lids of their makeshift casket seats and stood stupidly gaping at Lilah, nervously twisting their drink cans and cell phones in their shaking hands.

But one enterprising member of their group remained completely undaunted and had the sheer effrontery to raise his iPhone and snap several pictures of Lilah as she stood fuming before them.

"I don't know who you little fuckers all belong to," she growled, "but you're in some seriously deep shit." She grabbed a notepad and pen from a small desk near the doorway. "It's that fun part of the evening where we get to kick ass and take names. And we can do this the easy way—which means you each write down your name, address, and phone number. Or we can do it the hard way—which means I have our friends at the Winston-Salem Police Department come and confiscate your goddamn cell phones *and* the keys to the overpriced cars your clueless parents gave you for your sixteenth birthdays." She handed the notepad and pen to teen number one. "So. What's it gonna be, Scooter?"

Teen one took the pad from her and looked nervously at his pals.

"I'm doing it," he said. He quickly wrote down his information and passed the pad to a friend.

They all followed suit except for Ansel Adams, who continued to snap photos of the entire proceeding. When the pad was passed to him, he tossed it to the floor at Lilah's feet.

"Fuck you, Elvira. I didn't do anything wrong."

"Come on, Chad," one of the teens hissed. "Don't be an asshole."

"Fuck you, too, Jared. You're a pussy. I'm outta here."

He crossed the room until he stood face to face with Lilah. She thought fleetingly that it would've been a perfect moment if only someone could've spooled up the theme song from *The Good, the Bad, and the Ugly.*

"I'm not afraid of you, you freak," he hissed.

Lilah smiled at him. "You know what, Chaaaaaaaaad?" She dragged his name out like it had five syllables before stepping closer, so they were practically nose to nose. "You *should* be. I work *downstairs*. So hold my beer while I tidy up this mess you created, won't you?"

She saw the faintest glimmer of fear in his eyes. Then she stepped aside so he could exit the room.

"The rest of you can get out of here, too. But remember that one day, each one of you will end up naked and lying on a table in the basement of a place exactly like this. So be a bit more mindful of how you respect the merchandise that one day will be your permanent home."

They filed past her without speaking. Lilah watched them go with disgust and disappointment. She'd deal with the damage in here later. But now, she needed to reenter the sea of Shoaf hangers-on and make her way to the hot-baked buffet that, according to Kay Stover, was single-handedly saving their business.

No sooner had she closed and locked the door to the selection room than she saw Sparkle, making her way through the maze of people. Predictably, she was carrying another basket of those infernal cookies.

"Sink!" she bellowed.

Sparkle stopped and cast about until she saw Lilah, draped against the selection room door like a curtain of black crepe.

"Over here," Lilah hissed. "*Now.*"

Sparkle looked dubious, but artfully pushed her way through the throng, dispensing fresh cookies along the way, until she reached the spot where Lilah stood waiting on her.

"What is it?" she asked with shocking innocence.

"What *is* it?" Lilah repeated with incredulity. "Do you wake up in a new goddamn reality every day, Mary Poppins?"

Sparkle continued to stare at her with confusion, so Lilah unlocked the door to the showroom and ushered her inside.

"Give me those goddamn cookies." Lilah took the basket from Sparkle and sat it down on the desk. "Look. You have to

34

get this madness under control or we're going to lose our license to operate. We're violating about twenty-five building codes for occupant load and safe capacity in public assembly. We'll be lucky if we don't get our asses shut down before the close of business tonight."

Sparkle actually looked defeated. "I know. I had no idea Mrs. Shoaf had this many friends and family."

"Friends and family my ass." She threw out an arm to encompass the mob beyond the door. "Those people aren't here to mourn Opal Shoaf. They're here because of those damn hot-baked rocks of crack you call cookies."

"What?"

Lilah grabbed the basket of cookies and shook it in front of Sparkle's face. "*These. These.* What do you bake into these? Some kind of spice mixture laced with Fentanyl?"

"*Of course* not. We ran out of snickerdoodles in the first thirty minutes. These are my granny's secret recipe."

"Oh, really? And was your granny always wacked out on Lydia Pinkham's when she baked?"

For the first time, Lilah saw something flash behind Sparkle's legendary green eyes.

"I don't appreciate your tone." Sparkle's voice vibrated with umbrage. "I'm just trying to do a good job here. And in case you haven't noticed, it seems to be working." Sparkle snatched the basket of cookies out of Lilah's hand. "Now if you'll kindly excuse me, I've got a mortuary full of hungry Shoafs—and all of them are waiting to get their hands on another one of Granny Ellis's ginger chews. I don't know anything about your family traditions. But in mine, the needs of others come first."

Sparkle swung around and yanked open the door that led to the corridor. She cast a final glance back at Lilah before exiting.

"We can discuss your concerns at a more appropriate time. Right now, I have guests to attend to."

Lilah watched her leave. Her straight back and the affronted energy behind the delivery of her remonstrance were surprising. Lilah had always possessed an uncommon ability to find the right nerve—a skill honed through years of practical application in the commission of her work. But even she had to marvel at how quickly she'd managed to tap the jugular vein that ignited Sparkle's defense mechanisms.

Maybe there was more to the human bounce house than met the eye?

But the cookies? *Those fuckers had to go* . . . No matter what fantasies Kay Stover had about them.

Still, Sparkle had been right. That was a consideration for another day. Right now, she had to deal with finding a way to bring down the curtain on this absurd excuse for a visitation.

Even if that meant using a fire hose to clear the corridor . . .

All Lilah wanted to do when she finally got home was kick back with a cold drink and console herself by indulging in her favorite guilty pleasure: rewatching episodes of *Ted Lasso*.

She kept this proclivity a secret and divulged it to no one— not even her sister, Frankie, who probably knew her better than anyone. It was nobody's business how she spent her private time. And for her, watching the overly saccharine and always uplifting interactions of the characters was like a kind of twisted *schadenfreude*. The spectacle they all created with their earnest expressions of attachment and kindhearted camaraderie was sickening. Like witnessing a fifteen-car pileup on the highway.

Lilah couldn't look away because the relationship dynamics were simply so incomprehensible—like a sappy, idealized burlesque of Hallmark-infused human interaction.

Just like those fucking, addictive cookies.

Clearly, a disapproving god had thrown those cloying hunks of ginger-infused dough into her path to trip her up. To force her out of her carefully crafted posture of indifference and lead her to the one thing she eschewed the most: traffic with other human beings in what passed for *meaningful* discourse.

Her mortification increased. It was unseemly. Was she now going to be subjected to engaging in that worst of all interactions: *sensitive chats?*

It was not to be borne.

She turned up the volume on her TV set. Of course, this would *have* to be the damn Christmas episode—perhaps the most sickening of the lot. The overflowing expressions of love and acceptance that all but radiated from the pores of the characters were so over the top, Lilah nearly threw her remote control at the screen. She was reaching the breaking point and had all but resolved to switch over to Fox News because the self-proclaimed entertainment channel could always be relied upon to deliver more lurid and terrifying content than a triple feature of Hannibal Lecter movies. But before she could make the switch from one bogus reality to another, her phone erupted with a staccato barrage of text message alerts. They fired off in such rapid succession, she assumed that either her father had again managed to get stuck inside the garden shed (where he snuck out to watch NASCAR races without having to endure the disapproving glowers of her mother), or that Gee String had forgotten to switch off the blowers on the backup retort—an auxiliary cremation machine they only used when

37

business was . . . *heating up.*

She was wrong on both counts. The messages were coming in fast and furious, from a variety of colleagues and family members. As she scanned the preview screen, a sickening realization came over her.

That fucking little twat, Chad, who'd been frenetically snapping photos of her during their Come to Jesus encounter in the selection room appeared to have exacted his revenge in a picture-perfect way.

Lilah opened her phone with trepidation and started reading the actual messages. Each one carried a link to a lurid photo of her, all but hovering against a background of polished caskets. She looked like the demented ghost of Bertha Rochester, shopping a liquidation sale at Death's Hilton.

Her shock and consternation increased geometrically as she realized the scope of the revenge one pimple-faced, pampered pissant had carried out with the practiced economy of the 146-character post that appeared beneath the photograph.

> Diva of Death emerges from the corpse cooler to show her rage. Who knew psycho cryptoverts could be so hot? Bring it, mistress of the dark. I'd like to rest in a few of your pieces. #boneyardbabes, #divaofdeath, #StohlersMortuary

And then there were the text messages, which kept right on coming even as she stood, rooted in place, reading through the first wave.

> **Frankie Stohler**
> Hey, Li? Since when have you started haunting

the back rooms of Instagram? "Diva of Death"? Pretty nice moniker! Getting a jump start on this year's Saturnalia celebration? Give me a call and let's do lunch—if you can shake the paparazzi.

Kay Stover
Well, well. I had no idea you'd step up and embrace the whole e-commerce angle with such dispatch. Now if you can manage to look just a bit less murderous, we might actually have a shot at turning a profit for two consecutive quarters. And don't worry. Your father has already called me about this. Thrice.

Kate B. Reynolds Hospice Home
Damn, Stohler. Nice way to nuke the whole dignity of death concept. What's next? Mobile embalming vans?

Everhart Aftercare
Yo, Diva of Death? My kid wants to have goth-themed cupcakes for her school birthday party. How much notice do you need to whip those up? Or does somebody have to die first? lol

Rita Kitty
Hey, girl! Next time you plan on going viral, at least let me do something with your hair. You looked just like a pissed-off Ronnie Milsap. Friends tell friends.

Salem Cremations
Just so you know, my daughter showed this to
me and said, "Hey, Daddy? How come Nancy
Downs doesn't work at OUR funeral home?"
Cannot wait for your breakout session at next
month's NFDA conference in Vegas. After this
little preview, I predict they'll move you to the
main stage.

Abel Stohler
Li? I think we need to talk about this whole
Diva of Death thing. I'm not sure it sends a
very welcoming message. Could you give me
a call when you get this? I can't get the shed
door open and Mom will be home in an hour.
–Dad

Sebastian Sprinkle
I told you that black bustier would make
you famous. So, my voluptuous Diva of Death,
can I borrow this outfit for Saturday night?
ROTFLMAO

Sparkle Lee Sink
Sorry to bother you at home, but I thought
you should know about this. I already
contacted the site administrators, but they
said only a complaint from you could elevate
the request to have the post removed. I'd act
quickly. It's already had 32,000 views and 875
shares.

She threw her phone across the room in disgust.

Diva of Death.

That pampered little shit, Chad. She wished she'd gotten the ingrate's address. She'd fire up one of the meat wagons and pay him a house call he'd never forget.

The messages kept coming in fast and furious. Finally, she shut off her phone so she didn't have to listen to any more of the alerts. And leave it to Sparkle to be the only one who'd tried to get the offensive post taken down. Not even Kay Stover seemed to care that Lilah'd been made the brunt of a cruel smear campaign. *And what the fuck was a cryptovert, anyway?*

She grudgingly had to admit that she actually *liked* that term—and it made her resent fucking Chad even more for being the one to come up with it.

Trying to settle back into the macabre fantasy world of *Ted Lasso* would be pointless. There was really only one thing she could think of to do that was guaranteed to keep her from continuing to check her phone messages. Or she could sit down and try to make more progress on her current, insightful treatise about fast-acting fungi use in burial applications for the upcoming issue of *Southern Funeral Director* magazine.

She grabbed her car keys and headed for the West End, so she could let her father out of his damn man cave before her mother got home.

Jerry Dean Crotty
May 11, 1994 – November 4, 2023

One of God's finest creations has passed away. In the early evening hours of Saturday, November 4, 2023, Jerry Dean Crotty, 29, left this life for the next, leaving behind a legacy of love, faith, and service to others. Jerry Dean lived his life humbly and placed God first in all areas of his life. Always giving a warm smile and a solid handshake, he never met a stranger. Jerry Dean proudly served as a Deacon at Speedwell Baptist. He taught Sunday School for a long time, except during race season. He also worked in various Church ministries such as Youth Club, VBS, Prayer Partners, ushering, and serving as a pallbearer when folks couldn't find anyone else to step up.

Jerry Dean was a very respected and beloved Modified stock car driver for many years. At the track, he witnessed with Bible verses on his cars, talking Jesus with other drivers and fans, leading in prayer on pit row, and giving his trophies to young fans after a quick witness. Racing with integrity was a top priority—right up until that fateful final turn at the "Madhouse" (Bowman Gray) track. Jerry Dean left this mortal coil and blazed a path to Glory behind the wheel of Number 12—his beloved blue Chevy—known by friends and fans as Jerry Dean's Chariot of Fire.

Jerry Dean was a man of many talents, maintaining the fuel tank farm at the Greensboro airport all the while proclaiming his faith through his words and deeds. He is survived by his wife, Teresa June (Snipes) and baby daughter, and a lot of other relatives and race fans who knew him to be a kindly soul.

The family will receive friends from 3 p.m. until 5 p.m. on Thursday, November 9, at Stohler's Funeral Home in Winston-Salem.

Posted by Stohler's Funeral Home, Winston-Salem, NC

600 Degrees of Separation

Lilah couldn't remember the last time she'd skipped work—or showed up late. But it was Thursday, and for once, they had no pickups. In fact, they had only one service scheduled for that day—the one for the young stock car driver who'd been tragically killed while racing his modified Chevy on the asphalt short track at "The Madhouse," or what locals called the NASCAR venue at Bowman Gray Stadium. Crotty's untimely death had dominated local news headlines for several days, so they were expecting another standing-room only event.

So, Lilah, uncharacteristically, allowed herself to take the morning off. When she finally arrived at the mortuary—*late*—she was surprised to see that Hambone and Gee String had already set out thirty tidy rows of folding chairs, all festooned with ribbons sporting the racing colors of top drivers in the modified class of racing. Lilah supposed they thought the attendees would choose to honor Crotty by showing up wearing their fan gear. The funeral promised to be a Technicolor spectacle.

She wondered what manner of baked goods Sparkle had

spooled up for the occasion. Probably sugar cookies cut out in the shape of tiny stock cars—each flooded with royal icing, dyed to match the racing club colors.

What the fuck is the matter with me? I'm starting to think like Sink.

And tomorrow, the two of them had to meet with those delusional cookie moguls at Salem Baking Company to discuss the feasibility of marketing Sparkle's heirloom cookies under the ridiculous name *Stohler's Eternally Delicious Ginger Chews.*

She navigated the halls of the mortuary like a cat burglar focused on avoiding detection. She didn't want to run into anyone who would remind her of the whole "Diva of Death" craziness that, against all reason, was still trending on Instagram. The last time she'd checked—about forty-five minutes ago—the post had had more than 79,000 views and been shared more times than she could count.

That rat bastard, Chad, was probably already planning his launch of a line of death merch.

It occurred to her to suggest to the denizens of Salem Baking that they'd do better to hire a slew of Gen Alpha marketing gurus than go with whatever brain trust had come up with the cringe-worthy "Eternally Delicious" brand.

But what did she know about marketing? Her idea of progressive thinking was considering a switch to compostable transport boxes for families interested in the low-cost benefits of green burial—an idea that had gained traction for her after that whole birdbath fiasco. It turned out there was no amount of bleach that could remove that regrettable rinse of FCF Blue No. 2 from the white interior upholstery of that Titan Oracle casket. The best they could do was dye the entire damn interior and hope for the advent of some grief-stricken romantic with deep pockets and a pronounced lack of aesthetic discrimination.

Too bad she hadn't known before that Jerry Dean Crotty's beloved stock car had been blue. Now *that* was what Kay Stover would've called a missed opportunity.

She cautiously peered around the corner toward Kay's office. The door was open, but no one was in sight. Curious. Where was everyone? Even Sparkle wasn't buzzing around, clutching her ubiquitous clipboard and talking through her headset to some florist or quick-copy printer.

She knew Wardell had the day off. His son, Lamar, was traveling with his middle school football team to the playoffs in Roanoke Rapids, and Wardell and his wife, Wanda, were driving two of the buses.

That meant the embalming suite would be deserted, too.

Lilah was nearly disappointed that no one had been on hand to tease or upbraid her about her unwitting, instant celebrity. She decided to venture out back to the crematory to see what Hambone and Gee String were up to. She was unprepared for what greeted her when she stepped inside.

The sound of laughter and talking drew her toward the conference room, where she found Hambone, Gee String, Rita Kitty, Kay Stover, and Sparkle all seated around the big board table, playing cards.

Cards? At (Lilah consulted her watch) 10:30 a.m.?

"So let me guess," she said from the doorway. "Nobody died?"

"Well, if it ain't the Diva of Death herself," Hambone bellowed. "We thought you might've lit out for Hollywood, what with all that overnight celebrity."

Gee String was nodding energetically. "Didn't expect to see hide nor hair of you until after dark."

"That ain't no surprise." Rita Kitty nudged him. "That *is* when them Divas of Death mostly come out to wreak mayhem on the world."

Kay Stover cleared her throat. "Are you gonna discard, Sparkle? It's your turn."

"Sorry." Sparkle had been looking at Lilah with a mixture of curiosity and concern, but quickly returned her attention to the game. She deftly withdrew a card and placed it on the discard pile.

Everyone groaned.

Lilah inched closer to the table to see what the problem was.

They were playing Uno—hardly the most mentally challenging game. And Sparkle had just off-loaded a green two.

"What's the deal with this card," Lilah asked. "Everybody out of twos—or green cards?"

"Naw," Hambone explained. "This here is a *special* version of Uno. One where a two of green card is kindly like a big ole sabotage. When it gets played, ever body else has to draw six cards."

"The *two* of *green*?" Lilah quoted. "Aren't there only two per deck?"

Kay Stover laughed. "Not when you use three decks."

To be fair, they did have an impressive draw pile in the center of the table.

"Who on earth came up with this random idea?" Lilah asked.

Hambone and Gee String exchanged glances.

"Yer daddy," Gee String volunteered. "The idea come to him back when we was dealin' with that whole train derailment and was movin' them poor souls through here back-to-back-to-back. 'Member as how we only had that one retort back in them days, and we was runnin' it flat out, twenty-four hours a day. Me'n Hambone was pretty much livin' out here and goin' crazy sittin' around and tryin' to stay awake between firings. So, yer daddy come out here with this little deck a cards and set down with us to kill some time."

"That's right," Hambone agreed. "An' we been doin' it ever since."

"Let me get something straight." Lilah pulled out a chair and sat down between Kay Stover and Sparkle. "*My* father invented this two of greens sabotage?"

Hambone chuckled. "No, ma'am. That'un there was added on later by Kay Stover."

"It figures." Lilah faced Kay with a raised eyebrow.

"What?" Kay responded. "I like to introduce a bit of mystery from time to time. It keeps things fresh and flexible—which should be appealing to you, Diva of Death."

Lilah rolled her eyes. "Good thing you don't apply these same techniques to bookkeeping."

"Oh, really?" Kay regarded Lilah with a smug expression. "You think I don't?"

"Then I suppose it was also your idea to color code the seating for the Crotty funeral?"

"Nope." Kay nodded at Sparkle. "You can thank Ms. Sink for that innovation."

Lilah wasn't sure, but she thought Sparkle looked almost embarrassed.

"It seemed like something they might like," she offered in a tone that was almost apologetic. "I didn't think about asking you first. I hope that was okay. I didn't want to trouble you last night after all the . . ." She didn't finish her statement.

"After all the . . . what?" Lilah followed up. "Could you

possibly be referring to the unhappy aftermath of my encounter with nature's Axe-infused, best argument for mercy killing?"

"Something like that," Sparkle agreed. "Did you try to have the post taken down?"

"Sure." Lilah gave a bitter-sounding laugh. "Right after I folded space and enjoyed a lovely dinner on Planet Kolob. There's a quaint bistro there called The Throne of God. They serve umbrage with a heaping side of who-gives-a-flying-fuck. Which, by the way, deftly summarizes the reaction of the powers that be at that hellscape called Instagram."

Sparkle looked genuinely sorry. "Try not to give it too much credence. These things never last more than a day or two. No one will even remember it by the weekend."

Lilah sat back against her chair. "Well, that blows chunks. I just had all my monograms changed."

"Don't worry none about that, boss," Hambone chimed in. "I think that there nickname fits you to a T. Me'n Gee String was real proud when we read about it this morning in the paper."

"The *paper?*" Lilah was incredulous. "*What* paper?"

"The *Journal.*" Rita Kitty hauled her massive bag up from the floor beside her chair. "Hold on. I got a copy of it right here." She pulled out the folded bit of newsprint and passed it across the table to Lilah. "You gotta admit that even when you're havin' a bad hair day, you still take a good photo."

Lilah's face grew hot as she scanned the article. Never before had mortification felt . . . bad. She'd always carefully curated her modestly goth appearance to avoid precisely this outcome. When you were dark and aloof, people tended not to notice you—in the same way they instantly become obsessed with dusting their dashboards to avoid making eye contact with the homeless person standing near a stoplight. It had never occurred to her that one day, her dour presentation would be viewed as a *commodity*.

"Not the way I'd prefer to make headlines," she said to cover her consternation.

"Well," Kay Stover observed, "I'll agree it doesn't have the same pizzazz as reports about that time you got caught breaking into Party City."

"Hey. At least I didn't steal anything."

"No." Kay conceded. "You were a tad more creative."

"So what? It was Halloween and they had a lame-ass window display."

"That is true," Kay agreed. "But even you have to admit that a re-creation of the Jonestown Massacre was an eclectic choice, at best."

Lilah shrugged.

"To be fair, Miz Stover, them bodies did look real lifelike."

"They should have." Kay shot Hambone a withering look. "If memory serves, *you* were the one who got her the bags of sawdust."

Lilah turned her attention back to Sparkle.

"So, to return to our previous topic—you genuinely thought asking the resident Diva of Death for permission to festoon thirty rows of folding chairs with brightly colored ribbons made any kind of sense?"

"When you present it in those terms, I suppose not."

Lilah gave a bitter-sounding laugh. "I just wish you'd had the foresight to sell that damn $2,800 blue-lined Oracle casket to dear Mrs. Crotty. It would've been the ultimate homage to the passion of her dearly departed's short life."

Hambone and Gee String exchanged amused glances.

Kay Stover cleared her throat.

Rita Kitty, who could never tolerate a vacuum, leaned toward Lilah and explained in hushed, confidential tones, that Sparkle had already seen to that.

"Wait a minute." Lilah turned in her seat to face Sparkle. "You sold that hideous, tie-dyed, *damaged* floor model to a young widow in the throes of grief?"

"I am afraid so."

"And for *cash*," Kay Stover added. She tossed a red number two card onto the discard pile.

"Well, hells bells." Lilah sat back and crossed her long arms. "Toss in a box or two of *Eternally Delicious* cookies and we've got ourselves a brand-new redneck special. We can call it The Blessed Slumber Package." She laughed. "What do you think we could get for that, Kay?"

"Four grand, easy."

"Don't be forgettin' all them ribbons. I done cleaned out that aisle at Hobby Lobby."

"You're right, Hambone," Kay added. "Make that $4,350."

"Necessity is the mother of invention." Rita Kitty drew a card and grinned. "Sorry, Gee String." She tossed a draw four card onto the discard pile.

"Well, I swannny." Gee String carefully drew four cards. "I need me an extra set of hands to hold all these dern cards."

"I could rustle you up a pair to use today," Hambone offered. "But we'd need to stitch 'em back onto that Miz Toddy Rock who just come in, before her service."

"Don't be crazy, Hambone." Rita Kitty chastised him. "You know Gee String would never wear that color nail polish."

Everyone laughed.

"And with that," Rita Kitty laid down all the cards in her hand, "I'm out." She grinned at Gee String. "I don't reckon you'll be needing them extra hands now, brother Freeman."

"Well, glory be to God." Gee String started counting up his points. "I was hopin' somebody would put me outta my dern misery."

"Why don't you join us, Lilah?" Kay Stover asked. "We've got another two hours before that PBR crowd starts arriving."

"You should," Sparkle added. "It would be nice to engage in something less confrontational—for a change."

"You mean besides an exchange of gunfire?" Lilah asked.

"Yes. Something like that."

Lilah thought about it. "Okay. But only if I get to choose the game."

Kay Stover was smart enough to be suspicious. "What kind of game?"

"Oh, don't worry. It's another card game. One of my favorites."

"I think I smell a rat," Kay replied.

"Honey," Rita Kitty leaned toward her and raised a hand to smooth out a swath of Kay's frizzy hair. "That ain't no rat. I told you. It's the aftermath of leavin' them perm rods in too long."

Kay swatted her hand away and glared at Lilah. "So, what is this game of yours?"

Lilah grinned at her. "Ever played Exploding Kittens?"

The mourners attending the Crotty funeral looked like a collection of extras from a Skittles commercial. But brand loyalty appeared to run deep and there was no co-mingling of team colors. That meant the Skeeter Bodine fans, all wearing hats emblazoned with bold number 44s, sat in the yellow section. The red section was occupied by die hard Travis Walthrop fans. Cody Briscoe, who'd just won the coveted Short Track Supernational at Afton Falls, commanded the most seats: six entire rows of chairs—so many followers that Sparkle had to dispatch Hambone to make an emergency run to Michael's for more blue ribbon. That left old-school drivers like Nick Mossback and Junior Teague to fill out the green and blaze orange sections, respectively. Sadly, the purple section only boasted three chairs.

When Lilah pointed that peculiarity out to Hambone, he slowly shook his head.

"That there's the section for that little Julie Ann Cobb." He lowered his voice. "Folks ain't really ready yet to rally behind them women drivers—even though this little gal come in fourth at Brushy Mountain."

Lilah had determined in advance that she'd beat a hasty retreat before the Crotty service got underway. But she did tarry long enough to get a good look at how Jerry Dean looked, resplendent in his racing kit, all decked out in the plush, baby blue confines of his Titan Oracle with the custom interior dye job.

Remarkably, the color was nearly a dead match with the nearly life-sized photo of Jerry Dean's hopped-up Chevy "modified" that had been mounted across two easels at the front of the reception room. She had to hand it to Rita Kitty, who'd mixed the fabric dye to exactly match the stain left during the regrettable birdbath incident.

Lilah felt a grudging respect for Sparkle's instinct and initiative when it came to off-loading the asset and even managing to turn a profit in the process. To be fair, the grieving widow, Teresa June, seemed to be taking great pride in pointing out the similarities, so it wasn't like they'd actually taken advantage of her. Not that Lilah would've had any scruples about that . . .

More than once, Lilah had editorialized about how her mentor, H.L. Mencken, had never underestimated the American public when it came to accepting inferior ideas or useless products. Her thesis was that most of the entrapments that defined the death industry were pretty useless. And those weaknesses all derived from a cultural conspiracy engineered to sanitize the end of life. Instead of embracing it as the logical and natural conclusion of living, consumers were encouraged to deify the experience and push it deeper into the uncharted realms of the mysterious and supernatural—always ensuring that its hardcore and base realities remained shrouded behind layers of pomp, prayer, and extreme excess.

She looked around the large room with its festooned rows of folding chairs and massive photo of a blazing blue stock car.

Yep. Funeral parlors *had* become the penultimate bastions of smoke and mirrors. And dark-robed practitioners like her were the commensurate sideshow barkers, offering up to their desperate, grief-stricken multitudes first-class access to gilded escape routes, guaranteed to shield them from any distasteful encounter with the raw, organic, and undeniable permanence of death.

At least, that's what dominated her thoughts during off hours, when there was nothing good streaming on TV or she wasn't consumed by working on her Vegas conference speech.

Or busy going viral on Instagram . . .

Once the human rainbow of mourners began arriving, Lilah retreated from the scene, intending to head back to the safety of the embalming suite. It was when she rounded the corner to approach the back stairs that she was blinded by the flash of a cell phone camera.

She reflexively raised her hands to shield her face.

"What the serious fuck *is* it with you people?" she bellowed.

By the time her vision rebounded from the realm of whiteout conditions, the photographer had already disappeared. She had no idea if the person had been part of the Crotty party or was simply some degenerate friend of Chad's, staking out the hallway to claim his own five seconds of fame.

Great. Just great. Maybe I'll get lucky, and Taylor Swift will start dating Elon Musk . . .

But she knew in her viscera that she was dreaming. There wasn't going to be any divine intervention to save her. She was sure to be served up to the scroll-and-click crowd again— another giant slice of burnt toast, trending with all the energy of the recipe for NyQuil Chicken and other deeply unimportant cultural phenomena. And why not?

After all, death *was* the new black . . .

And what the hell kind of hashtag would they gift her with this time? Somebody had to do better than Boneyard Babe, Hell's Hooters, or Diva of Death. Didn't these mentally myopic Gen Alphas have *standards?*

As she descended the stairs to seek solace in her cold and sterilized retreat, she knew she wouldn't have to wait long to find out.

The Black Bird of Chernobyl?

That's what was trending across three major social media platforms by the time Lilah emerged from the basement to join Kay Stover to discuss the upcoming lunch meeting with the Salem Baking gurus.

"It's probably best to go ahead and rip this Band-Aid off." Kay Stover passed her Android across the desk to Lilah.

Lilah's jaw dropped. The hallway photo of her had already been viewed 14,628 times.

"In *three* fucking hours?" She continued to scroll through the posts. "Don't these people have lives?"

"Apparently not. For some reason, my dear, you've become hotter'n a pot of necks."

Lilah sighed and handed the phone back to Kay. "If I knew what that meant, I'd come up with a blistering response."

"Don't let this get you down. Sparkle promises it will blow over soon."

Lilah glared at her.

"You know I blame her for this, right?"

"Sparkle? Why?"

"Because all of this craziness started as a result of her terminal pluckiness."

"I don't think we need to be casting blame around," Kay Stover admonished. "You bear a lot of responsibility for this, Morticia—flitting around like a store mannikin at Death R Us. It's a wonder that nobody thought to do something like this sooner."

"Just who in the hell would've done it sooner, Kay? A vengeful stiff with a cell phone?"

"We cannot police the actions of the crowds of people who attend services here, and you know it."

"That's my entire point. Before Dad hired a 'community outreach liaison,' we didn't *have* crowds of people attending anything here—not unless you count that year Dad let those Amway chapters hold their pyramid scam meetings here. On a good day, our services are lucky to draw about forty people, max—including the deceased."

"Which is precisely why we needed Sparkle."

"Putting butts in the seats doesn't increase our bottom line—no pun intended. And you know this as well as I do, Kay."

"No. But putting the Stohler name on tins of those branded cookies—*and* having your visage splashed across the screen of every cell phone in America sure as hell does."

"Have you been dipping into that top-shelf hooch you keep hidden beneath the stairs?"

Kay looked momentarily shell-shocked. "How did you . . . Never mind. Ever since last night, I've been fielding calls from every major funeral home conglomerate in the country—and even a few in Canada. And they all want one thing."

"Cookies?" Lilah quipped.

"No. God help us. They all want *you*."

"Me?"

"Yes. You. Well. Not *you*, exactly." She held up her phone to display the newest image of Lilah, resplendent in black and white, glowing like some refugee from a Vincent Price movie. "*Her.* They all want *her*: The Black Bird of Chernobyl. In less than twenty-four hours, you've become some kind of cultural icon. The new face of death. And the day that death starts trending? That's the day the crepe hangers of the world line up outside our crypt, clamoring to ride your tight-fitted shroud right into franchised bliss."

"Are you joking?"

Kay shook her head.

"You've been getting calls to acquire us?"

"Lock, stock, and bier pins."

"Jesus, Mary, and Joseph. What next?"

"That's up to you."

Lilah was immediately suspicious. "What's that supposed to mean?"

"It means, your father says it's your decision."

"Dad knows about this?"

"You're kidding me, right? He was copied on the first offer and exploded through my phone like one of those damn kitten cards in that sadistic game of yours."

Lilah raised a hand to her face. "I cannot deal with much more of this."

"Too bad, goth girl. Your dad says you're the one holding the keys to the family hearse, and you get to decide where to take it for a ride. So. What's it gonna be? Feast or famine? It's your choice. But don't deliberate too long. If Sparkle is right—and there's no reason to assume she isn't—this media feeding frenzy isn't likely to last long."

"I need a drink."

"Sorry, Lucretia. I'm fresh out of hemlock. But I do have some of this." She opened a desk drawer and withdrew a pint bottle. "Word on the street is that it's cheap, but gets the job done." She handed the half-empty bottle to Lilah.

"Old Grand-Dad? Seriously? Did you steal this from Rita Kitty?"

"Nope. Sparkle confiscated this from Hambone. She said he'd been using it to spike the punch. I actually tried it. It's not too bad if you can overlook those subtle notes of foundation on the back end."

"Foundation?"

"Oh, yes. Apparently, Rita Kitty re-purposes it after she cleans her makeup brushes."

"Dear god."

"Hey. Any port in a storm, right?" Kay retrieved two empty

coffee mugs from the credenza behind her desk. "Join me?"

Lilah realized that there was no way the day—or her entire fucking life—could get any more surreal.

"Why the hell not?"

Lilah picked up one of the mugs and held it out to her. Kay poured them each a generous glug of the astringent brew.

"To what should we toast?" Kay asked.

"How about to not running this damn meat wagon off a cliff?"

"Works for me." Kay clinked mugs with her. "As your father loves to say: it's *your* damn funeral."

It would've taken a calculator with quadruple precision decimal floating-points to count all the expletives contained in Lilah's response.

Lilah and Sparkle met the pitch team from Salem Baking Company for lunch at Six Hundred, a trendy live-fire restaurant rife with industrial chic, located in the old R.J. Reynolds Tobacco power station. The bistro's upscale menu focused on its specialty: wood-fired entrées, featuring notable standouts like burnt ends of pork belly, cast-iron venison, short ribs of bison, and a $120 bone-in ribeye.

A very meat-centric take on haute cuisine, Lilah noted after examining the oversized menu. She'd been doing her level best to ignore the outright stares they'd been receiving since they entered the high-priced eatery.

She'd been about on the verge of telling the Hardy Boys— what she'd dubbed their too-affable hosts—that she was a vegan but thought better of it when Sparkle seemed to read her mind and kicked her beneath the table.

"Trust me," Hardy Boy number one bragged to Lilah. "You haven't lived until you've sampled the food here. It's all about the heat. You may not realize it, but wood turns to ash and coals when it hits six hundred degrees Celsius. And that's the secret ingredient behind the success of every dish here."

"Amazing." Lilah sat with her chin resting on the back of her hand. "That's about 1100 degrees Fahrenheit isn't it? Imagine if they had access to one of *our* ovens. We let them reach 1500 degrees before we even think about adding any proteins."

Hardy Boy number two was looking a bit pale. Lilah wondered if he'd bypass the roasted meats and opt for one of the "Little Gem" salads with shiitake mushrooms and shredded celery.

"So, would you mind telling us a bit more about your plans to market the cookies?" Sparkle made a valiant attempt to steer the conversation into safer waters. "And do we have any flexibility with regard to the name of the product?"

"Oh?" Hardy Boy number two was busy eating a thick slice of hearth-baked yeast bread. "You don't like *Eternally Delicious?*"

"It sucks." Lilah passed the dish of whipped sorghum and thyme spread toward him. "More butter, Junior?"

"It's Jonas," he corrected. "And I'm sorry to hear you say that. We've had our most advanced marketing team work on the branding campaign for these."

"That may be, Jarvis, but *Eternally Delicious* sounds to me like something that keeps repeating on you—like radishes or cooked cabbage. Hardly the kinds of things you want to stuff into Granny's Christmas stocking."

"No, that's not what we meant to imply by the name."

They were all distracted by a series of blinding flashes coming

61

from the table beside theirs. Several coeds hurriedly tried to hide their cell phones behind their water glasses.

Lilah's agitation was increasing, but Sparkle stepped into the void.

"We were thinking maybe something a bit less beatific," she offered. "I mean, these are humble ginger chews—like you'd find at any country church picnic. They don't need to be . . ."

"Deified?" Lilah suggested. "I mean, it's not like we're hawking the cookie equivalents of *The Ecstasy of Saint Teresa.*"

"Well." Hardy Boy number one decided to join the fray. "We did have an alternative name that also tested well in our market research."

"Do tell?" Lilah beamed at him.

"Stohler's Heavenly Delights?" He said the name like it was the question at the end of a *Jeopardy!* clue.

"I think I saw that movie," Lilah pointed out. "But it was set in Scotland, and they were making curry."

"No. That was *Nina's Heavenly Delights.*"

Lilah looked at Sparkle with surprise.

She shrugged. "I saw it in college."

Of course, you did, Lilah thought. *Boy, you could just never tell these days . . .*

"I'm afraid we'll have to go back to the drawing board on names if neither of these is acceptable to you." Hardy Boy number two had nearly finished his bread and was nervously casting about for their server.

"Why not just call them Granny Stohler's Ginger Chews?" Sparkle rattled it off like it was the most natural thing in the world.

The Hardy Boys exchanged excited glances.

Another camera flash went off. It coincided nicely with the

branding epiphany the Hardy Boys were in the throes of.

"And would your family be okay with that?" Hardy Boy number two asked Lilah.

"Why the hell not, Jacko?"

"It's *Jonas*," he reminded her again. "So, you did have a Granny Stohler?"

"Of course." She eyed Sparkle. "Doesn't everyone?"

"Would you consent to let us use a photograph of her for the marketing?"

Lilah all but guffawed. "Sure. If I can find one taken when she was out of rehab."

Sparkle laid a hand on Lilah's arm. "Why don't we simplify matters and use a photo of *my* grandmother. After all, it *is* her recipe."

The Hardy Boys warmed to that idea.

"I think that could work," Hardy Boy number one said to his companion. "After all, there wasn't any real Betty Crocker. I mean, they've changed her portrait at least a dozen times in the last century."

"That's true," Lilah agreed. "Just like Lassie and Charlie the Tuna."

Hardy Boy number one blinked at her. "So, we'll get creative cranking on the branding."

"Wonderful." Sparkle picked up her menu. "We can review the particulars you gave us and get back to you within a week or so. How about we order some lunch now? We have to be back for a family consultation at two."

"We do?"

Sparkle kicked Lilah beneath the table again.

"Oh. That's right. *We do*," Lilah added, reaching down to rub her leg. "Big family. Tragic story. All six of them died in a freak hang gliding accident out at Kitty Hawk, practicing for some kind of Wright Brothers reenactment on the 17th."

"The centenary," Sparkle clarified. "They're a big reenactment family. Always do the Battle of Horsepen Creek remembrance, too—out at Guilford Courthouse. You've probably seen that one before, right?"

Both Hardy Boys nodded enthusiastically, even though it was abundantly clear to Lilah—and Sparkle—that they were lying.

The Hardy Boys really wanted this deal . . .

Those must be some goddamn good cookies, Lilah thought.

Their server arrived to take their lunch orders. As Lilah predicted, both Hardy Boys shied away from the 1100-degree Fahrenheit proteins and went with greener options.

Sparkle ordered a smashed kale salad with grilled chicken.

Lilah threw caution to the wind and ordered the bone-in ribeye with a side of truffle fries.

Why the fuck not? she mused.

She figured that all those people who had been not-so-discreetly snapping cell phone pictures of her ever since they'd walked into this inferno that passed for a restaurant should get what they paid for.

She could just imagine tonight's post: *Black Bird of Chernobyl takes her meat like her corpses: extra crispy.*

In fact, that wasn't far from the truth . . .

Fifteen minutes later, their server arrived with their lunch orders. Lilah sliced into her steak and was delighted to see that it was expertly prepared, with perfectly denatured proteins and the right viscosity to the juices. She decided to oblige her personal paparazzi and all but posed with a large forkful of rare, dry aged beef held aloft. It glistened in the amber glow of the gaslight shining above their table.

She counted half a dozen flashes before she slowly took a cautious bite.

It was perfection.

Just like that ridiculous hang gliding story they'd concocted on the fly. She was looking forward to the ride back to the mortuary so she could query Sparkle about being so quick on the uptake.

And about her taste in films. That one had been the biggest surprise of all. One of several, it seemed.

She took another bite of the ridiculously overpriced steak.

Who said life couldn't imitate art?

Lilah and Wardell had just finished up for the night when the phone rang.

"You want me to get it?" Wardell had already grabbed his backpack and was halfway up the stairs.

"No, It's fine. You go on." Lilah reached for the phone. "It's probably *60 Minutes.*"

Happily, for Lilah, it wasn't the news media, it was the county morgue. But the news was less happy for the indigent who'd been found dead in the dumpster behind the Harris Teeter market on Cloverdale Avenue. The county had kept her on ice for the requisite waiting period, but no positive identification occurred so the body had been released and was now en route to Stohler's for cremation. Lilah agreed to meet Dash outside their crematory to take possession of the remains.

"Want me to help you load this one into the reefer?" Dash used the slang term for their mortuary fridge.

"Sure."

The transfer didn't take long. Lilah signed all the requisite paperwork, and Jane Doe was tagged and safely stored on a shelf where she'd await cremation. The cremains would then be returned to the state for eventual disposition. She supposed that wouldn't happen anytime soon. The Freeman brothers had all they could do to manage the absurd, cookie-infused uptick in cases. And those numbers had been increasing steadily ever since Lilah herself had become the mortuary's latest hot commodity.

When they finished and closed the big reefer door, Lilah prepared to walk Dash back out to his beater transport van. But, uncharacteristically, Dash tarried.

"Got time for a smoke?" he asked.

"I don't smoke. Not unless you count those two rotisseries inside. You know that."

"I meant for *me*, Stohler. Life good at the center of the universe?"

"It's been . . . interesting."

"Yeah. No shit." Dash seemed to take her response as evidence of consent and at least some halfhearted willingness to talk, so he fished a pack of Camels out of his pocket and headed for the exit.

"It makes no goddamn kind of sense that you don't let anybody smoke in there."

"It does seem counterintuitive, I suppose."

"You think?" Dash sat down on a metal chair that was part of a small sitting area set up just behind the building. He didn't waste any time firing up a cigarette. "I was surprised to see you here tonight."

"Why?" That seemed like an odd supposition to Lilah. She was usually the one who met him when he stopped by with his nocturnal deliveries.

On the other hand . . . it wasn't exactly night. *Yet.*

"About that. What are you doing making drop-offs in the quasi-daylight? Doesn't the light burn your skin or something?"

Dash blew out a plume of smoke. Lilah had never been a smoker, although most people assumed she was because of her uncharacteristic, husky-sounding voice. Still, she found it interesting that the first drag off a cigarette always smelled good.

"I had to swap shifts with that loser, Benson. Asshole went to a Wake basketball game on Monday night and managed to fall off the bleachers. Clumsy as fuck in crowds. Probably more upset that he spilled his beer." He took another drag. "Damn moron."

"Yeah. We have our own problems here. There were close to two hundred people jammed into this place for each of our last two services. I have nightmares about somebody pulling a fire alarm and causing a stampede. It'd be like the aftermath of one of those Brazilian soccer matches."

"Shit, Stohler. That sounds like something you'd make popcorn for."

"Under normal circumstances it would be. But these services were more like progressive Last Suppers."

Dash nodded. "I have been hearing gossip about your change in fortunes since you started hawking those—what the hell are they called? Ginger snaps?"

"*Chews,*" Lilah corrected him. "Ginger chews. And I haven't been hawking anything. I'd rather harvest organs and sell them on eBay."

"No shortage of that." Dash laughed. "You'd have to get more creative."

Lilah crossed her long legs. "The boys at Salem Baking

Company are going to take care of that for us. Get ready for the launch of an all new, uniquely branded product line. If they're to be believed, these bits of magical dough will quickly replace human composting as the best innovation the death industry has seen in the last decade."

"Must be some pretty goddamn good cookies."

"Word on the street is they don't suck."

"Got any I can try?"

"Not on me."

Dash looked her over. "Too bad you don't have pockets in that damn fitted knife sheath you call an outfit."

"What the hell is that supposed to mean?"

"Don't get your Vickys in a wad, Elvira. I've seen *Project Runway*. I get that concessions to practical considerations like pockets would ruin the cut of your jib."

Lilah was incredulous. "Since when do you give a damn about how I dress?"

Dash stubbed his cigarette out on the bottom of his shoe. "Since I've started seeing your picture about a thousand times a night on my damn iPhone." He tapped out another cigarette. "*The Black Bird of Chernobyl?* Gotta say . . . sometimes those nomophobe freaks get it right."

"Again, I ask: what the hell is that supposed to mean?"

"Jesus, Stohler. Forget to take your Thorazine this morning? Don't you appreciate the searing metaphor at work here? Gotta hand it to the FOMO who coined that description for you. Of course, it didn't work out too well for the poor schmoes in Ukraine the first time the term got used. The locals who survived said their pre-reactor meltdown sightings of that freakish, supernatural black bird were harbingers of catastrophe. Seems like a mantra you'd have no trouble embracing. Just saying."

Lilah was half-tempted to ask Dash for a smoke.

"Yeah, well wreaking wholesale death and destruction wasn't in my long-range plan. I'd have been happier with a less expansive debris field—maybe just Ardmore and Old Salem."

Dash nodded. "What about all those golf-obsessed robber barons living in Buena Vista and Country Club Forest?"

"Them, too."

"I kind of figured. So, what the fuck happened, Stohler?"

"It's a long story."

"I got nowhere else to be. This was my last drop-off."

Lilah got an idea that was uncharacteristically extroverted. Why not? What awaited her at home besides more hours of misery reading text messages from people dying to make sure she'd seen the latest Instagram posts about her instant celebrity—or working on her damn Vegas speech. "How do you feel about bad hooch?"

Dash shrugged. "It gets the job done just as well as the expensive kind."

Lilah stood up. "Follow me."

Ten minutes later, they were seated in comfy chairs near the sales desk in the selection room. Lilah found that space to be more accommodating than her office, which had all the rustic charm of an abandoned rabbit hutch.

Dash sipped at his tumbler of Old Grand-Dad. "This really is some nasty shit, isn't it? Reminds me of the Isopropyl and 7-Up cocktails we made as kids."

"Jesus, Dash. Where'd you grow up? Dogpatch?"

"Close. Baltimore."

"Go Terps."

"Yeah. Never really followed that ACC bullshit much."

"I guess that accounts for your disdain for poor Benson,

your unfortunate coworker."

"No. That guy is pretty much an asshole all the time. The basketball stupidity just added richness to the story."

"So, tell me. What's a scholar like you doing ferrying dead bodies around for a living?"

"Nice try, Jerry Springer. I'm not here to spill *my* guts. This little prayer meeting is about your entrails."

"Trust me, Dash. Nobody wants to see my entrails."

"I think you underestimate yourself."

Lilah looked at him like he had two heads—which would've provided the mortuary with a unique opportunity for double billing. "Rarely."

Dash tossed back the rest of his Old Grand-Dad and held out his tumbler. "Any more of this paint thinner?"

Lilah handed him the bottle. "Help yourself."

"So, tell me about this brand-enhancement person your father hired. Is she responsible for the joint's newfound celebrity?"

Lilah was intrigued by his question. "How'd you hear about that, Dash? You cruising Junior League luncheons again?"

"Yeah. Right after my pickleball matches and volunteer service at the food pantry. As. If. I heard about it from Dan Raskin over at Kate B. Reynolds. Apparently, Stohler's is the talk of the local Crepe Hanger's Guild."

"It makes no fucking sense. I have a BS in mortuary science from Pitt—and a graduate degree in anatomy and physiology from George Washington. I followed that up with a two-year residency in the chief medical examiner's office in Cleveland, dealing with horrors that cannot even be imagined—and I can imagine an awful lot, believe me. Since then, I've spent most of my life here, following in my old-school father's footsteps, and trying my best, in fits and starts, to drag this family albatross toward a more environmentally responsible and less antiquated approach to aftercare. Adding the crematory was the first big step—that only took *nine* years. But still, the old methods are the ones people want. Pump 'em full of antifreeze, deck them out in one of these high-priced single-wides, and plant them inside concrete condos replete with HOAs, forever and amen." She drained her glass. "*God.* This stuff is more like drinking Old Grand-Dad's *bile.*"

"No arguments. You wanna call it a night?"

"Nah. I'll have another glass."

Dash laughed.

"Why not?" Lilah quipped, "Can't walk on one leg."

Dash looked around the selection room. "You know, normally I'd think sitting in here drinking cheap-ass swill would be pretty damn degenerate."

"But?"

"But, those open caskets do exude a certain warmth. I find them . . . calming."

"I'll remember that when your time comes. We've been doing some very innovative modifications on the interior appointments lately, too. I like to think of it as chromatherapy for the dead."

"You mean something like all that rainbow bridge bullshit?"

"Correct. Only this relates to color-coordinated casket liners vs. the afterlife of household pets."

"I do *not* understand this end of the business. I think I'll stick to my stop, drop, and roll right on half of the equation."

"Well, lately, I don't think I understand it, either. I used to spend what passed for free time reading journal articles and writing op-eds about advancements in green burial and the environmental benefits of human composting. But now? Now

I spend my time hiding from every goddamn person with a cell phone who is determined to post another shocking exposé about the secret life of some vertebrate called 'The Black Bird of Chernobyl.' I blame *her* for this."

"Her? Who is her?"

"That fluffy marketing ingénue Dad hired. *Sparkle Lee Sink*. She's like a cross between Reese Witherspoon and Martha Stewart. Being around her for more than five seconds is like having a bolt of sunshine rammed up your ass. What really pisses me off is that she's managed to do in six weeks what I've been struggling to pull off for more than a decade."

"Bake a better ginger cookie?"

Lilah gave him a withering look. "*No*. Turn a damn profit at this place."

"By baking a better ginger cookie?"

"Feel free to laugh it up. But those damn cookies have managed to put this place on the radar of the largest funeral home operators in the country. We're sitting on three bona fide purchase offers right now—and all because of those cookies and her themed approaches to bereavement services."

"At the risk of pissing you off, I think your recent celebrity has probably sweetened the pot, too."

"I seriously doubt that. Corporations like FSI don't invest capital marketing their services to twenty-somethings with hyperactive index fingers and the attention spans of lobotomized gnats."

"That is true. But still . . . there's no such thing as bad publicity."

"Unless you're Tiger Woods."

"I see your point. So, what are you going to do?"

"About what?"

"About this place. You going to off-load it or stay the course?"

Lilah thought about his question. There was no easy answer. Her father said it would have to be her decision. But right now, she had no idea how to make it. Or even if she wanted to try.

"If you had asked me that a month ago, I'd have said hell no."

"But now?"

"Now, I'm not sure about anything. To tell the truth, I don't even recognize the landscape anymore. It's like I fell asleep and woke up on the set of *Severance*."

"Hey, it's always scary when you think about making a career change. That's normal."

"Who said anything about making a career change? I'll never do anything but deal with dead people. They're the only kind I can stand. It's all these burgeoning, happy-go-lucky interactions with the living that I cannot stomach. If that's the cost of running a successful business, then I need to pack my winding sheets and move on down the line."

"Well," Dash stood up and downed the rest of his drink, "I guess you have your answer, then."

Lilah looked up at him. "To what question?"

"The only one that matters, my dark sister. What do you plan to do with your one wild and precious life. Me? I'm gonna go home, heat up a frozen pizza, and watch porn."

"Not what I expected from such a scholar, Dash."

"Hey . . . it's like Joni Mitchell said, Stohler. 'Leave 'em laughing when you go.'" He gave her a salute. "I'm outta here."

"Dash?"

He stopped and waited.

"One thing before you go. What the hell is your real name, anyway?"

He gave her a crooked smile. "Saul Rubenstein."

"Seriously?"

"'Fraid so. And just so you know," he wagged an index finger back and forth to take in all the overpriced death merch in the room, "my tribe doesn't cotton to any of this bullshit."

"I'll be sure to order your cardboard box at Walmart. They offer same day delivery."

"Good to know."

Lilah watched him leave, then continued to sit alone in the selection room.

No place on earth was as quiet as a funeral home after hours.

Except maybe a Baptist church on race day.

She looked around at the tidy phalanx of caskets, arrayed like shiny soldiers, ready to do battle with time and the elements. Maybe there *were* worse places to spend eternity.

Like the cheap seats at a Wake Forest basketball game . . .

Dash is right, she thought. *It really* is *calming in here.*

She propped her feet up on a deluxe, Lincoln Solid Copper XL model and settled in to finish off the rest of Rita Kitty's hooch. Maybe she'd luck out, and 80 proof would cut through more than mortician's wax. If not? Well. By the time she finished the bottle, she wouldn't much care.

Beatrice "Toddy" Marjorie Purvis Rock

May 15, 1941 – November 18, 2023

Beatrice "Toddy" Marjorie Purvis Rock, 82, was carried home on the very wings of angels into the waiting arms of her Lord and Savior, Jesus Christ, on Saturday evening, November 18, 2023.

Toddy Rock was born on May 15, 1941, in Horseheads, NY to the late Farcel "Pal" and Patsy "Pim-Pom" Frank Purvis. She spent more than 20 years working in a glass factory where she excelled in blowing and rolling molten glass. She was recognized for her commitment to her craft by receiving the highest pay grade for a non-management employee. In her personal life she was known for being honest yet feisty with a sense of humor that always made people laugh hard. She was a very loving mother and grandmother that was always seen with an open pack of cigarettes in her hand. Her hobbies included knitting, extreme ironing, and watching Rusty Wallace win his NASCAR races.

In addition to her parents, Toddy was preceded in death by her brother, Wren "Pickles" Purvis; and a sister, Ida Mae "Jitterbug" Purvis Dunn.

She is survived by her son, James "Bug" Rock, and granddaughter, Molly "Chipmunk" Rock.

There will be a 2 p.m. service held on Wednesday, November 22, 2023, at Stohler's Funeral Home with Pastor Roscoe "Pancake" Handsy officiating.

Posted by Stohler's Funeral Home, Winston-Salem, NC

Viral Instincts

Paybacks.

That was the concept that kept trolling the back alleys of Lilah's mind as she scrolled through the latest Instagram posts.

Beginning with all the things she could do to the bloated body of that human cipher, Chad. She allowed herself a few moments of happy indulgence recalling some of the more creative examples she'd witnessed during her two years in Cleveland.

Those Buckeyes didn't fuck around when it came to messing up a body.

Contrary to the promises Sparkle had made, the Instagram feeding frenzy hadn't slacked off one bit. The posts were still coming fast and furious.

> Black Bird roasts at 600 Degrees—the only place in town that's hot enough for the Diva of Death to spread her wings. #backbirdofchernobyl, #divaofdeath, #SixHundredWS, #StohlersMortuary

"Fear of death is why we build cathedrals, declare war, and watch cat videos at 3 in the morning." It's also why the world needs death divas like Caitlin Doughty and The Black Bird of Chernobyl. #backbirdofchernobyl, #thegooddeath, #askamortician, #StohlersMortuary

Diva of Death stocking up on antifreeze. Mixers for the office holiday party? #backbirdofchernobyl, #divaofdeath, #AutoZone, #StohlersMortuary

Death Drives a Mini. Black Bird of Chernobyl parks her Mini meat wagon in front of the ice cream shop on Trade Street. Two scoops of Death by Chocolate, please. #backbirdofchernobyl, #divaofdeath, #Ben&Jerrys, #StohlersMortuary

She'd had enough of this insanity. She was a prisoner in her own life. She couldn't go anyplace. Not the post office. Not the grocery store. Not the dry cleaner. Not ACE Hardware, when she had to make a last-minute run to pick up a set of replacement strap hinges. Not even the frickin' DMV.

Oh, yeah. Her personal paparazzi had caught up with her *there*, too.

Black Birds might be First in Flight, but they still have to wait In line at the DMV. #backbirdofchernobyl, #divaofdeath, #StohlersMortuary

It didn't help her mood that she was still trying to get her head around attending an infernal Jaycees luncheon tomorrow—*with Sparkle*. For Lilah, it was tantamount to being forced to spend her afternoon munching on crudités at Café Plutus, conveniently located in the fourth circle of hell.

She wondered if the Underworld God of Wealth allowed for separate checks . . .

When Kay Stover had briefed her about the event—a euphemism for threatening to revoke her corporate Amex card if she failed to show up—she explained that it was a golden opportunity for Stohler's to cultivate relationships with up-and-coming business leaders in the community.

Lilah told her she'd rather be flayed alive with knives.

Kay said she could probably arrange that if the venue changed to one of those Japanese steak houses. She pointed out that, ever since Covid, some of those chefs had been replaced by personnel who were less than adept at their craft. Only last week, her cousin, Darius, had lost part of his collar when it got sliced off by a flying hibachi knife. She added that the place did consent to comp his drinks—but noted that she couldn't do much to improve Lilah's odds today with such short notice.

Lilah agreed to accompany Sparkle, mostly because she didn't want to listen to any more stories about Cousin Darius and his monstrous bad luck when it came to eating out. Kay was warming to her theme and had just launched into a tale about Darius and some third-degree burns he'd sustained from an incident involving a hot skillet of hush puppies at a fire department fish fry when Lilah cried uncle and agreed to go with Sparkle.

Now she was stuck.

And what the fuck was she going to *wear?* She knew if she opted for one of her normal outfits, she'd be recognized in about two seconds by some Internet crazy. It was time to resort to extreme measures—even if that meant changing her appearance to conceal her identity.

Sadly, her closet afforded few options for anything other than bereavement wear. Even her "casual" clothing reposed in a suburb of funereal. She liked to think of those garments as belonging to her "death light" collection. She was able to find one cream-colored blouse her mother had given to her several years ago. Lilah had been obliged to wear it—*once*—just to appease her parents. But she'd artfully contrived to dump an entire ladle of arrabbiata sauce across the left breast while helping to serve dinner at their place, and that effectively took the garment out of rotation.

She wondered, idly, if Rita Kitty could dye the entire thing crimson . . .

No. She tossed the garment aside. She still had partiality for how the expansive stain made her look like she'd been stabbed in the heart.

After ten more minutes of searching, she gave up. It was hopeless. She'd have to borrow something from Frankie—and pray to God it wasn't one of the carjacking outfits picked out for her by Sebastian, whose tastes always gravitated to the realm of . . . slutty.

She looked at herself in the bathroom mirror—an activity she normally disdained.

Okay. So, makeup could conceal some of her natural, pale pallor. But her hair?

She lifted one of the black, rope-like tresses that could've doubled as a garrote.

Yeah. This was a job for Servpro—which meant there was only one place to go for help.

It wasn't usual for Lilah to visit Shear Elegance, her mother's upscale salon on Hawthorne Road. But extreme circumstances called for extreme measures. Lilah waited until closing time to make her appearance. She wanted to catch her mother alone. She took care to park her black Mini behind the building and enter through the employee entrance.

Janet Stohler was surprised to see her. She was busy putting a load of towels into the salon's oversized washing machine when Lilah found her.

"Hi, honey. What brings you to this part of town? Did you run out of bonding oil?"

"Hi, Mom." Lilah kissed her mother on the cheek. "No. I, um . . . need a favor."

"Sure. What kind of favor?"

"I don't suppose Frankie told you about any of the Instagram posts about me. Did she?"

"No." Janet Stohler smiled. "But every other customer who's been in here for the past week has. You haven't had this much publicity since you were ten and came in second at that county fair competition for the fastest time properly field dressing a deer."

"That thing was rigged. Those judges were totally biased toward those Cabela sponsors. They couldn't handle that a girl could do a better job than sixteen men, using just her scout knife."

"That may be true. Your father always did say you had the hands of a surgeon and the tenacity of a serial killer."

"Dad always was a smooth talker." Lilah glanced at the wall clock. "Do you have to be anywhere right now? I don't want to keep you late."

"No, honey. I've got some time. But why didn't you call me and make an appointment? You know I'll always fit you in."

"I know that. But this was a kind of last-minute decision. And I was afraid that if I scheduled it, I'd have too much time to talk myself out of it."

Her mother leaned against the washing machine and folded her arms. "That sounds ominous."

"It's this whole Black Bird of Chernobyl thing. I'm literally being stalked by hordes of Gen Alphas with cell phones. They follow me everyplace. I have no privacy and it's driving me crazy. And to make matters worse, I have to attend a damn Jaycees luncheon tomorrow because, according to Kay Stover, it's 'good for business.'"

"Now, why do you think that'll be so horrible?"

"Mom? Have you ever seen *Dawn of the Dead?*"

"Of course, I have, honey. We had to watch it—*twice*—at every one of your birthday parties."

"Well, that's what these women are like—pencil-thin designer zombies who subsist on diets of plant-forward Hello Fresh meals and spend their days in hetero consumer comas, blindly driving their Teslas from store to store to shop for the best prices on Tory Burch bags."

Janet sighed. "Come in and take a seat in the chair, and we'll discuss what you want to change."

"That won't be hard. *Everything.*"

"Lilah."

"Mom."

"Honey ..."

Oh, great. Lilah could tell her mother was settling in to deliver one of her ubiquitous pep talks. *Here it comes,* she thought.

"There's never been a day in your life that you shied away from who you are. It didn't matter what anyone else said or thought. You always went your own way. Granted, that did lead to some rather unique fashion choices throughout the years. But your father and I always trusted your instincts and understood that the choices you made were driven by something deeper than a desire to shock or rebel." She reached out a hand to smooth Lilah's hair. "You had something else. You had an awareness of who you were—in your viscera—and what your unique place in the world was. That manifested itself in some incredible ways, too. You were never afraid of anything. You never gave up once you made your mind up to try something. And you never ran away from a problem—not one time. So, before I fasten this gown around your neck and consent to alter anything, I want you to tell me right now what about *you* has changed."

And just like the aftermath of every other one of her mother's *The Mountain Is You* homilies she'd had to sit through, Lilah felt her insides clench.

She looked morosely at her mother's reflection in the big mirror.

Janet Stohler was still one of the most beautiful women she'd ever known.

And Lilah had spent a *lot* of time studying the features of women—at all stages of their lives in every type of condition—so she felt eminently qualified to make such an assessment. It was her mother's steadiness, constancy, and downright decency that added such distinction to her appearance. She was, and had always been, a truth-teller. And that's what she was doing right now.

And just like every other damn time in her life before today, Lilah knew she'd been busted.

83

Her mother gave her a full minute to consider her response—which can be a long damn time when you're trying like hell to avoid something. When it became clear that no answer was forthcoming, she opened a drawer and pulled out her cell phone.

"What are you doing?" Lilah asked.

"I'm texting Frankie. I think it's time for the Stohler women to get drunk together."

Lilah wasn't inclined to disagree.

Lilah's younger sister, Frankie, was a third-grade schoolteacher who moonlighted as a repo agent for a fly-by-night asset recovery agency in a nearby town called K-Vegas.

It was a long story . . .

She and her partner, Vera—nicknamed Nick—had met when they'd each taken temp jobs at the skeevy joint to make fast extra money. Frankie needed it to continue to afford school supplies—and provide lunches—for her kids. Nick had been trying to make headway paying off the law school student loans that were driving her into penury. The only magic that emanated from that experience had been finding each other. They were so sickeningly sweet as a couple that Lilah compared them to a pair of the marzipan figurines that danced and frolicked across the idealized village squares of all those snow-covered, candy Christmas villages.

They, like marzipan, usually made her want to barf.

Frankie met them at the door holding out two bottles of wine.

"White or red?"

"One of each?" Janet kissed her daughter before glancing

back at Lilah. "Make that two of each?"

"That can happen." Frankie hugged her sister.

Lilah must've held on to Frankie a nanosecond longer than usual—which was not at all—because Frankie drew back and looked at her with narrowed eyes.

"What's going on, Li?"

"What do you mean?"

"Something's different about you."

"What? Did I cut myself shaving or something?"

"No. It's more ineffable than that."

"Ineffable? Are you playing *Words with Friends* again?"

"Nice try. Come on in, you two, and get comfy. Nick is out with Sebastian for a girls' night."

"Which means they're at drag bingo?" Lilah asked.

"More than likely."

"What on earth is drag bingo?" their mother asked.

"Use your imagination," Lilah and Frankie replied in unison.

Janet Stohler laughed. "You two never change."

Frankie handed a bottle and a wine opener to Lilah. "You do this one and I'll get the other."

"No fair. Yours has a screw cap."

"Sucks being you, Li."

"Hey. My hands are my livelihood. I cannot risk accidental injury by trifling with inferior implements like this dime store corkscrew."

"Seriously? Don't you have a bag of highly sophisticated tools always at the ready—like death's avenging girl scout?"

"Contrary to popular opinion, I do *not* chase ambulances. I don't have to. They come to me voluntarily."

"Well then, why not put your raspiest Dirty Harry impression to good use and intimidate the shit out of it. I'm sure the cork will surrender without a fight."

"I don't care which of you does what." Janet Stohler dropped into an oversized armchair and kicked off her shoes. "Just give me a glass of something."

"Rough day, Mom?" Frankie handed her mother a glass of chilled Chardonnay. It was a generous pour.

"Holiday parties," Janet explained. "In the past week, we've created more French twists than a Parisian pretzel bakery."

Lilah extracted her cork with a satisfying pop. "They have pretzels in France?"

"*Oui*," Frankie answered. "But they're more butter forward and not as crunchy as ours."

"That's a pretty apt description of the hairdos, too." Janet sipped her chilled wine with pleasure. "I don't know what I'd do without Barry. He's a whiz at all these retro hairstyles."

"Isn't that kind of *de rigueur* for gay hair stylists?" Lilah asked. "But then, I don't get out all that much."

"Until tonight," Frankie quipped. "What's up, Li? Nothing good trending on Instagram?"

"Very funny, Pippi Longstocking."

"So why don't you fill me in on what's been happening? Dad said something about how those miracle cookies Sparkle's been whipping up are driving attendance at services into the stratosphere. I gather that experiment has been successful?"

"*Sparkle?*" Lilah replied. "That sounds like you know her."

"I do, in fact."

That was news. "How the hell do *you* know her?"

"Believe it or not, she was in my class at St. Mary's."

That figured, Lilah thought. St. Mary's: the bastion of knotted tennis sweaters. "Were you the one who introduced her to Dad?"

"Nope. He found her on his own. So, you can't blame that

one on me."

"What makes you think I want to blame anyone?" Lilah's tone was a tad too aggressive for their mother's liking.

"How about you take it down a notch, Lilah. No one here is your antagonist."

"You're right." Lilah faced Frankie. "I'm sorry, Gidget. The Instagram thing is getting to me."

A massively obese cat waddled into the room and made a beeline for Lilah.

Oh, Jesus fucking Christ. Not this thing. Again.

It was Sebastian's beloved cat, Carol Jenkins—who held nothing but disdain for every living mortal—except Lilah. Carol Jenkins proceeded to rub her voluminous rolls of fat affectionately against Lilah's black-clad legs.

Lilah tried to discourage the attention, but it only made the cat more insistent in her expressions of attachment.

"What the hell is *she* doing here?" Lilah tried again to push Carol Jenkins away. "I thought she lived with Sebastian now, since Nick moved in with you."

"She does. Mostly. Sebastian and Nick worked out a co-parenting arrangement. One week we have Carol Jenkins, the next week Sebastian takes her, and we get Penny Morgan."

Penny Morgan was Sebastian's other cat—one Frankie and Nick had rescued during one of their more infamous repo jobs.

That was another long story . . .

"I have *no* idea why this obese tabby finds me so . . ." Lilah didn't finish her sentence.

"Alluring?" Their mother supplied.

"I was going to say something less revolting—like *interesting*."

"Face it, Li. It was love at first sight as soon as Carol Jenkins found out that you share her passion for streaming back-to-back episodes of *Locked Up Abroad.*"

"I'll never forgive that bastard Sebastian for ratting me out." She gave up on trying to push Carol Jenkins away. That was tantamount to moving a solid brass catafalque without a dolly. "Don't you have something to distract her—like a hunk of brisket or a family-sized Stouffer's lasagna?"

"Nope. Not at the moment."

"Great." Lilah tucked her legs beneath herself to remove them from Carol Jenkins' reach. There was zero chance the fat tabby would be able to jump onto the sofa without the assistance of a Hoyer lift.

Eventually, Carol Jenkins gave up on her unrequited quest for love and waddled back out of the room—but not before turning around in the doorway to hiss at them all.

"'Love has pitched his mansion in the place of excrement,'" Lilah quoted.

"Robert Frost?" Their mother asked.

"Robert Frost? The Norman Rockwell of poets?" Lilah tsked. "Seriously, Mom?"

"It's Yeats." Frankie topped off her mother's wine. "Right, Li?"

"I'm impressed, Pippi. I figured Yeats had been banned in public schools—along with all those other bodice-rippers like *A Journal of the Plague Year* and *The Bible.*"

"Not quite. Have you forgotten how you always recited 'Crazy Jane Talks to the Bishop' and 'The Widening Gyre' in your sleep? That was why I moved to the summer porch."

"Is that why? Your father and I thought it was because of Lilah's science experiments."

"Mom. I wouldn't call injecting roadkill with Borax a science experiment."

88

Lilah took offense to her mother's characterization. "It was bona fide research. You cannot call it *experimental.*"

"Well, what on earth *would* you call it?" Janet asked.

"Pathological comes to mind." Frankie interjected.

Lilah tossed her head dismissively. "You say potato . . ."

"Girls. Really? We're here to discuss Lilah's dilemma. Not to air family grievances."

"True," Lilah agreed. "Besides, I left the Festivus pole in my other suit."

"Nice one, Li. So, how about you describe this 'dilemma' for us?"

"You've seen the Instagram posts. What else do you need to know?"

"Oh. Silly me. I thought the dilemma had more to do with Sparkle and the SRO funeral services that are making your life hell."

"That, too," Lilah agreed. "The woman is rapidly replacing Michael Bublé as the bane of my existence."

"He annoys me, too," Frankie agreed. "He's like the precursor to AI-generated music. But I never found Sparkle to be *annoying*. On the contrary, she was always rather easygoing and likable. She did a lot of tutoring, as I recall. And volunteered on weekends at the local Women's Center in Raleigh."

"Does Rome know about this? Surely she's a candidate for sainthood by now."

"Be nice, Lilah. She sounds like a lovely young woman. No wonder your father was so impressed with her."

"How'd he find out about her, Mom? I thought she was working in High Point for the Market Authority."

"I gather she was until her marriage broke up. She moved back to Winston-Salem after the divorce was finalized."

"She was married?" Lilah was incredulous. "To a *man?*"

Frankie didn't miss the significance of Lilah's overreaction. "Why not, Li? It happens to the best of us."

"Whatever." Lilah ignored her sister's reference to her own tenure being married to a man. "That still doesn't explain how she got on Dad's radar."

"I was just getting to that," their mother continued. "She'd been working for Common Giant Branding, and that's how your father met her. The agency was doing some campaign work for the local movement to save Civitan Park, and he was very impressed by her creative energy and initiative. He's very proud of the fact that he lured her away to work at our mortuary."

"Right," Lilah added. "Because there's such an obvious overlap between preserving wetlands and planning NASCAR-themed funerals."

"Honey? Would you rather have the opposite problem? *No* bodies at the services besides the decedent?"

"Come on, Mom. It wasn't that bad before, and you know it."

"Here's what I *do* know, honey. Ever since Dad hired Sparkle, Kay Stover has been in a *very* good mood. And that hasn't happened since that Cat 5 blizzard killed 154 people back in '96. *That's* what I know."

Frankie looked back and forth between her mother and sister.

"Until this moment, it never really occurred to me what an epically fucked-up family we really are."

"Why?" Lilah asked. "Because we have a healthy perspective on the business of death?"

"*No.* Because we consistently use words like 'healthy' and 'business' in the same sentence *with* 'death.' That's one twisted perspective I've never shared with any of you."

"Evidenced by that night you and Nick accidentally jacked a hearse that was, shall we say, occupied?"

"Hey . . . we took it back as soon as we found out about the . . . you know . . ."

"Stiff in the trunk?" Lilah offered. "And I recall how respectfully you did it, too—a ring and run in the middle of the night."

"That's not fair. We left a condolence card."

"I'm sure that gave great comfort to the family of the dead man you took joyriding. But on the bright side—he was only about eighteen hours late for the barbecue."

"That's just messed up, Li."

"Well, for what it's worth, I think the sainted Sparkle shares your illusory perspective on death. She didn't *plan* for those cookies to turn our fortunes around. She genuinely thought serving them at funerals was just *nice*."

"That might be true, Lilah. But your father said that the Crotty funeral was attended by 174 people. They didn't all show up because of a few platters of ginger chews. They showed up because Sparkle understands that making the services relevant to the lives of the deceased stands the best chance of increasing Stohler's market share of the area's business. And according to Kay, it's been working like a charm."

"Did Dad also tell you about the offers to sell out we've received? Do you think that was also part of Sparkle's master plan for success?"

She could tell her question surprised her mother. "No. He did not tell me that. How many offers?"

"Three at last count. And all of them from very reputable conglomerates. We'd be allowed to keep our name and some of our staff. The only change would be in management and methods. And probably procurement. We'd have to adopt their processes and sell their product lines."

"Would they let you stay on?" Frankie asked. "Would you want to?"

Lilah had been asking herself those same questions ever since Kay had shown her the purchase offers.

"I honestly do not know. But right now, with this Instagram craziness plaguing my every waking hour, I have to say the potential to disappear from sight has great appeal. So, maybe I wouldn't elect to stay on? At least, not longer than the transition period they'd require."

"What would you do, Li? I honestly cannot imagine you in any other kind of work."

"Oh, don't worry about that part, Pippi. I'll never stray too far from the family body farm. There are a couple of states now where composting has become legal—and I've always had a keen interest in that as an alternative pursuit. So, I might consider making a move to that kind of career track."

"Composting?" Frankie looked confused. "You mean—farming?"

"Earth to planet Stohler." Lilah snapped her fingers in front of Frankie's face. "I'm talking about *human* composting. As in, you give us custody of Granny's cold, dead corpse—six weeks later, we hand you back a bag of topsoil guaranteed to yield the best 'maters you ever 'et."

"Dear god." Frankie's eyes were like saucers. "That's actually a thing?"

"It's been a thing, little sister. In fact, I'm going to a trade show in Vegas next week where there'll be practical demonstrations of the process. I predict they'll find plenty of volunteers slumped over the slot machines in Bally's." She looked at her mother. "They know they're dead when they stop ordering free drinks."

"I think I'm with Frankie in the concerns department, Lilah."

"Really, Mom? You're creeped out by human composting? I'd have thought a keen gardener like you would've been all over it as a humane and natural way for each of us to return to the earth."

"Not *that* part. The part where any business would encourage people to keep gambling until they dropped dead."

"Ever been to Vegas, Mom?" Frankie asked.

"No. But it can't possibly be as bad as you both think—can it?"

"Hell, fuck yes," both girls said in unison.

Janet shook her head. "Did we ever decide which one of us is the DD for tonight?"

Lilah raised her hand. "I think it's my turn."

"Good." Janet held her glass out to Frankie. "I'll take another glass. And this time, fill it to the rim, please."

As Frankie got up to fetch more of the chilled wine, she touched Lilah on the shoulder. "If you want to keep drinking, I can always have Nick run Mom home." Lilah was more than halfway poised to take her up on her offer until she added, "You can share the guest room with Carol Jenkins."

While it might be true that Lilah'd had her fair share of looking for love in all the wrong places, she knew with confidence that a fling with Carol Jenkins would only end badly.

No matter how many episodes of *Locked Up Abroad* they binge watched.

Sparkle agreed without question when Lilah asked her to drive them to the Jaycees luncheon. Lilah didn't bother sharing her belief that the drone car would be less recognizable than her black Mini—which, to be fair, really did look like a miniature hearse.

This time, the lunch meeting was being held in one of the banquet rooms at Milner's Restaurant, a place known for its Southern cuisine. Lilah was relieved that at least she wouldn't have to listen to any more sophomoric lectures about how to properly roast meat.

Sparkle tried, gently, to coach her on the way to the venue. Lilah could tell she was interested in keeping their interactions with the aspiring future business leaders friendly and engaging. Which could only mean she'd found Lilah's demeanor to be caustic and combative in their recent *tête-à-tête* with the Hardy Boys. She thought about apologizing but decided it would seem even more uncharacteristic than her churlish behavior the other day.

"Tell me what you hope to accomplish by sucking up to these not-quite-ready-for-prime-time players."

"I don't think that's much of a mystery," Sparkle replied. "How would it not benefit us to be on good terms with other business leaders in the community?"

"Other?"

"Yes. I regard you as a business leader, too. I think there could be opportunities for you to engage with some of these members as a mentor."

Lilah laughed heartily. "Honey, nobody in this county

regards me as anything approximating a leader."

Sparkle glanced at her briefly before returning her eyes to the road.

She had a nice ride. A Volvo X40 Recharge. Electric. Of course. It seemed like a very appropriate choice for her. Comfortable but practical. Efficient but still stylish. Sturdy but refined. Not small, but not large either. Kind of cute, actually.

All the things she was.

Lilah felt a twinge of panic about her assessment. *What the fuck was that?*

It had to be that near miss with Carol Jenkins. She'd make Grendel's mother look good.

"So," she began to cover her momentary lapse, "what misguided information leads you to think of me as any kind of leader? And on what planet do you think I would be effective mentoring anyone? Unless it's an advanced course in how to convert your crematorium into an air fryer for fun and profit. Because, hey? It's eco-friendly and eliminates a shit ton of saturated fats."

Sparkle actually smiled.

"Don't think I didn't see that lightbulb of yours go off," Lilah told her. "We're *not* trying it."

"Maybe not. But it is precisely the kind of innovation I was talking about."

"You call *that* innovation? Well, hell. I got a million ideas exactly like it."

"I am sure at least some of them are practical applications that we could implement."

"Do yourself a favor and don't share that opinion with Kay Stover. She tends to start swilling Maalox by the quart whenever

I try talking with her about my ideas for streamlining operations."

"Really? What kinds of ideas?"

"You don't want to know."

"Maybe I do."

"Let's talk about something of greater importance."

"Okay . . ."

"Will they be serving alcohol at this shindig or are all of our future leaders in danger of getting carded?"

Sparkle smiled again. "I daresay they'll have an open bar."

"Oh, goodie." She shot Sparkle a sidelong glance. "You *do* drink, don't you? I mean, *something* besides Crystal Light spiked with Old Grand-Dad?"

"Well. That *is* an acquired taste."

"I know. I found out the hard way. Dash and I killed the rest of Hambone's stolen bottle the night of the Crotty 500."

"Why on earth did you do that?"

"I could lie and invent an excuse, but the truth is easier. I was in the throes of an existential dilemma."

"How many guesses do I get in this game of professional *Jeopardy!*?"

"How many do you need?"

"Only one. I'll go with, 'What is Instagram?'"

"She shoots, she scores."

"I really am so sorry about that, Lilah. The continuing popularity of those posts defies logic—and all demographic trends."

"Well, when you're popular . . ."

"Is this why you asked me to drive today?"

"You were an honor student at St. Mary's, weren't you?"

"Who told you I went to St. Mary's?"

"One guess. See if your perfect record holds."

"Frankie?"

"Correct. You're on a roll. Why didn't you tell me you knew her?"

Sparkle shrugged. "It didn't seem relevant. And I doubted it would improve anything."

"Still. Small world, and all that."

They arrived at Milner's, and Sparkle parked the car.

"Ready to face the music?" she asked.

Lilah unclipped her seatbelt. "We who are about to dye salute you."

Sparkle was busy collecting her purse and notepad.

"You don't really think it'll be *that* bad, do you?"

"This?" Lilah jerked a thumb toward the restaurant where they could see smartly attired young professionals making their way toward the entrance. It was worth noting that every one of them was checking their cell phones while they walked. Probably looking at absurd new posts about *her*. "Hell, no. I was referring to dyeing more of those casket liners. I think we may have stumbled upon a cottage industry gold mine."

"I never know when you're serious."

"Good. That means my plan is working."

Inside the restaurant, they were directed to a large, private room located off the back of the main dining area. It was already full of fresh faced, earnest looking upstarts sporting two hundred-dollar haircuts. And every one of them could've been ripped from the pages of a J.Crew catalog.

"Jesus, take the wheel," Lilah muttered under her breath.

"Come on." Sparkle touched her arm. "Let's go mingle."

Mingle?

"I'd rather be stuffed with paraformaldehyde." When Sparkle looked confused, Lilah added, "Specially formulated sawdust—or, as Hambone calls it, kitty litter."

"Oh? Is that what you used to lend authenticity to that display at Party City?"

"Do I know you?"

"No. In fact, you really don't."

Lilah had been about to make a response when someone clapped her soundly on the shoulder.

"Lilah Stohler! There must be an 'r' in the month—or some kind of eclipse. What brings you out in the broad daylight?"

Lilah sighed and turned around to face the smiling countenance of Julius Kernodle, who owned a chain of medical supply stores that fleeced Medicare recipients across four counties. He had an idiot son by the same name who'd barely managed to graduate from High Point University—a boutique college that catered to idiot children of business scions—and who had joined him working the family grift, so papa Kernodle was just known around town as "Big Julie."

"Hi ya, Big Julie. Didn't expect to see you at this meet-n-greet. Got a hankering for some rubber duckie? I hear it's very good here."

Big Julie reared back on the heels of his wingtips and roared. "You always were the kidder in the family. Never forget that time you served us all a round of drinks you called 'Purple Jesus,' and your daddy grabbed the glasses away before we had a chance to taste 'em. What was that stuff again?"

"Introfiant arterial formaldehyde. I find its deep amethyst color to be very—festive."

Big Julie had been not-so-subtly staring at Sparkle the entire time they'd been talking. To be more accurate, he'd been staring at Sparkle's décolletage.

"Forgive my rudeness, Big Julie. This is my associate, Sparkle

Lee Sink. Sparkle, please meet Julius Kernodle, purveyor of all things that regularly exceed Part B coverages."

Sparkle extended a manicured hand. "How nice to meet you, Mr. Kernodle."

"Well, if you ain't the cutest little thing I seen in about a month of Sundays. Where they been hidin' you, Miss Sparkle?"

"It's actually Mrs. Sink. But thank you for the compliment. And I haven't been hiding, Mr. Kernodle. I assure you. I've just been busy learning the ins and outs of aftercare by spending a lot of time working with Lilah—*downstairs.*"

That seemed to take some of the wind out of the old lecher's sails. Not many of these geezers got hot and bothered at the prospect of getting horizontal with anyone who spent their days performing unspeakable acts beneath the fluorescent lights of a mortuary's embalming suite.

Lilah was pretty sure he'd soon be headed for the men's room to wash his hands—four or five times, minimum.

"Well, if that don't beat all." Big Julie craned his tree-stump-sized neck to look beyond them. "I see they're fixing to start this meeting, so I'd best go claim my seat. It was real nice to meet you, Mrs. Sink. See you around the chaparral, Lilah. Tell your daddy I said hey."

He hurried off.

"*Downstairs?*" Lilah quoted, once he was out of earshot.

"It seemed like . . . an *expeditious* choice."

"You think? Poor pathetic Lothario is probably going to soak his hand in Purell for a week."

"He'd do better to soak his delusions. What a creep."

"Get used to it, lamb chop. This here be the lion's den. You think I adopted this outward persona because black is so slimming?"

"I never actually thought about it."

"Right." Lilah laughed. "And I sell Mary Kay Cosmetics on the weekends. Come on, let's go find seats near the bar."

"Before we do . . . they don't serve Purple Jesus here, do they?"

Lilah took hold of her elbow. "There's only one way to find out."

The funeral for Beatrice "Toddy" Rock wasn't exceptional in any of the more dramatic ways they'd seen recently—except for one oddity. Well. Make that two.

It wasn't uncommon for folks in the South to have nicknames, but Mrs. Rock's family carried that practice to an extreme. And for some reason, the immediate family members all insisted on wearing name tags. Lilah had never seen so many Pals, Pim-Poms, Pickles, and Pancakes in one place in her life.

Although, in the case of the officiating pastor, Roscoe Handsy, the nickname "Pancake" could only be an improvement. When he'd approached her before the service and introduced himself as "Handsy," she had to fight an impulse to reply, "After a couple of drinks, I am, too."

The other oddity was something she'd had to seek Sparkle about to ask for an explanation. She found her in the kitchen, of course, pulling a tray of ginger chews out of the oven.

"That Toddy Rock service going on up front . . ." she began.

"Yes?"

"Why in the world is there an ironing board set up near the casket? Are they going to do some ritual straightening of her hair before interment?"

"Oh, that." Sparkle closed the oven door and began transferring the hot cookies to a cloth-lined basket. "Apparently, Ms. Rock was a champion at extreme ironing and was very proud of her successes. The family wanted to honor her by presenting her grand national trophy at the end of the service."

"Before we get to the trophy part, just what in the serious fuck is extreme ironing?"

"I'd never heard of it before, either. But during our consultation, the family explained that their aunt Toddy had always been a thrill-seeker and got into the sport naturally one time when her brother, Pickles, took her to a ham radio operators convention on Roan Mountain. Apparently, there were some extreme ironing practitioners competing out on one of the steeper balds, and Toddy became mesmerized watching one contestant complete seamless rotations on the yoke of a white dress shirt while balancing the board on a forty-five-degree rock outcropping."

Lilah narrowed her dark eyes. "You're totally making this shit up, right?"

"Oh, no. It's a real thing, I assure you. They even have national competitions—including the freestyle series, which Ms. Rock won back in 1996. I gather she ironed an entire pleated polyester midi that required damping—and utilizing the steam setting on her traditional one-iron."

"Do I want to hear where she was when this occurred?"

"Hanging upside down by a bungee cord, 876 feet in the air, over the New River Gorge in West Virginia. The ironing board was attached to her harness."

"Oh. My. *Fucking*. God. That wizened little woman up there in the Batesville Economy Silver?"

"That would be she."

"You said there's a . . . trophy?"

Sparkle nodded.

"Do I even want to know what that looks like?"

"Oh," Sparkle walked over to a large, velvet-covered box that sat on the break room table, "I think you do."

Sparkle opened the box and carefully withdrew a shiny bronze replica of a standard steam iron, replete with a wreath of embossed flames and a braided cord painted to resemble iron. It was fantastic and horrifying in nearly equal parts. Lilah felt like she was staring at an artifact that had been forged by the ubiquitous fires that swept through after a natural disaster—some obsolete Meghalayan Age tool that had been uncovered during the excavation for a new shopping mall in suburban Hoboken.

She held it in her hands gently, like a modern-day Rosetta Stone—an encoded message that, if ever translated, could explain the mysteries and contradictions of contemporary life.

"For the first time in my life, I have no words."

Sparkle nodded sympathetically. "I know exactly what you mean. Even Jerry Dean Crotty's life-sized Number 12 poster paled in comparison to this."

"Do you ever have those times when you feel like you showed up for work and ended up in *The Twilight Zone*?"

"Every single day."

"Yet, you continue to bake those cookies." Lilah returned the *objet* to its box. "What are they? Some kind of hedge against madness?"

"Why don't you try one and find out?" Sparkle picked up the still-steaming basket of ginger chews.

"I think I'll pass. I'm allergic to sweetness."

"Well, to answer your question, I suppose, for me, these

cookies *are* some kind of hedge against madness—against sadness, certainly. They're like a lifeline to something simpler: a time in my life when any fear, any hurt, any loss could be made better—even if just for a few minutes—by a big, soft ginger cookie. One baked especially for me by someone older and wiser—who understood my failings but loved me anyway."

"You can't say it much better than that." Lilah took the basket from her. "I'll take these to the Rock family for you."

Sparkle was surprised by her offer. "You don't have to do that."

"It's fine. Besides, I don't think it's safe for you to get too close to Pastor Handsy."

"Knock, knock." Lilah stood outside Kay Stover's open office door.

Kay looked up from her computer. "Come on in. I'm just cooking the books, like always."

"How's that bottom line shaping up?" Lilah dropped into a chair. "Still trending in the right direction?"

"My sources say yes."

"I see you're still using that Magic 8 Ball for all your prognostications."

"Why quit a winning strategy?"

"True. Wardell said you were looking for me?"

"I was." Kay nodded.

"I only stepped outside for two seconds. Why didn't you wait on me?"

"You know I can't stand being down there. All that white tile and fluorescent light give me the yips."

103

"Kay . . ."

"Don't even start with me."

"Do you whistle past the graveyard, too?"

"In fact, I do. At my age, the last thing I need to see is DoorDash in my rear view mirror."

"Afraid he might be chasing you down with a fresh bottle of Rita Kitty's elixir?"

"That mess is just foul. And you tell those Freeman brothers to stay the hell out of my stash."

"That reminds me," Lilah folded her arms. "Why do you keep that stuff hidden beneath the stairs, anyway?"

"Would you rather I keep it all in here, artfully lined up along the windowsill?"

Lilah considered Kay's windowsill. It was crowded with potted plants in various stages of neglect, and a dozen or so fossilized rocks—probably on hand so Kay could throw them at people who annoyed the piss out of her.

"I don't much care where you keep it. I'm just curious about why you have it. You've never been that much of a drinker."

"I'm not. But back in 2007, your daddy got the bright idea that we needed to have a bar set up for 'higher profile' clients." She made air quotes around higher profile. "He'd become addicted to that damn show, *Mad Men*, and got it in his head that all successful executives had drink carts in their offices. It was enough to drive your mother crazy. Clients started calling her at the salon to express concerns about poor Abel's 'problem.' After a month of that craziness, your mother came down here one afternoon, collected all the bottles out of his office, and stashed them in that old filing cabinet in the closet beneath the stairs."

Lilah laughed. "Didn't Dad ask what had happened to his makeshift bar?"

"Of course, he did." Kay nodded. "I made up some story about how we'd been busted for being in violation of about ten Alcoholic Beverage Control permits for dispensing liquor without a license—and that we were looking at fines of a thousand dollars per infraction if we continued. He sulked for a while, but soon moved on to his next obsession: switching our hearses out for models built on SUV chassis—so they could handle bigger caskets without damaging the floral sprays. As he put it, 'You know, Kay . . . more and more of our customers are eating steady diets of beans-n-taters, and we need to be able to accommodate the increased size of those XL caskets.'"

"Dear god. We should add espionage to your job description."

"Tell me about it." She sifted through some papers. "This is what I wanted to give you." She passed the documents over to Lilah. "We finally got the detailed offer of acquisition from FSI. It's pretty impressive. You need to take your time looking this over. I also sent a copy over to Kirk so he can review for any legal sticking points." Kay took up her worry stone.

That thing is like a tell, Lilah thought. *I guess we're getting to the rat killing.*

She flipped through the pages. "What do they say about personnel?"

"About what you'd expect. They'll centralize most functions regionally with the three other facilities they own in the state, so no on-site procurement or bookkeeping. They'll bring in contract embalmers but will keep the crematory—although they will likely want to replace the Freeman brothers with company types. And they want to keep Sparkle—and, of course, our resident Instagram influencer."

"Wait a minute." Lilah looked at her with alarm. "They'll get rid of Wardell, the Freeman brothers, and—you?"

"Pretty much. It's standard practice for these takeovers. They always want to place their own people and consolidate operations to cut overhead costs. I think, in our case, what they really want is a big ol' ginger-flavored slice of the cookie revenues *and* the chance to hitch their corporate cortege to the coattails of our reigning social media icon."

"That's the stupidest thing I've ever heard."

"Which part?"

"Take your pick. Losing the people who made this a success. Any of it. All of it."

Kay seemed amused. "Not sure I agree with your police work there, Marge."

"On, come on, Kay. For starters, why the hell would any staid and dour death industry stalwart want to taint its carefully crafted veneer of dignity by laying claim to the reigning poster child for *Beetlejuice?*"

"Can't help you with that one."

Lilah dropped the papers to her lap in frustration and closed her eyes. "Tell me what to do?"

Kay regarded her in silence for a few moments. "I always thought this day would come. But I imagined a different scenario when you finally asked me this question."

"Different? Like how?"

"I don't know." Kay shrugged. "You facing a seven to ten stretch in the crowbar hotel for committing some unspeakable act."

"Unspeakable act?" Lilah was intrigued. "What manner of unspeakable act?"

"I'll agree that in your case, the list could be fairly long. But take your pick. With you, it could be as simple as that time you pretended to cut a finger off the hand of a cadaver and ate it in front of a mortuary intern. Poor boy was so busy laying a patch out of here, he never did find out it was a Vienna sausage."

"I remember that. Rita Kitty had brought a crockpot full of those disgusting things for our holiday party. Weren't they cooked in grape jelly or something equally noxious?"

"I don't know." Kay mused. "Some people say they're addictive—like having sex with the lights on."

"Okay. That's too much information."

"Oh, grow up, Lilah. Don't tell me I offended your delicate sensibilities. Have you never tried it?"

"Kay? I have zero desire to discuss my sex life with you—or anyone. And besides, if sex with the lights on is anything remotely like Vienna sausages marinating in a vat of grape jelly, I'll happily pass on the experience."

"What a weenie." Kay smiled at her own joke. "No pun intended."

"Why this sudden prurient interest in my private life?"

"Oh?" Kay leaned forward and rested her chin on her hand. "Do you mean to imply that you have a sex life?"

"What the hell has gotten into you? Are you binge eating those ginger chews? It's widely known that imbibing too many nightshade derivatives can exacerbate IBS."

"Since when does irritable bowel syndrome lead to well-intentioned curiosity about a colleague's romantic inclinations?"

Lilah was uncomfortable as fuck with the turn the conversation had taken, and Kay knew her well enough to realize it and press her advantage.

"Not that I owe you any kind of response, but you'll be glad to know that I *have* no romantic inclinations."

"That is good news. It means you'll have no problems with this."

Lilah smelled a rat. "With what?"

Kay passed her a fat envelope. "Here are all the travel documents for your trip to Vegas for the NFDA convention and expo next week."

"Okay. What's the catch?"

"You're not going alone."

Oh, Jesus Christ . . . "You cannot be serious."

"Do I not look serious?"

"Kay."

"Lilah."

"I absolutely refuse to attend a death show shackled to Little Miss Sunshine, who'll be sure to have a fit of the vapors every two seconds. It's. Not. Happening."

"It's. Already. Happened. Suck it up, cupcake."

"Kay. You know what those conventions are like. They're nothing but hookup fests tinged with quasi-romantic hints of necrophilia. The only reason I'm going is because of the fucking keynote I have to deliver at a breakout session. I do not need a fluffy tagalong to keep out of harm's way."

"I think Sparkle can handle herself just fine without your intervention."

"Even if that's true, give me one good reason why she should go?"

"You're holding it in your lap. FSI has already stated that they want to include her in their future plans for this mortuary—and others. So, it behooves us to sweeten the pot by getting her greater exposure to the marketplace."

"I think you might be getting ahead of yourself. I haven't decided to sell yet."

"Oh, you're going to sell. I'd stake my Swingline stapler on it."

"What makes you so sure?"

"Once you have time to review the numbers they're tossing

around, you'll realize that taking this deal means you'll be walking away with enough cash to do whatever strikes your dark fancy—including opening one of those bizarre human composting facilities you're so enamored with."

"Even if that were true—and I'm not saying it is—I couldn't do that here."

"It's true that they'll hit you with a non-compete clause that will prevent you from starting any like business within sixty miles of one of their facilities."

"Added to the fact that natural organic reduction is illegal in North Carolina."

"Probably not for long," Kay added.

"I'm not as confident about that as you are. People can drive past a squirrel decomposing on the road every day and not give it a second thought. But any talk about allowing a human being to return to the earth in the same natural and unfettered way stirs up all of our deeply enmeshed, irrational fears and incites a reflexive retreat to the safe harbor of arcane religious teachings that elevate death to some kind of sacrament."

"Do yourself a favor when you speak with the FSI people and keep these opinions under wraps—at least until the ink is dry on the sales agreement."

"I already told you that I'm not sure I'll take their offer."

"Just remember my advice. And be nice to Sparkle. She's not the lightweight you take her for. She's got great instincts, a good mind and a bigger heart—all of which are assets to this business."

Lilah got up. "Whatever you say, boss. But you shouldn't continue to discount yourself in the Stohler's success story. It's been your steady hand on the tiller that has led us to this lauded land of opportunity."

"Uh huh. I'll take some modest credit for the colossal task of balancing the books here for the past three decades, but I am in no way responsible for the seismic changes our perky little St. Mary's grad has wrought during her brief tenure here. Nor am I responsible for your unique contributions."

"Mine? Pray tell what those might be?"

"Seen today's Instagram posts yet?"

"No."

"You'll get my gist later on, then."

"Great." Lilah left Kay's office imbued with a host of sinking feelings she knew would do battle for ascendancy throughout another sleepless night.

Rufina Magdalena Strub

November 30, 1933 – December 1, 2023

Rufina Magdalena Strub, 90, of Clemmons,
NC, passed away on December 1, 2023. She
was born in Baltimore, Maryland, to the late
John Paul and Deloria Matthews.

Rufina was a very large, loving, and
devoted woman who cherished her family
and her church community. She found great
joy in making chicken pies for Jesus and took
pride in teaching other Christians the fine art
of crimping the pie crust. Rufina's warm and
nurturing nature endeared her to all who knew
her and ate of her gravy.

She is survived by her son Ted, her
daughter Patty, and her stepdaughter
Betty. Rufina was also blessed with
nine grandchildren, twenty-two great-
grandchildren, and thirteen great-great-
grandchildren all of whom enjoyed her
chicken pie and brought immense happiness
to her life.

Rufina was preceded in death by her
brother, two husbands, and her parents.

Rufina was a blessed member of Calvary Moravian Church. A private memorial service will be held to honor her life and celebrate her favorite recipes at Stohler's Funeral Home in Winston-Salem.

Posted by Stohler's Funeral Home, Winston-Salem, NC

Smoke and Mirrors

For some reason, Kay Stover had seen fit to upgrade their seats on the long flight to Vegas. Lilah didn't mind the extravagance. She had long legs, and it was nice to be able to stretch them out—especially on a six hour flight. They were flying on Delta, so they had the requisite short layover in Atlanta—which gave proof to the adage that even if you *died* on a Delta flight, you had to stop over in Atlanta on your way to heaven. The other benefit of having a seat near the front of the plane was that it shielded Lilah from the enterprising stares—and cell phones—of potential Instagram groupies.

More or less.

Their seats were situated only a few rows behind the forward lavatory, and more than one passenger made good use of the return trip to try and sneak a clandestine photo of the infamous Black Bird, who apparently had a Sky Miles account, and flew Delta on longer trips to rack up points for use on those international trips foretelling wholesale death and destruction.

Maybe it was a lot simpler, and she was just interested in those free drinks . . .

Their premium seats *did* come with a free cocktail, which Lilah didn't waste time waiting to order—although Finlandia was hardly her idea of an upgraded spirit. It was more like something she'd find stashed in Rita Kitty's makeup bag. Still . . . any port in a storm.

Sparkle was less adventurous and went with a glass of indifferent white wine. *Of course.*

Lilah would've even managed to halfway enjoy her drink if there hadn't been an obnoxious ten-year-old seated behind her, rhythmically banging his foot against her seatback. She did her best to ignore it for the first twenty-five minutes of the flight but gave up when he slammed into the back of her seat so hard it caused her to slosh half of her drink all over the armrest separating her from Sparkle.

"Goddamnittofuckinghell!" She tried to brush the liquid off her sleeve and handed what remained of her cocktail to Sparkle. "This shit ends now." She unfastened her seatbelt and prepared to stand up to confront the passengers in the row behind them.

Sparkle quickly reached out a hand to stop her.

"No. Let me do this, okay?"

Lilah only consented to allow Sparkle to attempt to deal with the nuisance since she was seated by the window and didn't relish the idea of having to climb over her to get out.

Sparkle stood in the aisle with one arm extended along the headrest of her seat and addressed the pair of travelers behind them, using her sweetest Southern voice. Lilah had to work not to take advantage of the close-range opportunity to consider the full-length view of her *assets.*

"Hi there," Sparkle said to the adult traveling with the youngster behind Lilah. "My name's Sparkle, and I'm sitting here in front of you on this plane. If you don't mind, I'd like to speak with your little boy?" When the parent consented, Sparkle directed her comments to the energetic youngster. "Long plane rides are really boring, huh? It's hard to be stuck in your seat, I know. But I have to tell you something. You are kicking the back of my friend's seat with your feet. It really bothers her, and I need you to stop. And I have an idea that might help you with that. Why don't you change seats with me so you can meet her and let her tell you about her job? That would be different. She works in the basement of a funeral home and makes dead people ready to be buried. Wouldn't that be a fun thing to learn about to take your mind off kicking her seat?"

Lilah couldn't see the little boy's face, but she clearly heard him say he'd stop kicking the seat if he didn't have to meet the scary lady.

Sparkle thanked them both and asked the little boy if she could buy him a special treat, like some Pringles or a coloring book. He took her up on both.

"That was a pretty damn good intervention," Lilah complimented her when she reclaimed her seat.

"Don't thank me. You provided the real incentive." She pushed the call button to ask the flight attendant to deliver the bribery booty to their companion. She also ordered Lilah another Finlandia to replenish the one she'd mostly ended up wearing.

"That *was* a rather inspired idea. I'm glad I wore one of my most intimidating mix-n-match ensembles from the Grim Reaper collection."

"I think you'll be happy to hear that I packed more somber attire for the conference. I didn't want to stand out like a sore thumb—or spray of zinnias at a December funeral."

115

"Decorum *is* so very overlooked these days," Lilah said thoughtfully. "Especially at those NASCAR-themed funerals."

"Death in the fast lane," Sparkle quipped.

Lilah laughed. "Why aren't you this funny at work?"

Sparkle regarded her with an amused look.

"I guess I'm still new to gallows humor."

"Stick with me, kid. You'll be an ardent practitioner in no time."

"Oh, I will. That is, unless you ditch me as soon as we reach the conference venue."

Lilah hoped her face didn't show how near the truth Sparkle's suggestion was. Was the woman some kind of clairvoyant? Or was Lilah's plan of attack simply that transparent?

"Why, Mrs. Sink . . . I'd never do a thing like that."

"Please don't call me that."

"Why not?" Lilah was surprised. "I thought that's what you wanted to be called."

"Only by lecherous old men with more arrogance than sense."

"Oh, I wouldn't have called Kernodle's attentions arrogant."

"No? What *would* you have called them?"

"Aspirational comes to mind. Clearly the old geezer thought he was tall enough for this ride."

Sparkle actually blushed. It wasn't unbecoming.

"Did I embarrass you?" Lilah asked. "I'd apologize, but it's the truth."

When Sparkle didn't make any response, Lilah decided to go for broke. "Mom told me you'd been married and are recently divorced. I'm sorry about that."

"Do I need to ask why you were discussing my private life with your mother?"

"Probably not."

"Why is every conversation with you like a fencing match?"

"Is it?"

"Yes." Sparkle nodded. "And usually without protective tips."

"Combat rules. My favorite."

"I'm sure it's no accident that you haven't answered my question."

"Which one?"

"The one about your interest in my private life."

Lilah considered her response. "I wouldn't call it interest, exactly. It's more like curiosity."

"About?"

The flight attendant appeared with Lilah's replacement vodka tonic. The cheap airline booze must've been giving her false courage. She weighed her options. She could plead ignorance and say it was just anecdotal information shared during a general discussion of how her father came to hire Sparkle—which was the truth. Or she could indulge a whim to be a bit more daring and ask Sparkle to address some of the seeming contradictions in her character.

Okay. One of the contradictions. There was that whole movie thing, too . . .

She went with a third option: changing the subject.

"Ever been to Vegas before?"

Sparkle looked genuinely confused but chose to answer her question anyway. "Yes. Once."

"Convention? Or spring break gambling trip with your sorority sisters?"

"I'll do you a favor and ignore that last part. *Neither.* I got married there."

"Oh." Lilah hadn't expected that response. "Would you like

another glass of wine?"

Sparkle glanced down at her nearly half-full glass. "Why?"

"Because I think this is going to be a longer conversation."

In fact, it was.

Sparkle ended up telling Lilah about how she'd met Tommy Sink right after graduation and had made the gargantuan mistake of accompanying him on a buying trip to Las Vegas during the Home Furnishing Market Show. Tommy was then employed by Furnitureland South, the largest retail furniture store in the United States. One misguided night, after too many margaritas, they ended up standing before Elvis in one of Sin City's all-night wedding chapels.

"To this day, I cannot think about that without mortification. Thankfully, I never showed my parents what passed for the wedding photo. We looked like two drunken deer, standing in the high beams of an oncoming tractor trailer."

"How long did it last?" Lilah asked.

"Not long. I knew it was a mistake and so did he. Stupidly, we tried to make it work. But it was pointless. Neither of us was temperamentally suited for that kind of relationship."

Lilah was tempted to ask what kind of relationship Sparkle thought she *was* suited for—but chose the better part of valor. For once.

"I'm sorry that happened," she said instead. "It can't have been easy."

"No. It wasn't. What about you?"

"Me?"

"Yes. Ever been married?"

Lilah gave a bitter-sounding laugh. "Not even close."

"Forgive the impertinence, but that seems hard to believe."

"I know, right? I mean, who wouldn't jump at the chance

to pursue an intimate relationship with a goth wannabe who spends her days dealing with Dexter's leftovers?"

Sparkle had been looking at her intently. "I wouldn't exactly call your appearance goth."

"Oh, really?" Lilah was intrigued. "How *would* you describe it?"

"Maybe something approximating . . . Stygian chic."

"Oh, God." Lilah laughed merrily—which actually sounded more like an undulating vibrato played on the D string of a bass cello. "You should post that on Instagram."

"Don't think I haven't thought about it."

An alert *bonged* and the captain announced that they were making their initial descent into Atlanta.

Lilah knew this bout of easy camaraderie was at an end—at least for this leg of the journey. And that was beyond okay with her. She preferred keeping unexpected distractions like Sparkle Lee Sink at arm's length.

And she found that having to admit to the fact that Sparkle had *become* a distraction was the most distracting thing of all.

Welcome to a long day's journey into night, Lilah told herself as they crossed the threshold to Bally's Hotel and Casino, where they were immediately plunged from the blinding light and scorching heat of the desert into a climate-controlled, subzero no-man's land where time ceased to exist. There was no day or night once you passed through the revolving doors. There was only more of everything: more food, more drink, more noise, more miles of hideous carpet, and more waitresses wearing skimpy, low-cut tops and fishnet hosiery than you could shake a stick at.

And there was not a single wall clock to be found anyplace in the entire 3.2 million square feet the titanic monument to bad taste and excess took up on the Las Vegas strip.

Even though the iconic hotel that had staked its claim to a coveted spot in the city's highest-priced real estate market for decades had undergone massive renovation and was in the process of changing its name to "Horseshoe," the air quality inside its gilded walls was unchanged. It was just as thick with stale cigarette smoke and disappointed hopes as it had always been.

"God, I hate this place," Lilah muttered as they rolled their suitcases toward the check-in kiosk. It was notable that, unless you were looking for a free cocktail, high-priced companionship, or direction to one of the gaming tables, actual working personnel at the hotel were next to nonexistent. Bally's was essentially a self-serve facility.

It was a Vegas mainstay that you paid a premium for people not to care. Or to notice you, for that matter. This was the prime directive that underpinned the sacred pledge that what happened in Vegas, stayed in Vegas.

Just like Sparkle's ill-fated marriage.

They had to cross through the casino to get to the elevator bank. In fact, they had to cross through the casino to get to just about anything. It was part of the grand design of these places. They were like those old hand-held wooden mazes she played with as a child—the ones you had to rotate and twist to get a marble to roll around obstacles to find a way out. She understood that this design was intended to keep unsuspecting hotel guests on the gaming floor so they might stop and indulge in an innocent game—or fifty—at one of the tables or ubiquitous slot machines that whistled, flashed, and strobed all along the serpentine pathways that snaked through the cavernous space.

Sparkle had to stop several times along the way to respond to panicked text messages from Kay Stover. Apparently, preparations for the Rufina Strub service had gone off the rails—literally.

"We've got trouble back in River City," she shared with Lilah. "Kay estimates that there might be as many as one hundred and eighty attendees. I gather Mrs. Strub was very beloved by her Moravian congregation."

"We've got enough chairs in storage to set up for that. What is it now?"

"I gather that Mrs. Strub's family is determined to celebrate her life by giving everyone who attends the service a generous serving of her signature life accomplishment."

"Which is?"

"According to Kay, it's chicken pie ..."

Lilah chewed the inside of her cheek.

"... gravy," Sparkle added.

"Did you say *gravy?*"

Sparkle nodded.

"What the hell are they supposed to do with gravy? Toast her life by drinking a generous slug of it over ice with a jalapeño and celery garnish?"

"Rita Kitty has some thoughts."

"Oh, I am *sure* she does."

"Apparently, Hambone's men's group makes the Brunswick stew at his church, and he has access to one of the twenty-gallon cauldrons they use. Rita Kitty thought he could set one of those up in the parking lot to make sure they have enough to go around. Apparently, they're propane-fired so there won't be any drop cords."

Lilah closed her eyes. "Oh, dear god."

"Kay just wants to keep us in the loop."

"Yeah. I'm sure she's already been on the horn with Kirk to discuss the limits of our liability." Lilah took hold of her elbow. "Let's go find our rooms. We can sort this looming mess out later."

As they made their way across the seizure-inducing décor of the lobby, Lilah began to notice something out of the ordinary—even more out of the ordinary than the usual out of the ordinary it was customary to encounter at a casino in Vegas. There were people dressed in *animal* costumes . . . very good ones . . . energetically pulling levers and pushing buttons on slot machines with their puffy hosts of furry paws.

What fresh hell is this?

Apparently, Sparkle had noticed the strange phenomenon at about the same time. Lilah felt a tug on her sleeve and Sparkle bent close to whisper, "Do you see that giant . . . *rabbit* . . . over there at the blackjack table? Or am I hallucinating?"

"No. I see it, too. The Horseshoe must have lower standards than Bally's had. I mean—some of the regulars here are sleazeballs—but catering to Leporidae is a bridge too far. I only see four of them right now, but I predict that by morning, they'll outnumber all the big-bellied Jersey Teamsters in here by about two hundred."

"Oh, look!" Sparkle pointed at a roulette wheel with excitement. "Isn't that Avatar Kyoshi?"

"What is that—and where am I looking?"

"Over there," Lilah pointed. "Standing next to Harley Quinn."

Lilah squinted in the direction Sparkle was pointing. "No. I think that's Boy George."

Sparkle slugged her on the arm. "I gather you're not a fan of anime?"

"Is that a country singer?"

"Oh, my *god*. Come on. Let's find the elevators."

They passed a large placard mounted on a tripod, announcing that the hotel was proud to be hosting the Annual Cosplay America Conference.

"Okay," Sparkle observed. "That accounts for the costumes."

"I wonder who in this establishment thought it was a good idea to book these events together—Hunter S. Thompson?"

Ten minutes later, they'd finally made their circuitous way to a bank of elevators that led to the Jubilee tower rooms. Once they were aboard, Lilah pointed out a placard that was posted inside the elevator doors.

IF YOUR HEADPIECES ARE MORE THAN SEVEN FEET HIGH, PLEASE REMOVE THEM BEFORE LEAVING THE LOBBY AND ENTERING THE ELEVATORS.

"I guess they don't want them mistaken for any of the main stage showgirls," Lilah quipped.

They'd been assigned rooms 2207 and 2209, respectively. If Lilah remembered the mind-numbingly slow speed of the elevators accurately, that meant they were billeted on a high enough floor to require packing trail mix for sustenance during the long trips to and from the conference venue.

As they walked the absurdly long corridor to reach their rooms, they passed at least five more cosplay practitioners. Their elaborate costumes made them look eerily like cartoon characters that had come to life—right down to a scantily clad and extremely well-endowed Asuna the Bunny Girl, who was like a cross between Betty Boop and Debbie Harry—during her years working for *Playboy*.

"Clearly I need to watch more cartoons," Lilah whispered.

Sparkle rolled her eyes and tugged her forward. "Come on. It can't be much farther."

After yet two more minutes of walking, Sparkle asked Lilah what the plan for the afternoon was.

"Do we unpack and head back downstairs to the convention area? Try to connect with some of the other attendees?"

"You're joking, right? By now, any of those coffin-dodgers who are already here are either drunk and passed out over slot machines, or drunk and passed out over call girls they met on their way to the slot machines."

"I hope you're joking."

"Sadly, I'm not."

"That's . . . disappointing."

"Had higher standards for these stalwarts of eternal security, did you?"

"Can we at least tour the exhibits?"

"Those won't open until tomorrow."

Sparkle looked at her watch. "It's only two o'clock. What are we going to do all afternoon?"

Lilah was tempted to say she wanted to get a hunting license and go scouting for that bunny named Asuna. Instead, she made a more magnanimous choice—one she knew in her viscera she'd live to regret.

"Do you want to try to get into a show?"

Sparkle's eyes widened. "They have those at two in the afternoon?"

"There is no two in the afternoon in here. There is no time at all. There is only one never-ending, amphetamine-fueled, psychotic carousel ride beneath the big tent at the Fellini circus called Las Vegas." When Sparkle didn't reply, she added, "That means, yes. There *are* shows here at two in the afternoon."

They'd reached their rooms. Finally.

Sparkle swiped her key card and the green light illuminated. When she pushed the door open, she gasped.

"What is it?" Lilah asked. "Is the room not made up?"

"No. It's . . ." She didn't finish her statement.

"Let me see." Lilah pushed past her to look inside. "*Oh, my god.* Well. I see that Kay scored us rooms in the bordello wing of the hotel."

The room had walls covered in bright crimson, faux-velvet flocked wallpaper accented with shiny gold interlocking circles. The carpet was a darker shade of red with random slashes of taupe running through it. To make matters worse, the round bed had a cream-colored, padded headboard that took up half of one wall.

"Is that a . . . *spa tub* . . . in the middle of the room?" Sparkle asked with wonder.

"Yes. Yes. I daresay it is. It seems the Horseshoe renovation architects hail from the literal end of the *en suite* gene pool."

"Oh, my."

"Well. When in Rome. Or Gomorrah, as the case may be. Get settled and give me a ring when you're ready to head back downstairs. We'll look around and find one of the Vegas hallmarks to distract us."

"You mean like Wayne Newton?"

Lilah looked at her with amusement. "I doubt it. Wayne Newton is one of the headliners in the Embalming and Restorative Arts Seminar tomorrow. I was thinking of something less cringe worthy—like maybe a comedy show? We're stuck inside this fun house for the next two days. Why not stock up on some good coping strategies to survive it? You could think of it as psychological carb loading."

Sparkle did not disagree. Twenty minutes later, she tapped on Lilah's door.

Lilah opened it with a flourish and stepped back so Sparkle could see that the room was an exact replica of Sparkle's.

"Look—twins! Who said you couldn't step into the same river twice?"

"Dear god. Do you think every room on the floor is like this?"

"Probably. They tend to command steep discounts on these materials."

"I wonder how many miles of this wallpaper the hotel has?" Sparkle asked.

"Probably enough to stretch from here to Lake Mead, where its regrettable designer should be rewarded by resting in peace wearing a brand new pair of concrete boots."

Sparkle looked at her quizzically.

"Where there is no hope, the people perish."

"By the way," Sparkle said, "I turned on the spa tub, just to see if it worked."

"And?"

"Oh, it does. It has colored lights that strobe. Apparently, you can sync them via Bluetooth to your Spotify playlist."

"See? *Innovation.* We should totally steal that idea to add to the options roster for our next NASCAR-themed funeral. Imagine a casket that plays 'God Bless the USA,' with deluxe red, white, and blue chromatherapy lighting." Lilah was lost in thought for a moment as she considered her brainstorm. "I wonder what Kay would say."

Sparkle smirked at her. "Probably $6,950."

"She's a wise woman."

"You'll get no argument from me on that one."

Lilah held the door open for her. "If we head down now we might just make a five thirty show."

"Five-thirty? It's barely three o'clock."

They began to retrace their steps toward the elevators.

"I told you about these elevators, right? They're slower than Dante's descent through the nine circles of hell. And, ironically, when the doors open you emerge into an oddly similar place."

Lilah hadn't exaggerated. Their elevator stopped on virtually every floor during the long ride down. An endless succession of what Lilah called slam-and-click businessmen, tired-looking tourists with hyperactive kids, more businessmen accompanied by high-priced afternoon companions, and all manner of woodland beings—some dutifully carrying their headpieces—got on and off their car as it made its halting journey down twenty-two floors to the casino level.

Once they emerged from the elevator, a cacophony of human, mechanical and digital noises hit them like a blast from a thousand loudspeakers.

"And they call New York the city that never sleeps? How can it possibly be like this twenty-four hours a day?"

"My mentor in mortuary science always said there are only *two* kinds of people in the world," Lilah explained, "the walking dead, and the ones who bury them."

"That seems . . . limiting."

"How so?"

"I don't know. It probably leaves out at least one other state of being."

"Such as?"

Sparkle thought about it. "What about professional accordion players?"

"Okay. *Three* kinds of people."

The approached an illuminated "entertainment" kiosk.

"Now we search for something that won't bankrupt us, make our ears bleed, or dupe us into sitting through a floor show headlined by twenty-five of the strip's best Cher impersonators. And note to self: none of them can wear their headdresses on those elevators, either."

Lilah began scrolling through what appeared to be an endless list of entertainments and venues.

"Let me know if you see anything that strikes your fancy—as long as it doesn't involve anything related to Madam Tussaud's or Elvis."

Sparkle couldn't quite conceal her wince. Lilah immediately felt like a cad.

"Shit. I'm sorry. Nice way to make you feel right at home. Not."

"It's okay."

"No, it isn't. I can be such an ass sometimes. I'm sorry for my lack of sensitivity. I wasn't even thinking about what you shared."

"It's really okay. Don't worry about it." Sparkle pointed at something on the screen in an obvious attempt to divert attention from her reaction to Lilah's faux pas. "An illusionist? How about that? Have you ever seen one?"

"You mean besides Miss Rita Kitty and her Technicolor dream kit?"

Sparkle smiled. "Yes. Besides that."

"Only once. When I was about seven, my father took me to see a magician who was performing at the Dixie Classic Fair. He mostly did bad card tricks. It only took me about two minutes to realize he was using a pinochle deck. I gathered that twist made it a lot easier for him to identify the face cards most of his volunteers randomly selected."

"Never since then? Some of them are real showmen."

"I'm game if you are. Pick one."

They spent a few minutes reading the various show descriptions.

"How about this one? Nathan Burton. I've seen him on some late night TV shows. He's pretty entertaining to watch. And his act includes a stable of showgirls who could give that Asuna character you're so fascinated with a run for her money."

Lilah chose to ignore Sparkle's insinuation.

On the other hand—who cared what she thought?

"This says his show is at Planet Hollywood."

"How far a walk is that?" Sparkle asked.

"This is Vegas. Nobody walks. We'll get a cab."

"Won't that blow our per diem?"

"Do you think I care? Obviously, Kay Stover wasn't too concerned about making us do this trip on the cheap. Upgrades to business class. High-roller rooms with the premium hooker upgrade. I don't think she'll quibble with cab fare to another hotel."

"Wait a minute." Sparkle was reading something on the kiosk. "This says that Planet Hollywood is a six-minute walk from Bally's via a walkway through Paris."

"Then let's hoof it."

They wound their way through the casino en route to the walkway that led through Paris, the Las Vegas monument to the City of Lights. They tried to pay attention to the hundreds of eating establishments they passed along the way, hoping they'd find an appealing dinner destination.

"What about this place?" Sparkle pointed out a restaurant that seemed to be doing a robust business.

"Luke's Lobster?" Lilah asked.

It had a giant sandwich board out front that proclaimed, *Get your own Noah's Ark for $52 at Luke's.*

"I wonder what a Noah's ark is?" Sparkle asked.

"I'm guessing—two of everything?"

"Makes sense, I guess."

They walked on.

"Although, this special does beg the age-old question," Lilah observed.

"What's that?"

"Noah had three sons. Shem, Ham, and Japheth. Right?"

"That's what I recall from Sunday school."

"So doesn't it make you question the veracity of a story that has an obedient Jew naming one of his sons after breakfast meat?"

"I don't think the proscription on pork products had been handed down yet."

"You can be a real buzzkill sometimes."

A twenty-something walking toward them carrying a shopping bag with *Planet Hollywood Miracle Mile* emblazoned on it stopped dead in her tracks, right in front of them.

"Ohmygod! The Black Bird of Chernobyl!" she exclaimed, before raising her cell phone and snapping half a dozen photos of Lilah.

"*Seriously?*" Lilah cried out, belatedly trying to shield her face.

"Thank you!" the young woman gushed before hurrying along her way.

"I am so totally fucking over this thing," Lilah complained.

"Look on the bright side," Sparkle suggested. "Maybe you can ask the illusionist to make it disappear."

"What? Instagram?"

"Why not?"

"As if. I'd have better luck asking for world peace."

The line at Planet Hollywood was only modestly long, so it didn't take them long to purchase their tickets and find their seats inside the monster-sized theater.

Lilah overheard dozens of whispered *Oh my gods* and *Holy fucks* as they made their way to their seats.

I had to be in my dotage to think this was a good way to kill time, she thought.

Before the house lights dimmed, Sparkle quickly responded to another text from Kay Stover. Apparently, Hambone's inspired solution for cooking up twenty gallons of chicken pie gravy meant he'd first have to stew up thirty to forty whole chickens to get enough broth. According to Kay, he and Gee String figured it just made sense to go ahead and move the entire Walburg Baptist Church Brunswick stew operation from the church parking lot to Stohler's. Hambone also thought maybe some of the folks attending the Strub service might like to take home a quart of the triad's best stew.

"I guess Kay found out about it this morning when she arrived for work. She said the parking lot was full of pickup trucks and overweight men swilling coffee and eating donut holes."

Lilah was incredulous. "I can't even . . ."

"What do you want me to tell her?"

"Maybe that there's a redeye flight leaving Greensboro for Las Vegas at midnight tonight?" Lilah slowly shook her head. "Tell her to call Dad and see if he can come pinch hit."

"Lilah?"

"What?"

"Kay said your father was one of the men there this morning. Apparently, he brought the donut holes."

"Of *course* he did. Why couldn't he have picked this damn morning to get locked in his garden shed?"

"What?"

"Never mind. It's a long story. Tell Kay to handle it. She has carte blanche to figure out how."

"Roger." Sparkle sent the text and dutifully turned off her phone as the house lights began to dim.

"Thank God. Now no one can see me," Lilah whispered to Sparkle. "I can bask in blissful mortification under the comfort of darkness—as is my custom since I had the singular bad judgment to take over that house of horrors."

Sparkle couldn't make any reply because Burton's show began—and got off with a bang. He and his crew launched right into a series of monster illusions, making one of his shapely assistants—Sparkle had not misled Lilah about them— disappear and reappear with dazzling lights, upbeat music, and impressive pyrotechnics. His routine was seamless and deftly engineered to hold the short attention spans of a Vegas audience. After twenty-five minutes of fantastic feats and large-scale illusions, Burton took a brief intermission, and the house lights came back up.

"It's difficult to imagine what he can do to top all of that," Sparkle observed.

"Maybe he can resuscitate the June Taylor Dancers?"

"I have no idea what you're talking about . . ."

"I know. They were a bit before your time."

"And yours, too, I'll bet."

"What can I tell you?" Lilah replied. "I like to live in the past."

"Because the present is so terrifying?"

"Maybe. But not as terrifying as the future."

"True," Sparkle agreed. She held up her cell phone. "Should we see if proof of your Vegas adventures has made it to Instagram yet?"

"Let's not and say we did."

"You have no sense of adventure."

"Trolling Instagram is *not* adventurous. Adventurous is more like—ironing a pleated skirt while hanging by a bungee cord above the New River Gorge. Or playing cards with Kay Stover."

Sparkle shook her head. "I have to say that you're a lot more fun away from the funeral home."

"You know, you could probably cross-stitch that onto a tea towel, open up an Etsy store, and make a fortune selling them for $9.99 each."

"See? That's exactly my point."

"What point?"

"You. You're so much more—accessible."

Before Lilah could make another snappy reply, the house lights blinked to signify that the show was resuming.

For the second half of his program, Burton chose to bring the tone of the performance down from the high tech stratosphere and focus on audience participation. He approached the apron of the stage and walked down a short flight of steps into the audience.

"Ladies and gentlemen," he proclaimed. "We have a bona fide celebrity in our midst." He held a cell phone aloft. "How many of you are devoted followers of the infamous Black Bird of Chernobyl, who has been blazing a trail across Instagram feeds for the past month?"

The crowd went wild with applause.

"Well, as fate would have it, she's right here in our audience."

The roar from the crowd was deafening.

Lilah wanted nothing more than to disappear into her seat and pray for retro-abortion . . . whether for Burton or herself—she didn't much care. But it was too late. A key light from above had discovered her in the audience, and Burton was approaching where she was seated.

"Oh, dear god . . ." Sparkle looked at her with concern. "What are you going to do?"

"Do?" Lilah looked back at her. "In the words of old Pappy Stohler, I think it's time to make hay while the sun shines."

She got to her feet and greeted Nathan Burton with her best Diva of Death scowl.

Two minutes later, she was standing beside him on the stage feigning complete indifference while he set up his next stunt. He withdrew a deck of cards from his jacket and showed them to her.

"Card tricks? Seriously, Nathan? Can't you do better than that? These seats cost forty-six bucks." She faced the crowd. "Am I right?"

The audience clapped and cheered.

"Okay," Burton agreed, good-naturedly. "Dealer's choice. Whattaya have in mind, Black Bird?"

"How about you test your mettle on these?" Lilah withdrew a small package from the inside pocket of her own blazer.

Burton took it from her and looked it over with surprise. He gave her a sly smile before holding it up to the audience.

"Ladies and gentlemen . . . behold! A tarot deck."

The crowd whooped and cheered.

"So," he faced Lilah. "You travel with a deck of tarot cards in your jacket?"

"Doesn't everyone?" Lilah replied in her best Lorraine Bracco voice.

More whoops and hollers.

"Okay." Burton smiled a big Vegas smile and began shuffling the cards. "I'm game." When he finished, he fanned them out face down and held them out to Lilah. "Draw a card—any card. Look it over carefully and don't let me see it. I'll turn around so you can show it to our audience."

Lilah did as instructed and withdrew a shiny, oversized card. When she showed it to the audience, there were peals of laughter, but no one gave away her choice.

"Finished?" Burton asked.

"Oh, I am way beyond finished, Nathan."

He turned back around to face her. "Now place your card back into the deck.

"It's really okay, Nathan," Lilah drawled. "I've seen this movie before." She deftly replaced her card.

Burton reshuffled the deck. "Now there's one more crucial step."

"Of course there is."

He placed the deck face down on a table.

One of Burton's buxom double D assistants walked forward carrying a small tray. He retrieved a canister containing some kind of powder and proceeded to use it to liberally dust the top of the deck. Then he picked up a book of matches and struck one. When he dropped the match onto the deck of cards, a huge plume of rainbow-colored smoke shot up toward the rafters.

The crowd oohed and aahed.

When the smoke had dissipated, Burton smiled hugely at Lilah.

"Are you ready to see your card?"

"I am," Lilah replied. "Believe me when I tell you it's what I live for."

He approached his full-figured assistant and said, "Brittany? May I?"

"Of course, Nathan." she cooed before tucking her arms behind her back and thrusting her generous endowments forward.

Burton delicately reached into the recesses of her bodice and withdrew a shiny card.

The crowd went wild.

He showed the card to Lilah. "Is this your card?"

"Well, shiver me timbers, Nathan—it sure is."

Nathan showed the card to the audience. "Ladies and gentlemen, let the record show that the Black Bird of Chernobyl chose *Death!*" He winked at Lilah. "A somewhat ironic choice. Kind of typecasting, wouldn't you say?"

"Not at all, Nathan." Lilah picked the discarded deck up off the table and fanned the cards out before showing them to the audience. The deck contained 77 identical cards—all depicting the same image of the Grim Reaper. "I'd say, just like everyone else in here, you had a one hundred percent chance of getting exactly the same outcome."

Burton was a good enough showman to laugh like hell. His backstage producer had been right: this ad lib routine was going to make headlines from coast to coast.

"Bested by death!" he proclaimed.

"As are we all," Lilah agreed. "Besides . . . smoke and mirrors are good for business in *both* of our professions."

136

"Ladies and gentlemen," he placed a hand on Lilah's black-clad shoulder. "Give it up for the one, the only, the genuine Black Bird of Chernobyl!"

The place went wild.

"I still cannot believe you did that." Sparkle and Lilah were tucked into their booth at Luke's Lobster waiting on the arrival of their Noah's Ark entrées. "What possessed you?"

"Would you believe me if I said The Ghost of Christmas Future?"

"That's an unexpected response."

"It was for me, too. At first, I wanted to kick him in the nuts. But I figured a stunt like that would certainly make FSI less inclined to acquire Stohler's. So, I chose the path of least resistance." She took a sip from her glass of 2020 Le Haut-Lieu Moelleux—a bargain at the low, low Vegas sidewalk sale price of $185. It had been a wicked indulgence on her part, but after suffering through the ridiculous scene with Nathan Burton, she decided to treat herself—and Sparkle—with what she'd tell Kay was some well-deserved hazardous duty pay.

"So, where did the Christmas Future metaphor come in?"

"Can we just say there's no time like the past to make you thoughtful about the future?"

"I gather this means you've decided to accept FSI's offer?"

Lilah nodded. "More or less. "But only if I can negotiate concessions on a couple of their likely changes to personnel."

"Oh? Who might they be?"

"Kay Stover and the Freeman brothers. Wardell, too—although he could easily stay on if he joined the ranks of their

137

itinerant embalming corps."

"They'd replace Kay and the Freemans?"

"Yes."

Sparkle's face fell. "That's disheartening. I cannot imagine Stohler's without those three."

"Nor can I. Those sticking points are deal breakers for me."

"Even if you leave?"

"Especially if I leave."

Sparkle was quiet while she absorbed Lilah's revelation.

"Can I ask you something I've been wondering about?"

"Sure."

"It's about the Freeman brothers," Sparkle began. "They're not actually *brothers*. Are they?"

"You mean because one is white, and one is Black? Or because one is six-foot four, and the other is five-foot two?"

"Yes." Sparkle replied.

Lilah smiled. "They came to work as a set—actually applied for the job together. And it's worth knowing that, at the time, there was only *one* job opening. But Dad said they were two halves of a whole—right down to finishing each other's sentences. And it made no sense to him to try and separate them. So, he didn't. They've been there ever since I can remember. And they've grown right along with the business. Whenever anything needed done, it was always the Freeman brothers. Still is, really. They're like family. Better than family, actually, because they make no judgments. Ever. And I've never worked with anyone who dealt with the dead more respectfully than those two. It's like they know each person who passes through our doors personally— know their life stories and honor their pasts. The same thing is true for the indigents we know nothing about—not even their names. It doesn't matter to the Freemans. Every one of these souls matters to them. Every one of their lives—and deaths—is precious. So, to take those two out of the mixed-up equation that is Stohler's Funeral Home would upset the natural balance of the place. When you said losing them—and Kay—would be disheartening, you were right. Without the Freemans, without Kay—the heart of Stohler's would stop beating. I cannot let that happen."

Their entrées arrived in the nick of time for Lilah. She realized she'd been getting a tad too *authentic.*

It's fucking Vegas, she told herself. *I always get terminally moribund out here.*

"Would you answer one other question for me?" Sparkle's voice cut through her reverie.

Lilah looked across the table at her with a raised eyebrow. "Shoot."

"What possessed you to put that deck of tarot cards in your pocket?"

"Would you believe me if I told you they just happened to be in the pocket of that jacket?"

"No."

"Too bad. It's the truth."

"You're kidding. Right? You have to be . . ."

"Nope. I last wore that jacket to Frankie's birthday party on November 19th. The cards were part of a party gag. Nick wanted me to do a Tarot reading, and I thought it would add some gravitas to the event if every card I turned over was Death." She smiled. "Frankie failed to see the humor in it, of course."

"So, you just ad libbed that entire card trick thing?"

"Pretty much. Kay told me that I needed to stop whining about the social media frenzy and take control of it—start bending it to my advantage so I can finally have a forum to talk about things that really matter to me. So, standing up there in those klieg lights, I thought, no time like the present. That's when I realized those damn cards were still in my pocket."

"I can't even take that in. What are the odds? And that you decided just to go with it? Even more incredible."

"I suppose so. Kind of makes you wonder what my next act will be, doesn't it?"

"Oh, yeah. You might say that."

Lilah raised her wine glass. "Here's to finding out."

Sparkle lifted her glass so they could do a proper toast.

"Against my better judgment, I'll drink to that."

Conference activities began promptly at 9 a.m., so they got up early to have time for breakfast in the hotel before heading down to the convention level. It was clear they weren't the only ones with that idea. The restaurant was filled with austere-looking men dressed mostly in black. There were a few exceptions. One woman was attired flamboyantly, wearing a tight dress covered with a pastiche of brightly colored poppies reminiscent of a Van Gogh composition—if he'd ever painted on polyblend. Lilah figured she must be a vendor. Her ensemble was entirely too plucky for her to be a practitioner. There was a pronounced fashion hierarchy in play at these conventions. Funeral directors wore suits, usually ill-fitting, in either black, dark gray, or navy blue—with ties that were sold packaged with the shirts. Embalmers wore khaki slacks and polo shirts. Crematory operators sported ratty jeans and Skechers, and frequently had man buns. Cemetery caretakers tended to display lots of ink, and could usually be found in the hospitality suite, playing fantasy football and swilling free Jack & Coke.

Lilah scanned the menu. "Thirty-six dollars for Eggs Benedict? It's comforting to see that everything in this joint is marked down to retail."

"Maybe it's made with free-range hollandaise?"

"Oh, no. I doubt it. At this price, these eggs are clearly *de-*ranged."

Sparkle laughed. "What do we do first today?"

"The opening session kicks off at nine. Before that is the Meet & Greet, which is tantamount to being locked inside a vault with about two hundred insurance salesman."

"Charming."

"Just remember: if anyone asks you if you've ever thought about whole life, they're talking about a *different* kind of eternal premium."

"Noted. What time is your talk?"

Lilah raised an eyebrow. "Who told you about that?"

"Kay Stover did. But I'm sure it'll be listed in the program."

"Probably. It's at 10 a.m. tomorrow. But I don't expect you to attend."

"Are you nuts? After your performance last night, I wouldn't miss it."

"I have been avoiding my phone since last night."

"Really?" Sparkle sounded surprised. "I haven't. The response has been . . . epic."

"'Epic?'" Lilah quoted. "Epic is a word that should only be used when talking about the digestive tract of Joey Chestnut—or the filmography of Charlton Heston."

"Don't underestimate yourself." Sparkle withdrew her cell phone from her bag. "You made *The Las Vegas Review-Journal*, *TMZ*, and the news crawl at CNN."

"*What?*" Lilah took the phone from her and read the highlighted headline. *Death Becomes Her: Social Media Sensation Bests Vegas Illusionist in Live Performance.* She looked at Sparkle with resignation. "Never before have I uttered the words, 'I want to die' and meant them in anything other than an aspirational way."

Sparkle took back her phone. "Don't be so melodramatic. You were amazing. People are now talking about you like you're some kind of wisecracking death ambassador, versus an aloof and unwitting oddball."

"Oddball?" Lilah was amused by the term.

"Well . . ."

"It's okay. I get it." Lilah shook her dark head. "I feel like Lloyd Bridges in *Airplane!*—looks like I picked the wrong week to quit sniffing glue."

Lilah's dejected mood persisted when they descended to the convention level and followed the directional signs to the rooms that housed the NFDA Convention. She tried valiantly to persuade Sparkle that they'd really have a better time and cultivate more useful relationships at the Cosplay event going on at the opposite side of the cavernous space, but Sparkle didn't bite.

"I wonder if they have anime cremation containers yet?"

Sparkle laughed. "Thinking about a new product line?"

"Why not? We seem to be adept at tapping into up and coming market trends."

"I think 'up and coming' might be a stretch. Maybe wish fulfillment?"

"I have no desire to wish ill on any woodland beasties."

"That would've been welcome news to the ones you embalmed with Borax as a child."

Lilah looked at her with amusement. "Have you been

lurking around my LinkedIn page?"

"Not even close. Frankie told me."

"Of course she did. My little sister rivals the Google when it comes to freely dispensing information."

"It wasn't like that," Sparkle insisted. "We were playing a game of Never Have I Ever during a late study session."

"Really? More like a game of Which of These Things Is Not Like the Other."

They picked up glossy printed copies of the convention program from a rack outside the entrance to the vendor area.

"Oh, look," Lilah pointed out. "There are *five,* count 'em, hospitality suites set up this year. You know it's mandatory to visit every one of them."

"Why would we do that?"

"Because they give you these nifty little coffin stamps on the back of your hand. And if you get all five, you're automatically entered into a drawing to win a coveted door prize."

"Door prize? At a funeral show? That's . . . terrifying."

"I'll say." Lilah nodded energetically. "As I recall, the winner last year got a set of double old-fashioned glasses that read, 'Last Responder,' and a set of swizzle sticks shaped like trocar wands." Lilah was lost in thought for a moment. "That beat the hell out of the paltry thirty-six jars of mortician's wax they gave away in Phoenix. I actually won those."

"What on earth did you do with them?"

Lilah looked amused. "One guess."

"Oh."

Lilah laughed. "I gave them to Rita Kitty. I think she used them to seal up cracks around the foundation of their house. She said the stuff works better than Bondo—and it's easier to match colors."

Sparkle squinted at her. "Is it possible to participate and *not* get entered into the raffle?"

"You have no sense of adventure. Okay. Let's do this. How about we separate at the entrance and work both sides of the room? That'll cut our time in purgatory in half faster than a fistful of indulgences."

"Yeah. I don't think so," Sparkle replied.

Lilah was nonplussed. "Why not?"

Sparkle looked up at her. She really did have the most incredible green eyes.

"You think I'm not onto your reindeer games?"

"What's that supposed to mean?" Lilah feigned umbrage.

"We separate at the door, and then you disappear. This ain't my first rodeo, Black Bird."

"I am shocked and offended."

"By the fact that I stood up to you?"

"No," Lilah replied. "By the fact that I'm so damn transparent."

"Come on." Sparkle took hold of her elbow. "Let's get this party started."

Before they were two feet across the threshold of the room, Sparkle's phone exploded with a barrage of text messages, sent in rapid succession.

"This cannot be good." Sparkle pulled her phone out of her bag and quickly read the string of texts. "And . . . it's not." She faced Lilah. "Kay says the lot at the funeral home is so jammed with cars for the Strub service that people were having problems trying to find places to park without hitting the cauldrons of Brunswick stew and chicken gravy."

"Oh, Jesus Christ. Do I even want to know?"

"Well, Kay has a call in to Kirk, our attorney."

"Kirk?" Lilah's dark eyes grew wide. "What the fuck happened?"

"It seems that a pair of nearsighted octogenarians driving an ancient Delta 88 backed into one of the cauldrons and knocked it over."

Lilah was too shocked to speak.

"Kay said it was a perfect storm and the boiling vat of stewed meat and vegetables went everywhere. Her exact words were that it was like witnessing a 'tidal wave of chunky red death.'"

"We are so beyond fucked. Please, in the name of all things I hold sacred and profane, tell me that no one was hurt."

Sparkle demurred. "Kay said they didn't quite know the extent of potential injuries yet."

"*Yet?*" Lilah felt her blood pressure begin to soar higher than the headdresses of the cosplay practitioners strolling past them to attend their own opening Meet & Greet. "I'm going to spend the next twenty years paying off these legal settlements by working nights as a stiff-stacker at the county cold-cut pantry. You do know this, right?"

"Try not to awfulize. You told Kay to manage this—so let her manage it."

"Right. Because *that's* working out . . ."

"Lilah? We're twenty-five hundred miles away from Winston-Salem. There is nothing you can do to affect the outcome of this. You trust Kay. Let her handle it."

"You're right." Lilah expelled a deep breath. "As the Bible says, 'Sufficient unto the day is the evil thereof.' Let's go face another kind of music."

"Good idea," Sparkle agreed.

No sooner had they entered the room than cries of, "There she is— our reigning Diva of Death!" and "Behold, a Deathling has entered the chat!" rang out. So many people queued up to have selfies taken with Lilah, she was tempted to start charging for them.

They also peppered her with a nonstop litany of inane questions.

"What was it like to cut that slick sideshow hustler down to size?"

"Are the rumors true that you're getting your own show at Planet Hollywood?"

"Did the NFDA comp your registration fee? They should have. If the effing shroud of Turin could get up and walk through these doors, those blood-sucking bastards would charge it full freight, too."

"Where can I get my hands on some of those all-death Tarot decks?"

"Is it true your Mini Cooper cargo bay has aftermarket casket rollers and bier pins? Did those mods invalidate your warranty?"

"Is your skin naturally this pale or do you wear a special setting powder?"

"Have you heard you're edging out Selena Gomez for the most likes on Insta?"

"Do you know if these almond bear claws are gluten free?"

Lilah was thrilled to finally get a question she could answer.

"Listen buddy," she leaned toward the bewildered-looking little man. "Here's a ginormous clue: since they're stuffed with almond paste and covered with vanilla icing, it won't be the glutens that end up killing you."

As soon as she could wrest herself free, Lilah grabbed Sparkle by the sleeve and hissed, "Let's get the fuck outta here."

They quickly retraced their steps back to the lobby and made a beeline for the exhibit area.

Sparkle gaped when they stepped inside. Lilah realized that she'd probably never seen so many shiny, fantastic monuments to death on display in one place. To be fair, it *was* like walking smack into the middle of a necromaniac's wet dream.

"Oh. My. God."

"Kind of takes your breath away, doesn't it?" Lilah asked. "I remember how I felt the first time Dad brought me to one of these."

"How was that? Overwhelmed? Terrified?"

"No. More like I'd just been handed a get out of jail free card."

Sparkle gazed at her with wonder. "You're not joking, are you?"

"No." Lilah cast her gaze about the cavernous room. "I realized that no matter how extreme I was—no matter how dark and divorced from polite society I worked to become—the more important it was that there was something like *this*—something that could manage to make me seem—*normal*."

"Lilah? Believe me." Sparkle waved a hand to encompass the modern-day Pharaoh's tomb of otherworldly delights spread out before them. "*This* isn't what makes you seem normal."

"It isn't?"

"No. It's your humanity. Your self-deprecating humor. And the kindness you work so hard to keep concealed behind all those halfhearted scowls and nonstop declarations of not caring a whit about the people who pass through your capable hands every day."

"You're crazy."

"*I'm* crazy?" Sparkle asked.

"Pretty much, yeah."

"A strange thing to allege, when *I'm* not the one who's

prepared to walk away from an insanely lucrative offer if it means sacrificing the jobs of two lovable, but quirky, septuagenarian non-brothers with an incomprehensible roster of duties and an adherence to methods that are eclectic, to say the least."

Lilah considered her argument. "You forgot about Kay Stover."

"Her, too."

Lilah was obviously uncomfortable with the direction of the conversation. Mercifully, Sparkle took pity on her, and changed the subject. "Where do we start?"

"I find that internal combustion is always good to get your engine going. How about we explore innovations in hearses?"

"I'm game. Let's go."

It was a good display. There were upgraded Cadillac XTS models, Lincoln MKTs, Jaguar XJLs, and even a Rolls Royce Phantom B12—complete with suicide doors—that had a sticker price of $662,000.

"Now that's what I'd call one helluva high-priced Uber ride to eternity."

"Who in the world would even buy such a thing?"

"Whoever they are, they don't live in Winston-Salem."

Sparkle stopped dead in her tracks. "What in the world is *that?*"

Lilah followed her gaze to take in the unique spectacle of a motorcycle hearse. It featured an anniversary edition Harley Davidson Road King motorcycle attached to a glass enclosed, custom Fifth Wheel Tombstone hearse sidecar.

"That right there would be Charon's hog. The last hurrah for a weekend warrior." Lilah peered closer. "Although I have to say, this is the first time I've ever seen one with a six-foot rabbit inside the hearse compartment. I wonder if he had to take off his ears to fit?"

Sparkle looked closer. "Dear god. It's one of those cosplay actors."

"*Death Be Not Proud*," Lilah quoted.

"I think I've now seen everything."

"Oh, trust me. We're just getting started."

They walked on to an area that was like an amphitheater stacked with rows and tiers of caskets—in every color, shape, and size. Sparkle was impressed by a series of models that were woven like baskets—some had even been dyed with bright colors or hand-stenciled with patterns of leaves or flowers. There was even a special model called a PRIDE edition that had a rainbow flag surrounding its four sides. A craftsman sat at a table operating a mechanical loom that wove the natural materials into a variety of patterns.

Just beyond the basket display were a series of plant-based caskets that were advertised as one hundred percent compostable. But what dominated the majority of the floor space in the container area were the stalwarts of the industry: the gleaming solid wood and polished metal caskets that accounted for the lion's share of profit in the death industry.

"I feel like I'm in the last scene of *Reservoir Dogs*."

"There is a kind of Greek tragedy vibe to all of this, I'll grant you."

Sparkle pointed at a display of cremation urns. "But not to those."

"True. I am especially enamored with the mini replica of the *Pietà* and the KISS memorial pyramid."

"Okay. That one is just fucked up."

Lilah was surprised by Sparkle's use of the expletive. "Why, Mrs. Sink. I never thought I'd hear such language from you."

"Well *look* at that ridiculous thing," Sparkle said with disgust. "Don't you find the ring of flames around its base to be a bit ..."

"Prescient?" Lilah suggested.

"No. Lacking in taste comes to mind."

"You think all this is fantastic and unbelievable, wait until we get to the Aquamation display."

"Do I even want to know what that is?"

Lilah nodded energetically. "It's the wave of the future. Literally. Come on and I'll show you."

The imposing steel alkaline hydrolysis chamber looked like something you'd see in a large commercial laundromat.

"It's basic water cremation," Lilah explained. "A body is placed inside the heated tube with a solution that is ninety-five percent water and five percent everyday alkaline chemicals—the kind found in soaps or cosmetics. Within hours, everything gets dissolved—except bones, which are reduced to powder the same way they are in flame cremation."

"What happens to the organic matter?"

"It becomes like soapy water—which is compatible with any municipal wastewater treatment system. In fact, the discharged water is actually beneficial because it nourishes the bacteria that breaks down sewage."

"Is this legal in North Carolina?"

"Strangely enough, it is. We're one of twenty-six states that allow it. Acquiring one of these chambers was my top priority when I took over the business. But now ..."

"Now it would be up to FSI?"

"Correct. And believe me, green burial solutions are not in line with their strategies for protecting their bottom line. Aquamation costs about $1,500—far less than flame cremation and exponentially less than conventional embalming and burial.

But for the legions of people who understand that there *is* no Planet B when it comes to the climate-related danger we're facing as a species, solutions like aquamation and direct green burial are gaining ascendancy. More and more, people want to return to the earth in gentler, more eco-friendly ways."

"I think I've seen enough for one morning," Sparkle said. "I'm kind of on sensory overload."

"Do you us want to leave?"

"No. Not at all. I think you should stay and keep looking around. I just want to go clear my head and digest everything we've seen. I'll come back in a bit and find you, if that's okay. And I have a couple of calls to return related to the Winkler funeral. Rita Kitty is pinch-hitting for me on some of the special requests the family is asking for."

"Do I want to know what those are?"

"Um . . . no. It's best if you don't."

"Okay, then. You go do your thing and I'll find something here to distract myself."

"My turn to ask if I want to know how?"

"Um," Lilah quoted, "no. It's best if you don't."

"It's good we understand each other."

"I think we're beginning to."

It seemed to Lilah that Sparkle wanted to follow up on Lilah's observation but chose not to.

Lilah wasn't sure if she felt more relief or disappointment.

"You okay?" she asked.

"Yeah. Don't worry. It's just a lot to take in."

"Okay." Lilah decided not to press her. "Come and find me later. I'll be . . . around."

After Sparkle retreated from the vendor area, Lilah wandered around, doing her best to avoid interactions with anyone. She didn't fail to notice the occasional unmistakable shutter clicks of cell phones but did her best not to lapse into a homicidal rage and chase them down with a length of embalming tube.

Like it or not, Lilah knew she had to confront the jumbled mixture of unwelcome feelings that were beginning to characterize her interactions with the attractive brand identity professional who'd entered her system like a pernicious virus. One for which she had no vaccine—other than to feign indifference. A strategy that had worked at first. Sort of. But that was now coming up woefully short.

This does not happen to me. Not ever.

Not even after her first sexual encounter inside a commodious Titan XL, with that fast-talking Orion saleswoman, Doreen, who swore she'd keep in touch.

"Yeah, whatever, Doreen," Lilah recalled saying as she pushed the woman's head lower—more to shut her up than anything else.

Truth be told, that *had* been a useful exercise. Those models really were as accommodating as advertised for their plus-sized clients.

It wasn't that she hadn't had relationships after that. She had. Just not—meaningful ones. And that had always been by design. Romantic distractions were just that: *distractions*. And Lilah didn't need distractions. They didn't work out for her. And her horrifically named nemesis, Sparkle, was looming up before her as the ultimate distraction—one she could ill afford. Especially now, when she was thinking about changing everything—including where she lived.

Her professional passion had always been geared toward advancing the availability of eco-friendly and carbon neutral aftercare solutions. A tough sell, especially when your humble mortuary was sitting smack-dab in the middle of the Bible belt. That made her resolve to sell Stohler's and strike out for parts unknown gain greater traction. If she could change the script, return to her chosen life of solitude, advance the causes she cared about, *and* make a ton of money in the process—why the hell not jump at the opportunity?

No. She didn't need any shiny objects named *Sparkle* to distract her from pursuing her path of least resistance. Not ever. And, sure as hell, not now.

She advanced toward the Recompose exhibit. The opportunity to visit this particular site had been the driving force behind her desire to attend the conference this year. She'd actually had some correspondence with the director about visiting their human composting site in Seattle and looked forward to the chance to witness a practical demonstration of their process.

Recompose was the pioneer "natural organic reduction," or human recomposing, facility in the United States. Using the principles of nature, their process took a human body and, through entirely organic means, reduced it over a thirty-day period into about a cubic yard of nutrient-rich compost—allowing the deceased to return to the earth as healthy soil—vital for the survival of plants, animals, and future generations of human beings. The all-natural process allowed each participant the unique ability to give back to the same earth that nourished and sustained them throughout their lifetimes.

It was, for Lilah, a perfect system. One she was becoming passionate about championing.

There were only a few people milling about inside the Recompose exhibit when she approached it and introduced herself to the staff who were handling the demonstrations. That allowed her to monopolize more of their time with questions about the actual equipment and process. The staff had placed a mannequin inside the vessel used to transport the body of the deceased into the chamber where the natural decomposition process took place.

Lilah had a better idea . . .

Fifteen minutes later, she, herself, lay inside the vessel upon a soft bed of mulch, covered with an organic cotton blanket. The staff ran through their description of the process for the small crowd that had gathered to watch the demonstration. They covered her body with an assortment of wood chips, straw, and alfalfa—all designed to support and nurture the decomposition process. Lilah asked questions throughout the demonstration, as much for her own edification as for the satisfaction of the voyeuristic interests of the onlookers.

Predictably, there was no shortage of cell phones on hand to document her time inside the vessel—which, surprisingly, was quite comfortable, with its ambient scents of eucalyptus and wildflowers. She thought she could happily spend eternity in there—it was like reclining on an accommodating florist floor, which was the ethos behind the enterprise.

A loud cry of, "Oh, my GOD!" disrupted her reverie.

She sat up abruptly to see what had happened and realized that Sparkle was standing beside the vessel with her hand pressed against her mouth.

There was a medley of mixed gasps and titters of laughter at Lilah's sudden appearance when she bolted upright—and about half a dozen camera flashes.

Great. she thought. *I can hardly wait to see* these *headlines tomorrow.*

"What in the hell are you *doing* in there?" Sparkle asked.

"Would you believe, test-driving my final ride?"

"Oh, for god's sake. Get out of there." Sparkle pushed the stepladder over so Lilah could climb out of the composting vessel.

"Well, damn. Just when I was on the cusp of taking the best nap of my life . . ."

Lilah descended the ladder to a smattering of applause. She brushed bits of mulch and alfalfa sprouts off her clothing and faced the small crowd.

"They'll be here all week, folks. Tell your friends and share the love with a forest near you."

Sparkle rolled her eyes and grabbed Lilah by the arm.

"Let's get out of here. I need a drink."

For once, Lilah was happy to follow her lead

"You don't have to ask me twice."

"Oh," Sparkle said as they made their way toward the first hospitality suite, "I heard back from Kay."

"And?"

"And . . . not as bad as it could've been. Turns out there was only one minor burn reported— and that belonged to one of the men in Hambone's church group. Most of the damages sustained came from footwear stained by the stew. Fortunately, Rita Kitty was on hand with her industrial-sized bottle of Resolve, and she was able to ameliorate all evidence of misadventure. Hambone gifted everyone affected by the mishap with a free quart of the stew. It sounds like the chicken gravy was an unqualified success, and that dear Mrs. Strub got the savory sendoff she longed for."

"Well, praise Hestia."

"It gets better. One of the other men in Hambone's group works for Ray's Body Shop and he was able to pop out the dent in the Oldsmobile on site. Kay said Rita Kitty was able to match the pale pink paint color perfectly by mixing a tube of Maybelline New York Cheek Heat with some leftover white primer Hambone had on hand in the shed."

"Pink?"

Sparkle nodded. "I gather it had been a Mary Kay car in the eighties."

"Yeah," Lilah replied. "I'm going for all *five* of those coffin stamps . . ."

Juniata Winkler
November 30, 1946 – December 12, 2023

In the company of chosen family, Juniata
Winkler passed away peacefully at home
on the afternoon of Saturday, December
12, 2023, from late stage kidney disease.
She was 77. In her family of origin, Juniata
is survived by a sister and two nephews. In
Winston-Salem, NC, she was the matriarch
of a chosen family of women who cared for
her in the last years of her life. Juniata was
the "other" mother to Tammi Pill and Susan
Hope-May, with whom she lived. Additional
family included Patty, Maxene, and LaVerne,
her beloved golden retrievers, and lifelong
partner, Dorsey Pegram.

Juniata was a Southern belle with Yankee
sensibility. She was curious, kind, devoted,
and easily distracted. She loved Charo. She
was equal parts brilliance and innocence, and
she was as likely to view the world through the
eyes of a child as she was to be devastated
by the state of things. She was a prolific
poet, writing more than 60,000 metrical

compositions that survive to this day. She was always quick to take a moral stand on political issues and was tireless and funny. She stayed determined to keep up to date on current events right up until the end. One of the final sentences she uttered came during her final hours of life after a controversial congressional vote, when she rose up and asked, "Which one of those bastards caved?"

Juniata was proud to say that she voted in every single election. She always said she'd like to be remembered as a feminist, a voting rights advocate, a lover of animals, and a trickster.

A small private service honoring Juniata will be held on December 14th at Stohler's Funeral Home in Winston-Salem. In lieu of flowers, the family asks that donations be made to Planned Parenthood.

Posted by Stohler's Funeral Home, Winston-Salem, NC

Never Have I Ever

Lilah was scowling at her phone.

They were sitting in one of the hotel's five hospitality suites, drinking complimentary cocktails furnished by S&S, one of the conference's premier sponsors. Lilah chose this venue for their first stop after the day's programming had ended because S&S Superior Coach Company was the only platinum-level sponsor, and she knew that meant they'd be serving the top-shelf booze.

Under duress, Lilah made Sparkle consent to receive her first tiny coffin stamp of the evening.

But her mood turned sour after her phone pinged and she got a text message from the conference programming staff.

"I cannot *believe* this happened." Lilah grumbled.

"What?"

"They just told me that the time and location of my talk have changed."

"It's not tomorrow morning?"

"No. It's now at 4 p.m.—and they've moved it into some damn theater instead of the smaller meeting room it had been scheduled for."

"Lilah, that's fantastic news."

"Are you nuts? It's horrible."

"No, it isn't. It means the conference organizers are smart enough to understand they've got a feathered gold mine under their corporate wings—and they want to capitalize on your celebrity."

"How in the world will all of that social media insanity help them?"

"For starters," Sparkle was looking at her own phone examining details of the revised event, "this talk will now be open to the public—so it won't just be attended by conference-goers."

"Oh, great. So, any of those furry abominations wandering the hotel corridors can wander in and learn all about the benefits of carbon neutral burial systems and why they should be legalized in every state?"

"That, and any inquiring news media that might be interested in finding out what else the celebrated Black Bird of Chernobyl has stashed inside her ghoulish bag of tricks."

"I fail to see any humor in this."

"If morbid curiosity lands you behind a bully pulpit, why not embrace it and use it as a means to promote a topic that matters to you? Better to speak to a more diverse crowd that might actually listen with something other than the deaf ears you consistently encounter from industry practitioners who are more concerned with profits than sustainable, long-term solutions."

Lilah lifted her martini glass and examined it. "I wonder what the hell they're putting in these drinks?"

"Why? Is it not good?"

"No. It's fine. But something is clearly affecting my judgment because what you're saying is actually making sense."

"Well, then," Sparkle raised her own glass, "there's only one thing to do."

"Deny everything and demand a higher proof on the booze?"

"Nope. Drink up and order another round."

Three drinks and two additional coffin stamps later, they'd advanced beyond the safe parameters of shop talk and were swapping stories about their college years. Lilah learned some choice tidbits about her sister that she planned to remember and use to her advantage at their next family gathering. And it was clear that Sparkle had also had her own share of intrigues and indiscretions.

"There's one thing I've been dying to ask you . . . so to speak."

"What is it?" Sparkle asked.

"Your *name* . . ."

"Oh. That."

"Yeah. That. I mean . . . what the fuck? Who names their infant daughter 'Sparkle'?"

"Tell me about it. It wasn't an easy name to grow up with, believe me. I always felt like I'd been named after a packet of Jet Dry. Finally, when I was old enough to complain about it, my father explained how the name came about." She didn't continue.

"And are you going to share that story with our studio audience?"

"Since you *nearly* asked nicely, I will. My mother was stricken with postpartum eclampsia immediately after I was born. She developed pulmonary edema and, tragically, she didn't survive it. My father said she only got to hold me once before she died, and he remembered her saying I sparkled like a tiny jewel. So that's what he named me. So, every time I'm tempted to cringe when I hear my name, I try to think about her and tell myself it's okay."

Lilah didn't know what response to make so made none. Instead, she reached across the table and squeezed Sparkle's hand.

"It's okay. What do you say we finish these drinks and move on to the next little coffin stamp?"

"Works for me. I'm in."

"Tell the truth, Sink—you really want that door prize, don't you?"

Sparkle gave her an unreadable look. "More than you realize."

Two tiny coffin stamps later, they were feeling even less inhibited and decided to engage in a game of Never Have I Ever. In their version, the participant who ended up with *fewer* than ten check marks won the round.

It was Lilah's turn to test Sparkle.

"Never Have I Ever pretended to be someone else online."

"Oh, jeez. For real?" Sparkle picked up a pencil and drew another hash mark on her cocktail napkin.

"Oh, my. Looks like you're down to seven dares, Miz Sparkle. Now, who did you pretend to be and why?"

"That's not part of the game."

"Oh, didn't I tell you? We're playing by the Marquess of Queensberry Rules."

"Those are *boxing* rules!"

"I know that," Lilah countered. "This was a late addition to the canon."

"You're crazy."

"You say that a lot."

"I know. And I'm *still* not telling you who I impersonated

online. It's now my turn, smarty pants."

"Okay, Sink. Give it your best shot."

Sparkle leaned toward her. "Never Have I Ever had impure thoughts about someone in this room."

Lilah wasn't sure she'd heard her correctly. "Excuse me?"

"You heard me. C'mon, Stohler. 'Fess up."

Lilah anxiously cast about the bar. Her eyes landed on a cocktail waitress who had a rather nice . . . backyard.

Praise God for convenient safe harbors, she thought. Especially since Sparkle had decided to play dirty.

"Okay. You win." She picked up the pencil and added a hash mark to her own napkin. "Now we're officially tied."

"And who in this establishment has inspired such impure thoughts?"

"No way, Sink. If you don't have to dish the dirty details, neither do I."

"Coward."

"Oh, yeah? We'll see who's scared. Never Have I Ever had sex . . . *with a woman.*"

Sparkle stared back at her for more than ten full seconds before picking up her pencil and adding another tick to her napkin.

Well, well. It's always the quiet ones . . .

"Well shiver me timbers," Lilah said with amusement.

"Don't tell me you're surprised."

"In fact, I am. I thought that whole *Nina's Heavenly Delights* thing was an aberration. Are you saying it wasn't?"

"No. I'm not aware that I'm saying *anything*—except that it's now my turn. Never Have I Ever had a lap dance."

Lilah thought about it. "Does a hyperactive Pomeranian count?"

"Nope."

Lilah sighed and picked up her pencil. "Then I suppose her owner does." She added a hash mark to her total. It was her turn again, and she knew she was treading on dangerous ground. Her brain was already fuzzy from too many vodka martinis and too much proximity to all of Sparkle's charms on ready display in the confines of a closed environment—this goddamn, modern-day Babylon of a hotel full of fucked-up woodland creatures and the flashy iconography of death.

It was like the love child of Tim Burton and Federico Fellini—and their union had produced one hell of a twisted script.

And all that alfalfa was messing with her head, too.

She never should've allowed Kay Stover to Armstrong-arm her into making this trip with Sparkle It was bound to go this way. *She knew herself.* If fate decided to toss something guaranteed to blow up in the middle of her best laid plans like a Molotov cocktail, she could be relied upon to spread her arms wide and make herself a bigger target. It had always been that way. And it was why she stayed away from romantic or sexual entanglements with anyone.

And what the hell did Sparkle think *she* was doing, playing with this kind of fire? The two of them couldn't possibly be more opposite. Sparkle was a denizen of the light. Her life experience and aspirations were completely different from Lilah's. They had nothing in common. Except for some ancillary similarities in the whole sexual orientation realm and a pronounced lack of fear when it came to death. . . which was surreal enough without the overlay of any other inducements to mischief.

Because right now, the reactive parts of Lilah's psyche—and parts south—were entirely focused on a cavalcade of actions that would only lead to mischief. And not only was Lilah capable of imagining *lots* of mischief—she was losing the battle to drag herself to higher ground while she still had the wherewithal to escape.

None of it made any sense. For either of them. *Yet?*

Here they were, playing some ridiculous *Teen Vogue* game and acting like horny ingenues.

Well. *She* was acting like a horny ingenue. She wasn't sure what Sparkle was up to.

She stole another glance at her. Sparkle was still watching—and waiting. Waiting for—*what?* For Lilah to make a move? For Lilah to make the *first* move?

For another set of cocktail napkins because they both were racking up so many damn points in this infernal game of kiss and tell?

But nothing in Sparkle's demeanor suggested that she was at all concerned. On the contrary, she appeared to be having fun. How was it even possible for her to be enjoying the joyride along the road to certain ruin they were taking? There was nothing even remotely positive about the outcome of this scenario.

Well. Unless she included how goddamn hot Sparkle looked, sitting there in her form-fitting Junior League ensemble, all but daring Lilah to test her resolve one more time.

Of course, she could also be misreading everything. That had happened before—with disastrous results.

Never Have I Ever wanted so much to read another person's mind . . .

She finished her drink.

What could be the worst that could happen?

She had no idea whose voice was asking that question. She didn't quite recognize it as her own. It had too much of a

Romper Room quality to come from anyplace familiar. But right then, it was drowning out the dire and sonorous chants from the chorus of her familiar.

She inched closer to Sparkle within the confines of their already impossibly small booth. She knew she was casting a die she could not call back, but she was now past caring.

"Never Have I Ever kissed a mortician."

The words hung there between them.

Lilah flashed back to the time she'd been roped into going skydiving. It had been her mother's sixty-fifth birthday and they'd all accompanied her on the death-defying leap. Lilah was unprepared for the absolute euphoria that overtook her during the free fall. It was like nothing she'd ever experienced—those shockingly quiet moments hovering above the earth before her chute opened and returned her safely to land.

Waiting for Sparkle to respond felt the same way—equal parts anticipation and terror.

Sparkle took her time. Lilah wasn't sure which way the outcome of her dare would go until Sparkle reached up and slowly outlined Lilah's lips with the tip of her finger.

It was probably the most erotic thing Lilah had ever experienced.

Sparkle followed that slow survey with her mouth. She took her time. Quick, fleeting touches. A gentle nip. A soft lick. Then a firmer, more determined exploration. Lilah had to fight the impulse to take control. But she didn't have to worry. Once Sparkle had demonstrated her commitment to the task, they both tumbled deeper into the exchange, fighting for ascendancy. And in Lilah's case, fighting to breathe.

Against her will, she pulled herself away and gaped stupidly at Sparkle, whose eyes were shining like green fire.

"Do you think we should maybe take . . . *this* . . . someplace else?" Lilah scanned the suite as she waited for her breathing to return to normal. "I really don't want to see this on Instagram tomorrow."

"Good idea."

Standing up took a bit more effort than expected. Lilah was shocked at how weak her legs felt. She stood back and extended a hand to Sparkle. "Ready?"

"Oh, yeah. You might say that." Sparkle slid out of the booth to leave with her but tarried when she seemed to think of something. "One second . . ." She picked up her pencil with a shaking hand and added a hash mark to her napkin. "So that one's now a *big* ten-four."

Lilah woke up the next morning, expecting to have a hangover and cautiously elated that maybe she'd cheated that little death. She slowly took an inventory to be sure.

The first thing she noticed was that the bed was on the wrong side of the room.

The second thing she noticed was that she was naked beneath the sheets.

The third thing she noticed was that someone else was sound asleep beside her.

Oh, Jesus, Mary, and Schrödinger's damn cat.

She'd done it. *She'd done this thing.* And now the day after had come—as days after *always* came—and she'd have to deal with the consequences of her profoundly misguided actions.

She tested her recollections. *How drunk had she been?*

Not very, in fact. That admission was mortifying enough

without the barrage of other admissions that followed in quick succession.

Had she enjoyed herself?

The truth? *Hell, fuck yes.*

And how drunk had Sparkle been? Had Lilah taken advantage of her in an inebriated state?

Not so much.

Her thoughts swung back to the way they'd entered Sparkle's room—like two hormone-addled teens, about to embark on their first, lightning-fast sexual encounter. They slammed into each other as soon as the door closed behind them, deep kissing with ferocity and tearing at each other's clothing as they stumbled across the room to fall across the absurdly round bed.

Only it hadn't ended up being lightning fast—not once they got started. Sparkle proved to be as careful and thorough a practitioner in this exercise as she was in the commission of the rest of her duties. Lilah felt downright pliable in her hands— allowing Sparkle free reign to mix, roll, knead, and altogether infuse her with the same kind of magic she baked into every one of those sweet confections that had single-handedly changed the future for of all of them.

And it wasn't like Lilah had settled for accepting the role of passive bystander in their bake off Olympics. Oh, hell no. *Not a chance.*

She closed her eyes in mortification and wished she'd had at least *five* more martinis—enough to ensure that she wouldn't recall any of her own excesses. But recall them she did, in Technicolor detail. Flashes of all they'd done—all *she'd* done with Sparkle's breathless urging and consent—blazed across her mind like lightning in a summer storm.

Sparkle stirred beside her.

Ohdeargod. Lilah prayed to any deity that might be listening. *Don't wake up. Don't wake up. And for the love of God, please don't roll over, or I'll be totally fucked. Again.*

It was too late. Sparkle stretched, yawned, and rolled onto her back, exposing a broad swath of the minefield that spelled nothing but danger for Lilah.

"Oh," she said when she saw Lilah looking anxiously over at her. "So, I guess that wasn't a dream."

"Um. It appears not."

Sparkle looked down at her naked body. "I guess so."

"How do you feel?" Lilah couldn't summon the nerve to ask the real question that plagued her, which was some derivative of *What the serious fuck are we going to do?*

Sparkle stretched and tugged the sheet up over her chest.

Hell hath retreated to its box. Lilah was flooded with relief. Had Sparkle remained so gloriously ... *exposed* ... Lilah knew it would've taken a twenty-mule team to keep her rooted to her side of the bed.

"I think," Sparkle began, "I'm ... hungry."

"Hungry?" Lilah hadn't expected that response.

"Yes. You may recall that we never actually ate anything last night."

"Not unless you count . . ." Lilah reflexively quipped but, managed to stop in time. *Filters,* she reminded herself. *Use your fucking filters.* ". . . all those bowls of bar mix."

"Right," Sparkle noted. "I'm sure that's exactly what you meant."

Lilah shrugged. "I don't trust myself to say much of anything right now."

"Does that mean you regret what happened?"

Lilah shrugged. "Do you?"

"I'm not sure."

"And why do you say, 'what happened' like you're referring to some kind of oil spill off the coast of Alaska?"

"Okay." Sparkle sat up against the padded headboard. "I'm sensing some discord, here. How would *you* characterize it?"

"The truth?"

Sparkle nodded.

"I honestly have no idea."

Sparkle sighed. "Since we each were active and seemingly *willing* participants in whatever did take place last night, I'll try not to take offense at your obvious concern."

"Are you concerned about what this might mean for our working relationship?"

"Truthfully, our working relationship wasn't the first thing that crossed my mind this morning."

"What was?"

"That the only reason you allowed yourself to do this was because you knew you'd be leaving."

Sparkle's words hit Lilah like hammer blows. "I'd hope I'd never do something like that."

"I hope not, myself."

Lilah closed her eyes and leaned her head against the padded monstrosity that took up half the wall behind them. "I'm sorry I created a mess."

"You didn't create anything by yourself. And it doesn't have to be a mess."

"What do you mean?" Lilah asked.

"I mean it's up to us to figure out how we want to manage it."

Lilah opened one eye and looked at her. "You mean we pretend it never happened?"

"Is that what you want?" Sparkle asked.

"I honestly don't know right now."

"Then neither do I," Sparkle added.

"Okay. So instead of continuing to sit here naked on this bed, why don't we do something else until we figure it out." Lilah thought that was at least one thing that made sense in a world that had suddenly lost its grip on reason and rational behavior. "What do you want to do?" She asked Sparkle.

"How about we get dressed and go downstairs for some of those thirty-six-dollar eggs?"

"I'm game," Lilah replied with more enthusiasm than she felt. "Just not the free-range kind."

"Don't worry." Sparkle dared to reach out and pat her hand. "You're not stuck inside any prison you cannot escape."

"That's just it. I'm not sure I want to escape."

"I can't help you with that, Lilah. You have to figure it out on your own."

Lilah gave her a slow nod. "I know."

"Now which one of us is getting up first to do the walk of shame?"

"I'll flip you for it?"

"Well, technically, this is *my* room—so I think that means you're the one who needs to beat a hasty retreat."

"Fair enough." Lilah reached for her discarded jacket and donned it before getting out of bed. She made her way across the room, collecting her other articles of clothing along the way. Before she reached the door, she thought of something, and turned to face Sparkle.

"Hey . . . why did we come into your room instead of mine?"

"Don't you remember?"

"Not really. As I recall, I was kind of preoccupied with something."

Sparkle rubbed her neck. "I remember."

"Sorry. Hope I didn't leave a mark."

"Oh, you left a mark, believe me. But that's not why we came in here."

"No?"

"No. When we finally got here, there were a couple of . . . woodland furries engaged in some kind of direct. . . *commerce* . . . against your door."

"My door?"

"Uh huh." Sparkle nodded. "They were in the process of exchanging . . . assets."

"Assets? What *kind* of assets?"

"Use your imagination."

"Oh, dear god . . ."

"It was an impressive performance. I'm not likely to soon forget it."

"What is it with this fucking hotel? Do people enter and lose all sense of decorum?"

"Lilah?"

"What?"

"Your professions of moral outrage would ring truer if you weren't standing in the middle of my hotel room wearing only an open blazer and one sock."

Lilah looked down the landscape of her long, naked body.

"Good point."

"Meet you outside in twenty minutes?"

"Roger." Lilah checked the view through the peephole twice to be sure the coast was clear before quickly exiting Sparkle's room and hurriedly entering the sanctity of her own.

Lilah had no idea how they managed to navigate the rest of the day without being overcome by embarrassment or regret.

They decided to split up and attend different sessions, agreeing that it made the most sense to divide and conquer—and vowing they would share notes at dinner. But Sparkle did rejoin her a few minutes before her speech in the larger theater venue was scheduled to begin.

Lilah was still complaining about the last-minute change. The room was rapidly filling up, and her nerves about speaking increased each time another person entered and claimed a seat.

"Stop complaining," Sparkle enjoined her. "This is what you've wanted—a chance to get people to listen to something other than strategies for how to increase their profit margins by amping up services no one really needs. Take advantage of it."

"I suppose so."

"You know so. Quit being so tentative. Get out there and embrace the full force of your power to rage against the machine. Teach. Inform. Inspire. And if none of that works, scare the ever-loving shit out of them. Take no prisoners. Be the Black Bird. It's your time to soar."

Lilah eyed her with suspicion. "Who are you? Wayne Dwyer?"

"Just. Do. It." Sparkle impulsively kissed her on the cheek. "I'll be sitting in the back row."

Lilah raised a hand to her cheek. "Why? So you can be first out if the place catches on fire?"

"Something like that."

173

An aide came to fetch her, and it was time for Lilah to face the music.

In retrospect, it wasn't so bad. Once she got started, she quickly warmed to her topic and her enthusiasm for the message took over.

"Every year in this country alone," she shared, "the chemicals and materials buried along with bodies include thirty million board feet of choice hardwoods harvested from our forests, one hundred and forty thousand tons of steel, twenty-seven hundred tons of bronze and copper, and an estimated one million, six hundred and thirty-six thousand tons of reinforced concrete. Once viewed as our best hedge against these abuses of the environment, our increased dependence on flame cremations now pumps an additional three hundred and sixty thousand metric tons of carbon dioxide into the air we breathe—as well as contributing to toxic levels of mercury.

"New technologies for green and eco-friendly methods of dealing with our dead—processes like alkaline hydrolysis and human composting—provide our last, best carbon-neutral methods for giving back to the planet that has nourished and sustained us throughout our lifetimes. As finite humans who are steeped in centuries of religious and cultural teachings, our fatalistic understanding of death might be unavoidable. But it is up to each of us to teach that death is a natural part of life—and that completing the cycle of life means returning to the earth in our purest forms, as the organic matter we are and have always been.

"This is our sacred trust. The very organization sponsoring this conference surveyed nearly a thousand individuals aged forty and over and found that more than half of them—fifty-six percent—said they were open to considering green burial options. This is our charge. *This is our time.* Let us embrace the great responsibility we are heirs to and demonstrate the commitment and courage needed to rise to the occasion.

"After all, there is no Planet B. Thank you very much."

Lilah stepped back from the podium. The applause was modest at first, but gradually gained intensity until people were on their feet. Lilah was smart enough to realize that most of that approbation came from attendees who were not part of the death industry. But it was a start. She'd happily accept it as a launch point to help her introduce more cracks to the shiny veneer of an industry that was tone deaf to the needs of the planet—and the people who were beginning to clamor for more humane, responsible, and natural ways to deal with the loss of their loved ones.

She knew it was going to be a slog, but it was a cause she was ready to embrace.

And then there was the other thing she was in more of a quandary about embracing . . . the one that was now heading toward her with a huge smile on her face.

"That was incredible," Sparkle exclaimed. "You must be so elated about the response."

"You think so?" Lilah asked.

"Don't you? Half the crowd was on its feet when you finished."

"Yes. I noticed that, too. But, sadly, it was the half that doesn't work in the industry. They seemed blithely unmoved. As usual."

"Don't give up. Sooner or later, they'll cave to market pressure—just like they did with the increasing popularity of cremation. You just have to keep beating this drum."

"I was too preoccupied with staying on topic to notice if there were any of my paparazzi in attendance. Dare I ask if you saw any?"

"Before I answer, how would you feel about a little hair of the dog?"

"Feeling a bit queasy, are we?"

"No. I just think it might make a bitter pill easier for you to swallow."

Lilah felt suddenly deflated. "What is it now?"

Sparkle took hold of her arm. "Come on. Let's go to Paris."

Lilah did her best not to coerce Sparkle into sharing her news until they were seated at a corner table in Mon Ami Gabi, an upscale French bistro in the heart of Paris. Against her better judgment, she ordered a French 75 martini—but swore she'd limit herself to just one. After the first sip, she felt her resolve melt away faster than an ice cube tossed into a hot oven.

"My god, this drink is transcendent."

Sparkle was drinking a tea-infused, fussy gin concoction called an Aviation. "I agree. This is truly extraordinary, too."

"How'd you manage to score a reservation here?" Lilah looked around the swanky interior of the place that looked like it had been plucked from a location on the Rue Saint-Jacques in actual Paris and dropped into the middle of the Las Vegas strip.

"Well, believe it or not, most people in Vegas don't eat at such an obscenely early hour. And I might have booked the table before we left to come out here."

"I should've known. What made you think we'd be free at this hour to come here?"

"I didn't know that for sure. But it's always easier to cancel than to get in if you wait too late to try."

"Words to live by. I think that's the mantra of the Catholic Church, too."

Sparkle laughed.

"So." Lilah twirled her martini glass by its long, delicate stem. It had to be some kind of very good crystal—probably Schott Zwiesel or something equally ostentatious. She always found there to be a direct correlation between the quality of the stemware and the price of the cocktails. She could snap this one between her fingers like a twig—and she feared she might want to once Sparkle finally spilled her guts.

"When are you going to tell me what I first had to be anesthetized to hear?"

"It's not that bad."

"Okay. Then how bad is it?"

"Remember how I told you about the rabbit and the woodland nymph engaging in some subterranean discourse just outside your door last night?"

"I do. And either that fucking rabbit has about fifteen cosplay clones who shopped at the same online retailer, or he's preternaturally prolific. Where haven't we seen him since we got here?"

"True. But what I neglected to tell you was that they weren't the only ones in that corridor when we arrived back at our rooms last night."

"Do I want to know who else was there?"

Sparkle demurred.

"Uh oh. It's not good, is it?"

"It's . . . complicated." She withdrew her cell phone and navigated to a screen before continuing with her narrative. "There was also someone walking past us—with a phone. I don't know if it was the woodland nymph busily bobbing for apples that caught his eye or this . . ." She passed the phone across the table to Lilah.

Lilah looked down at the lurid Instagram post showcasing

quite a vintage Vegas tableau.

Yep. There she was, feasting away on Sparkle's neck like it was the last oasis in the middle of a cultural desert. She read the regrettable caption.

> Love at first bite? Black Bird munches on
> fresh meat during her stopover in Vegas.
> #BlackBirdOfChernobyl, #BallysLasVegas,
> #whathappensinvegas

She looked at Sparkle with incredulity. "How can this possibly get any worse?"

"If I were you, I wouldn't ask that question."

"Which means?"

"Kay called."

Lilah slumped back against her seat before signaling to their server. When he approached their table, Lilah held up her martini glass.

"Yeah. We're gonna need another pair of these."

The server nodded and faced Sparkle. "And the same for you, madam?"

"Oh," Lilah cut in. "Do you want another one, too?"

Sparkle laughed and told the server the same drink would be fine.

"Do you want to put me out of my misery and tell me what Kay had to say?" Lilah asked after he walked off. "I assume she saw it."

"Oh, she did."

"You know, I'm not entirely sure *she* isn't the one posting half of that shit. She's got a seriously twisted sense of humor."

"I kind of doubt it. Her reaction was more . . . proprietary."

Lilah smelled a rat. "In what sense?"

"Let's just say she was concerned about its possible impact on future contracts."

"That's ridiculous. Why would those slimy coffin jockeys at FSI give a flying fuck about anything I do? I'm not even part of their continuing equation."

"She wasn't talking about FSI, Lilah. She was talking about Salem Baking Company."

"Even so. I'm not part of that deal."

"No. You're not. But I am."

That brought Lilah's umbrage up short. "What do you mean?"

"Kay is concerned that press like this might tarnish the sainted legacy of dear Granny Stohler. She's afraid that images of the heir apparent—me—engaged in questionable conduct with an avowed social media iconoclast might diminish our chances of sealing that cookie deal."

"Well, sonofabitch." Lilah rubbed a hand across her forehead. "What the hell are we supposed to do to clean this mess up?"

"I wish I knew. The whole thing was a ridiculous lapse in judgment for both of us. I cannot believe I allowed myself to behave like a crazed wanton."

"Wanton? Isn't that a little strong?"

"Seriously?" Sparkle asked with some impatience. "Were you present for any part of what happened last night?"

"Yeah. I suppose there were some elements of wantonish behavior—by each of us."

"I don't think 'wantonish' is really a word . . ."

Lilah laughed. "You mean to tell me that you're fine with having sat on my . . . well . . . you know. But use of a questionable pseudoword elicits a formal protest?"

Sparkle looked shocked by Lilah's specific reference to an element of her performance the night before.

"You know, I could cite a few tricks of your own that stand—or lie—as equally noteworthy."

"Such as?" Lilah leaned toward her. "Go ahead. I'm all ears."

"Okay, wise guy. Such as the three times you put your . . ."

She was saved by the arrival of their server with their next round of cocktails.

"Do you see anything that strikes your fancy?" he asked as he replaced their glasses. "I'm happy to describe any items that require further explanation."

Lilah was tempted to ask him to pull up a chair.

"No, thank you," she said instead. "I think we can blunder our way through just fine."

"Of course. I'll be back to take your orders in a few minutes."

After he left, Lilah faced Sparkle with resignation. "Look. We did what we did and there's no denying it. The question now is what do we do to minimize fallout for Stohler's—but more importantly, for you?"

"I'm not worried about myself. I can handle it. But I don't want to ruin this franchise opportunity for the business."

"Here is one thing I know for sure: nobody is better than Kay Stover at navigating a minefield and emerging on the other side intact with a contract for how to build better minefields for fun and profit. Trust me—she will have half a dozen ideas about how to fix this. And we won't want to do any of them. But it's better for your long-term health and sanity to learn now that resistance is futile."

"Kay is your real mentor, isn't she? More, even, than your father."

Lilah thought about Sparkle's observation. "She's more like

my probation officer. Dad taught me about the practical side of the business. Kay taught me about life—and the value of keeping your personal attorney on speed dial."

Lilah's phone pinged.

"I wonder what fresh hell this is . . ." She pulled it out of her jacket pocket and checked the message. "Oh, my god." She smirked and looked up at Sparkle.

"What is it?"

"Guess who won the coveted hospitality door prize?"

"No . . ."

"Uh huh. Guess we'll have to go and claim it before heading to the airport in the morning."

"At least all that ink wasn't in vain."

"Which reminds me—were you able to wash all those coffin stamps off? I still have one that refuses to give up the ghost. I fear it may send the wrong message to clients."

"It took some scrubbing but, yes. I finally got them all to disappear."

"Maybe you'll luck out and the rest of what happened here will disappear, too."

Sparkle didn't look convinced or particularly fond of Lilah's suggestion—and Lilah began to wonder if she'd insulted her before Sparkle met her eyes and replied in a steady voice.

"Maybe so."

The flight back to North Carolina was remarkable only in that it was packed to the gills with tired-looking travelers who appeared to be as desperate to leave Las Vegas as they were. Who else would choose such an early flight, versus the die hards who would happily take a red-eye to gain a few more hours on the casino floor?

The only dramatic aspect of the trip home came when they had to figure out how to transport Sparkle's door prize: a 250-round case of 16 gauge, high-quality lead shot shells designed to contain the cremains of a deceased gun or sport shooting enthusiast. The manufacturer, Holy Smoke, LLC, provided a certificate entitling the bearer to engage Holy Smoke to hand-load the cremains into the shells when the blessed event occurred.

Sparkle was oddly excited about the quirky windfall. Her father, who'd been an enthusiastic lifelong hunter, was her . . . *target* . . . for the unique memorial gift.

"Don't you think it's a bit esoteric?" Lilah asked, when it became clear that Sparkle intended to keep the door prize.

"Not at all. And it beats the hell out of what I usually give him for Christmas."

"Which is?"

Sparkle sighed. "He has a serious chocolate addiction— but suffers from constant acid reflux. So, one year, I figured out how to make him big slabs of peppermint bark that wouldn't aggravate his digestive tract. Now it's what he wants every year."

"That sounds intriguing." Lilah was amused. "How'd you crack the GI code?"

"It's simple but effective. Instead of using crushed candy canes, I use peppermint Tums."

"Oh, dear god. This might be *your* get out of jail free card— with Salem Baking Company."

"It is pretty inspired."

As are most things about you, Lilah thought.

In the end, they decided to quit haggling with TSA in their

vain efforts to prove that the shells were not, and had in fact never been, loaded with live gunpowder. They were early enough for their flight that they had time to locate a post office in the airport and mail the box—although Lilah was the one tasked with lying to the counter agent about the contents of the ten-pound package.

"It's a mortician's deluxe tissue reducer set with two extra smoothing spatulas for wrinkles and saggy skin. Extremely fragile."

The clerk couldn't process the shipment fast enough.

Within minutes, they were though security and winging their way back to Winston-Salem. With luck, they'd arrive in time for Sparkle to check in on preparations for the Winkler funeral.

Lilah was blissfully unaware that Sparkle had chosen not to share any of the special arrangements requested by the family.

It had been a good decision because when they arrived at the funeral home about fifteen minutes before the start of the service, Lilah was stopped dead in her tracks by the barrage of sound that hit them like a rhythmic tsunami.

"Are those—conga drums?" she asked Sparkle.

"Unfortunately, yes."

"And . . ." Lilah listened more closely, "whistles?"

"Those, too."

"What exactly *is* this? And why is it playing at ear-splitting volume?"

"I think you'd call it contemporary Latin music?"

"That part I get. Are we holding a salsa dancing competition?"

"Not exactly."

Before Sparkle could explain the reason for the serenade, the vocals started.

We gotta get going.
Gotta get going.
What are we gonna do?
We're on our way to somewhere,
Cuchi Cuchi me and you.

"*Cuchi Cuchi?*"

Sparkle closed her eyes and nodded.

"Is that . . . *Charo?*"

"The one and only."

Lilah started to reply but gave up on it. "I'm going to need a moment. A lot of moments."

"I can't say I blame you. Remember when I told you I had to deal with some special requests for the Winkler funeral?"

Lilah nodded.

"Behold: special request number one."

"You mean there are more?"

"Oh, yeah. Several."

"Now I wish we'd packed those shotgun shells . . ."

Another special concession consisted of allowing Ms. Winkler's three beloved golden retrievers—Patty, Maxene, and LaVerne—to stand vigil beside the massive makeshift table containing her cremated remains. Apparently, Ms. Winkler had been an outspoken advocate for protecting the environment and had wanted her ashes interred inside a raised garden bed—which her chosen family had elected to bring to the funeral service—*in its entirety.* The thing had to weigh at least four hundred pounds. Sparkle explained that Gee String had set sturdy planks of solid hardwood across two sawhorses and draped it with black cloth. The raised garden had already been planted with wintergreen squash, kale, radicchio, and collard greens. A festive pot of coral peonies—favorites of the deceased—had been set in the center.

Ms. Winkler had been a prolific poet throughout her lifetime, and her collected works filled several bank boxes. The last concession the family had requested was making it possible for a designated number of friends and family members to approach a podium and read from the exhaustive collection of Ms. Winkler's heartfelt but indifferent poetry.

Sadly, the readers were miked-up, too, and the verse they shared—which could best be described as doggerel—could be heard all over the mortuary.

Judging by the content of the verse, it seemed that Ms. Winkler had been a zealous champion for combating climate change—as well as being a staunch supporter of reproductive freedom and the expansion of voting rights.

> I am prone to wonder
> As I wander in this sphere,
> How so much that was perfect
> Could now just disappear.
> Poppies no longer burst
> Into brilliant crimson hue.
> And legionnaires, they mourn,
> Along with all things true,
> As all their once fond icons
> Are now turned into glue.

The recitations were so bad that Wardell, who could withstand just about anything, complained to Lilah that if the readings continued much longer, he'd have to file a complaint with the Labor Relations Board. It wasn't exactly that the poetry was so bad, although it was—it was more that whenever the reader hit the end of a rhyming couplet, Ms. Winkler's three dogs would howl in unison like a canine homage to their namesake Andrews Sisters.

Lilah told Wardell just to crank up the volume on his Def Leppard Spotify playlist while she ventured upstairs to see if she could intervene and get Gee String to lower the volume on the makeshift poetry slam.

She ran into Kay Stover, literally, at the top of the stairs.

"Well, well," Kay exclaimed. "The infamous Black Bird has returned from her three-day stint of feasting on the blood of virgins—or in this case, contract employees."

"Don't start, Kay," Lilah growled. "I already feel like a schmuck."

"Good. If your inability to control your libido blows the Salem Baking deal, you'll feel more like a feathered wrecking ball than a schmuck."

Lilah looked around the hallway where they were standing. "Could we discuss this someplace a bit more private? I'd prefer not to have my dirty laundry compete for airtime with that greeting card drivel."

"Sure." Kay indicated the selection room. "How about in here? It's unoccupied right now."

"What's wrong with your office?"

"Hambone is in there right now, trying to fix the ceiling fan. It sounds like a washing machine on tilt. That's why I was looking for a quieter place to work."

"Fine. I do some of my best thinking in here, anyway."

"Hang on." Kay approached the door near the stairs and entered the supply closet. She emerged with a bottle of Baileys

Irish Cream liqueur.

"Isn't it a little early for that?" Lilah asked.

"You're kidding, right? I put this on my Cheerios."

"And you're worried about my reputation?"

"No. Not yours. Yours has been irredeemable for decades." They entered the selection room and closed the door behind them. "I'm concerned about Sparkle's reputation."

Lilah dropped into an upholstered chair. "I don't know how to explain what happened. Believe me. It wasn't scripted."

Kay had retrieved two plastic cups from the water cooler and poured them each a generous portion of the Baileys.

"Spare me the Monday morning quarterback routine." She handed Lilah her plastic cup. "I'm not your shrink. I gave up on trying to analyze your motivations eons ago. Besides, it doesn't take a Mensa baby to see that you two have had the hots for each other since *forever*."

"What?"

"Seriously? Are you going to deny that you haven't wanted to tiddle her winks ever since she got here?"

"Her what?"

"Never mind. It's before your time. Suffice it to say you've been wanting to get into her pants for more than a month now."

"That's absurd. I have *not*."

"Okay, then. So, what happened in Las Vegas was just— what? Some alcohol-induced lapse in judgment?"

"We weren't drunk," Lilah muttered.

That fact seemed to surprise Kay. "No?"

Lilah shook her head.

"Who knew? Maybe there's hope for you after all."

Lilah was ready to reply with a snappy rejoinder when something caught her eye. She leaned forward to get a closer view.

"What the hell is *that?*" She pointed to a brand-new Batesville economy model with a lurid liner.

"Rita Kitty is trying out a new color palette."

"*Puce?*"

Kay shrugged. "Why not?"

"Who the hell is going to buy that? It looks like it's been used to store cheap silverware."

"Funny you should mention that. It's already been purchased by the Camel Pawn Shop family."

"Of course it has."

"Now quit trying to change the subject. You were about to explain to me how an image of you and Sparkle, clearly en route to a night of making whoopee, ended up on about sixty thousand cell phone screens."

"No. I don't believe I was."

"Oh? So, you both were on your way to review your remarks for the breakout session on green burial?"

"Well . . ."

"And were looking for the notes you'd accidentally dropped down the front of her blouse? Because that happens . . ."

"Something like that."

"Lilah? Don't misunderstand the nature of my concern."

Lilah threw up her hands. "I get it, Kay. You're worried I'll blow up the Salem Baking deal—and ruin Sparkle's reputation in the process. She already shared your concerns with me."

"Did she? It's true those were the perspectives I shared with her. Did she also tell you she said she didn't give a rat's ass?"

Lilah was stunned. "She said that?"

"Well, words to that effect. By the sheepish look now ruining your normally stone-faced expression, I gather she did *not* share that part of our conversation."

"Again, I ask—what's your point, Kay? Do you want me to vow to stay away from her? I already have."

"Lilah? There's what's good for business, and there's what's good for your life. The tragedy is that you've never been able to tell the difference. Now you have a chance to change that."

"Is this still about the cookies?"

"Oh, for god's sake." Kay poured herself another drink. "Fuck the cookies, Lilah. I'm talking about your future."

There was a gentle tap on the door.

"Come on in," Lilah called out. She was relieved by the interruption. She hated it when Kay launched into one of her ubiquitous sensitive chats. And this one had the earmarks of a doozie.

The door pushed open, and Sparkle peeked around it.

"I've been looking for you," she said before noticing Kay perched on another chair beside the now-reinforced urn display. "Sorry, Kay. I don't mean to interrupt."

"No. Come on in," Lilah encouraged her. "Kay and I were just shooting the breeze to escape the Winkler poetry slam. What did you need?"

Sparkle looked at Kay. "Are you sure it's okay?"

"Absolutely." Kay got up to grab another plastic cup. "Come in and join us. We were just solving some first-world problems."

Sparkle took in the open bottle of Baileys. "So, I see. Isn't this becoming a thing in here?"

"And it's about time, if you ask me." Lilah looked around the space filled with caskets, urns, and other memorial keepsakes. "I honestly think we should turn this joint into a vodka bar. We could get around the liquor laws by making it a private club. We'd cater to a very exclusive clientele: you just have to be connected to someone freshly dead to enter."

"That stands about as much of a chance of success as most of your ideas." Kay handed Sparkle her drink.

"I really didn't mean to interrupt." Sparkle sat on a folding chair near the door. "I just had some interesting news to share with Lilah."

"Oh?" Lilah was intrigued. "What is it? Did we get busted for mailing that case of shotgun shells?"

Kay choked on her Baileys.

"I'll explain later, Kay," Lilah told her. "It involves a button of martinis and ten tiny coffin stamps." She returned her attention to Sparkle. "You were saying?"

"Well, I just got a call from the hotel. They've been trying to reach you. It turns out that I wasn't the only one who won a door prize. You did, too."

"Me?" Lilah was immediately suspicious. "What the hell did I win?"

"Brace yourself. It appears you were unanimously selected to win the coveted Best of Show Cosplay Award at the anime convention."

"*What?*" Lilah blurted with disbelief. "Those people are certifiable."

"Cosplay?" Kay Stover asked. "What the hell is that?"

"It's a portmanteau of 'costume play,'" Sparkle explained. "Participants create and wear fantastic and intricate costumes to represent their favorite characters from movies and animated—or 'anime'—cartoons."

"It even goes beyond that," Lilah added. "They actually get into role-playing and acting like they're the real characters come to life—sometimes very convincingly, too—right down to this randy, giant rabbit who we saw getting a blow—"

Sparkle loudly cleared her throat to stop Lilah's recitation.

"I think Kay gets your drift about role-playing."

"Yeah," Kay agreed. "It helped me remember why I always hated going to Vegas. But you?" She regarded Lilah. "I didn't realize you took costumes along."

"I *didn't.*"

"That's kind of the point, Kay," Sparkle explained. "Apparently, the organizers of the anime convention thought Lilah was role-playing."

"Role-playing?" Lilah asked. "Role-playing as what?"

"As the Black Bird of Chernobyl. In other words, as *yourself.*"

"Wow." Kay's tone was dripping with admiration. "It's true that nobody does the whole Diva of Death thing with the panache you bring to the role. And let's face it—you *have* nearly attained pop icon status."

"Well, not *yourself*, exactly. Your online persona. They thought you were cosplaying and role-playing as the Black Bird of Chernobyl."

"Let me get this straight." Lilah remained unconvinced. "All those furries running around and jacking up the light fixtures with their eight-foot headdresses thought I was impersonating some Instagram fantasy that didn't even exist a month ago?"

"The times, they are a -changin','" Kay Stover chanted.

"Yeah. *Whatever*, Bob Dylan." Lilah looked at Sparkle. "So, what'd I win?"

"It's a surprisingly significant prize. Fifteen thousand dollars in cash and a trophy that makes this new Batesville economy look understated."

"Fifteen large? For real?"

"Apparently. They said they needed your tax information before sending the check."

"Well, shit. Imagine the impression I could've made if I'd

remembered to pack my black lace bustier."

"If you two will excuse me." Kay got to her feet. "Hambone should be finished with my ceiling fan by now." Kay was still chuckling as she walked to the door. "Thank god it can't get any weirder than this."

She opened the door and a deafening reprise of the Charo classic was making the paintings of long-dead Stohlers that lined the walls of the corridor vibrate.

Lilah and Sparkle exchanged glances.

"Wrong," they replied in unison.

Teeter Rowan

April 10, 1929 – December 14, 2023

Mr. Teeter Rowan, 94, of Winston-Salem, went
to the big grain silo in the sky on Thursday,
December 14, at his home in Winston-
Salem, NC. He was born April 10, 1929, on
his family farm in Winston-Salem. He was
the second youngest of 14 children born to
Lucy Jane Ziglar and Henry Love Rowan of
Forsyth County. Teeter graduated from Atkins
High School in Winston-Salem with perfect
attendance, a fact that he would proudly
proclaim at any opportunity. Teeter was a
farmer all his life, taking over the family farm
when he was just 23. In later years, he took
a job with the Postal Service as a substitute
rural mail carrier, delivering the mail in the
morning and then returning to the farm and
continuing his work until supper time, his
favorite meal of the day.

Teeter is survived by five grandchildren
and four great-grandchildren who he loved
like family. He farmed with his best friend,
Blue "Red" Hanes until Red passed away.
Every night at exactly 9 p.m., the phone
on the wall would ring, and they would

discuss farming and weather, most evenings talking for over an hour. Teeter and his wife, Dot Goins Rowan, celebrated their 67th anniversary days before she preceded him in death. Also surviving is his beloved "therapy" dog, his Jack Russell terrier, Levi, who he loved so much and was by his side when he passed. So were his cats, Fuzz, the blind cat, and Mouthy, the stray cat that adopted him.

Teeter wanted to return to the earth he loved in a simple way without any fuss, so he chose to be buried right away, next to his wife in the woods behind his house. He asked for his body to be wrapped in the wedding ring pattern quilt his granny Rowan gave him when he married Dot Goins. He said that quilt kept them warm every night for 67 years, and he figured it would continue to do the job just fine in the afterlife, too.

A simple service of remembrance will be held at 11 a.m. Saturday, December 16, 2023, at Stohler's Funeral Home with Brother Trevor Priddy Smith officiating.

Posted by Stohler's Funeral Home, Winston-Salem, NC

Death Takes a Holiday

"Do you mind explaining *this?*" Lilah threw a fat envelope emblazoned with a *Forbes* magazine logo and a declarative, KNOW YOUR VALUE onto Kay's desk. "This was waiting for me when I arrived this morning."

"Take a seat, Lilah."

"What if I don't *feel* like sitting down? Not right now, and sure as hell not with Mika Brzezinski."

"Lilah, I shouldn't have to tell you that this opportunity is like manna from heaven. She wants to interview you because, practically overnight, you've joined Caitlin Doughty as the face of the Good Death movement. Read my lips: this is not a bad thing."

"It's absurd. How the hell does getting tagged in an Instagram post by some pencil-dick teenager with a pissant grudge suddenly elevate me to this realm of rarified air?"

"Her producers also cited the remarks you gave at the NFDA conference. Apparently, your online celebrity led reporters from several mainstream media outlets—including *Forbes*—to attend the event. The fact that you, as a young woman, run a successful funeral home that is becoming noticed for its offbeat and experimental approaches—*and* you're an outspoken advocate for change within a twenty-eight billion dollar a year industry that stubbornly remains wedded to antiquated methods and traditions that serve only one purpose: swelling their bank accounts. Like it or not, you have become a leading voice for change."

"I can't do any of those things if I stay on here below-stairs, doing endless successions of full poke and props on mee-maw and pawpaw for the patrons of this house of mourning glories."

"I know. That's why you need to take FSI's offer and go someplace where you *can* make a difference."

"You want me to sell this place? Leave Stohler's? What would my father do? Turn all the portraits of the ghoulish Stohlers who came before me to the wall? How can I do this to his legacy?"

"Your job is not to prolong your father's legacy—or anyone else's. Your job is to live your own life."

"What about the lives of Hambone and Gee String? What about *your* life, Kay? You already said they won't retain you."

"Lilah, I'm seventy-two years old. I've done my stint as death's handmaiden. It's time for me to hang up my abacus and see how the other half lives—you know—the people who cleave to the daylight. So don't worry one bit about me. I'll be just fine."

Lilah wasn't yet ready to capitulate. She dragged out a chair and dropped down on it in frustration.

"Even if that were true, Kay, I don't have the slightest inclination to be interviewed for inclusion in some glorified talk show homage to rich and famous do-gooders. In case you haven't noticed, I am neither."

"Lilah . . . it's already set up. Brzezinski is in the area for another event, so they're arriving tomorrow afternoon. You're *doing* the interview. If you care, as you say you do, about the future of this industry, you'll put on your big girl surplice, suck it up, and deal with it."

Lilah gave up. It was pointless to continue arguing with Kay when she had her mind made up. It had always been that way, ever since Kay came to work at Stohler's when Lilah was seven years old and could only dream of one day having unfettered access to the charms of the embalming suite.

"Okay, okay. You win. But paybacks for this will be hell, Kay. I'm not even kidding."

"Oh, really? What are you going to do that's worse than the time you dumped a quart of formaldehyde into my gas tank?"

"Hey—that was well-intentioned. You'd been complaining nonstop about that old Chevy of yours constantly dying on you and I thought it would prolong its vitality."

"Right."

"I still don't think it was reasonable for you to have made me hand wash all the hearses—for six weeks."

"It built character."

"I was *seven*, Kay. I couldn't even reach the landau bars without standing on a gurney."

"Do you know what formaldehyde does to a car engine, Lilah?"

"No. But as I recall, you started driving a Yugo shortly after that and seemed very happy with it."

"Desperate measures." Kay dismissed Lilah's observation. "With you as a constant in my life, I knew I'd need a car that was impervious to chemical interventions. Ironically, that thing probably would've gotten better gas mileage with an occasional dose of preservative."

"Necessity is the mother of invention."

"Which is precisely why Sparkle is going to prep you for your interview."

That caught Lilah off guard. "She is?"

Kay nodded. "Turns out she actually knows Mika."

"What? How?"

"Apparently, Brzezinski gave a commencement address at Johns Hopkins when Sparkle was working on a graduate certificate there, and Sparkle was her campus aide-de-camp. I gather they developed quite a rapport. So that makes her uniquely suited to help you prepare for the interview."

"That's . . . surprising."

"As are most things about Sparkle. But I'm sure I don't have to tell you that."

"No comment." Lilah got to her feet. "I suppose she's expecting me?"

Kay nodded. "She's in the kitchen getting a jump start on a fresh batch of cookies. Apparently, they're interested in touching on that aspect of your inspired leadership, too."

"Mine?"

"Who was I to correct the misperception? So go forth and prepare, Young Skywalker. Your Yoda awaits."

Lilah made a rude gesture before leaving Kay's office and heading for the kitchen, where she found Sparkle, bent over a row of cookie sheets, dropping batter with a small ice cream scoop.

Sparkle looked surprised to see her. "What brings you into this space you describe as a hellscape of artery-blocking coagulants?"

"Who told you that?"

"I refuse to reveal my source."

"It figures. Kay told me you were going to prep me for the

Brzezinski interview tomorrow."

"Oh? So that means you've agreed to do it?"

"I think 'agreed' might be a stretch."

"Oh, really? What method did she use?"

"Extortion comes to mind."

Sparkle laughed and put the two sheets of cookies into the oven.

"Are you ever going to break down and actually try one of these cookies?"

"Not if I can help it. You know the old adage: 'Mithridates, he died old.'"

"I think that was about ingesting poison."

Lilah raised an eyebrow. "And your point would be?"

"Right . . ." Sparkle tucked an errant twist of hair behind her ear. "These will take about twelve minutes to bake; then I'll be free. When are you able to get together to talk about this?"

"No time like the present." Lilah consulted her watch. "It's nearly 5.30. Do you have dinner plans?"

Sparkle seemed surprised by her suggestion.

"No. I was planning to heat up some of the Brunswick stew Hambone gave me. Care to join me?"

Lilah thought about the wisdom of going to Sparkle's house to do . . . , *anything*, but quickly derided herself for being ridiculous. They were both high-functioning adults—not alley cats in heat. And she didn't want to appear prudish by rejecting Sparkle's hospitality out of hand.

"Sure. That's very generous of you. Are you sure it's safe to eat?"

"I take it you haven't read any of the comments posted on Rufina Strub's memorial page?"

"Not yet . . ."

Sparkle smiled. "Suffice it to say that accolades for Walburg Baptist's Brunswick stew rivaled the superlatives expressed for Rufina's lauded chicken pie gravy."

"Please tell me you're not compounding either of those things into a new breed of cookie."

"Not just yet, no." Sparkle began washing out her mixing bowl and scoop. "Are you ever going to relent and try one of these?"

"Not if I can help it."

"Why not? Are you clinging to some kind of stubborn principle?"

"Maybe I'm clinging to my ghoulish figure."

"Isn't that 'girlish'?"

"No. It ceased being girlish when I could no longer find all-black mix-n-match on the Junior Terrace at Belk."

Sparkle gave up. "Do you want to meet me in the parking lot in fifteen minutes? You can follow me to my house. It's not far—only about a ten minute drive."

Lilah agreed and headed to her office to collect her things. The dark chorus in her head was cranking up its prognostications of doom. *What the hell are you doing?* it chanted. *This isn't the way to keep yourself out of the shitter. It's giving in to this kind of self-destructive behavior that will dig you in deeper than you already are. Be smart. Be vigilant. Run the fuck away . . .*

She snapped up her keys and messenger bag.

Black Bird my ass. I am such a goddamn weenie.

Sparkle lived in a small house in the Ardmore section of Winston-Salem, not far from Baptist Hospital. It was an historic neighborhood filled with Queen Anne craftsman-style homes built mostly in the early years of the twentieth century. Lilah had been surprised to see that Sparkle's house was located less than a mile from her parents' home on Glade Street, in the West End neighborhood where she and Frankie had grown up.

In fact, Lilah had fond memories of scouting for roadkill in this very neighborhood . . .

Small world, she thought as she parked her car to join Sparkle at the entrance to her bungalow. This part of Ardmore was revered for its quiet streets lined with big shade trees, and houses with wide front porches. Sparkle's masonry house was painted a pretty shade of salmon with dark gray trim—a color combination that would've made Rita Kitty quiver with glee, since it matched her recent foray into the fine art of retouching boo-boos on hoopties.

"Nice place," Lilah commented when she joined Sparkle. "How long have you lived here?"

"Less than a year." Sparkle unlocked the big front door so they could enter. "The only reason I got it was because I lucked into it before the new crop of hospital residents flooded the market and snapped up everything in sight."

Inside, the place was every bit as tidy and well put together as Lilah expected it to be. Sparkle had arguably good taste—befitting an acknowledged pro at marketing and brand identity. The place looked like a monument to Pottery Barn.

"Make yourself at home. I'm just going to ditch these things and change clothes. I'll be right back."

Change clothes? Didn't Sparkle lounge in the same J. Crew mix-n-match that she wore to the office?

When she was left alone, Lilah wandered about the room looking over Sparkle's books and the few framed photographs that

201

sat atop her built-in bookcase. There was a lot of contemporary fiction—probably titles that topped the lists compiled by Oprah Winfrey or Reese Witherspoon. There were also a bunch of older books with faded and worn cloth covers. Classics, mostly. She assumed those were heirlooms or books she'd picked up at yard sales. She pulled out a copy of *The Heart Is a Lonely Hunter* by Carson McCullers and opened it. An inscription on the title page read, *For Lee Ann Ellis, 1987.* There was a bookmark inserted at the beginning of chapter fourteen.

"That was my mother's." Sparkle's voice surprised her.

Lilah lowered the book. "Sorry. I wasn't snooping."

"No worries. She'd been reading that book while she was pregnant with me. She never got to finish it."

"I'm sorry." Lilah placed the book back into its spot on the shelf.

"I keep telling myself that one day, I need to read the rest of it for her. But I haven't been able yet to make myself do it."

"I can understand that. It would be like another kind of finality, I guess."

"That's what I think, too. It's almost like she's not really gone if she still has something left to finish. Irrational, I know. I can't tell you how many times I've picked it up intending to finish reading it. But I always stop myself."

"Have you read the book before?"

"Only to that very point. Do you know how it ends?"

"Yes. There might be a metaphor in the fact that your mother stopped reading it before it became even more depressingly bleak and hopeless."

"Good to know. Thank you for sharing that with me. I won't torture myself anymore for not finishing it."

"Don't. Sometimes things should end in the middle. What

we don't know can often be more comforting than what we might eventually find out."

"I'll try to remember that." Sparkle indicated that Lilah should follow her. "Would you like something to drink?"

Lilah had a hard time not laughing at her suggestion. After all, they didn't have the greatest track record when it came to sitting down with alcoholic beverages. But they were there to work, not to indulge in any more ridiculous parlor games.

"Sure. What did you have in mind?"

"I was going to open some wine, if that sounds appealing." When Lilah nodded her assent, Sparkle asked, "What kind do you think goes best with kettle-cooked, Southern Baptist stew?"

"Um," Lilah thought about it. "Got anything tinged with vinegar and gall?"

"Are you channeling the Brunswick stew or the prep session for your interview tomorrow?"

"Yes."

Sparkle laughed and headed for her small kitchen. "Let's see what we have." She began to pull bottles out of a narrow wine fridge and line them up on the counter top.

"I've got a Bardolino, a Beaujolais, and a decent Côtes du Rhône. Or we can always crack into this." She slammed a mason jar filled with clear liquid onto the counter. "It was a gift from Gee String during my first week. I haven't had the courage to break the seal on it yet."

"Are you kidding me?" Lilah picked it up to examine it. "Do you think he made it?"

"I was afraid to ask. I thought about gifting it to Rita Kitty to see if it would do a better job cleaning her makeup brushes, but I didn't want to risk hurting Gee String's feelings if he accidentally stole it back from her and recognized the jar."

"I see you've gotten to know the Freeman brothers well."

"I think they're adorable—like big hearts with feet."

Lilah perched on a stool. "That's a pretty apt description of them. I have always thought of them as the heartbeat of the mortuary."

Sparkle took a corkscrew out of a drawer. "Do you think they'll get jobs with another—*long term firm*—when you sell Stohler's to FSI?"

Lilah laughed at her description. "Where'd you hear that term?"

"I pay attention."

"Funeral humor is a specialized and oft misunderstood pursuit."

"I gather that. I guess it takes the sting out of the work if you can make fun of it."

"True." Lilah thought about Sparkle's comment. "But I think it goes deeper than that, too. It's only when we learn to make light of things that scare the bejesus out of us that we can begin to defuse their power. Death is like that for most people— it's the most terrifying and mysterious unknown we'll ever have to confront. It's the only thing in life that lasts forever—so it's the one event we fear more than just about anything else. And because we keep it that way—shrouded in mystery and hostage to rigid, archaic traditions—it wields incredible power over us. So, we learn how to joke about it to knock it down to size." She smiled. "At least, I do."

"See? You're already set for the interview tomorrow. I don't think you need any coaching at all."

"She isn't going to want to hear drivel like that."

"That's where you're wrong. This is precisely what she'll want to hear. It's why she's coming."

"Oh?" Lilah batted her eyes. "You mean she's not coming because of my manifold charms? The Black Bird of Chernobyl who awakens the deceased moon and thumbs her beak at decent society?"

"Her, too." Sparkle held up a bottle. "How about this one?"

It was the Beaujolais.

"A good choice," Lilah agreed. "A wine fermented in whole clusters and gassed with carbon dioxide. What's not to love?"

"Yes. That's exactly what I thought, too."

"It so is *not* what you thought."

Sparkle set about opening the wine. "Is this another one of those Truth or Dare games?"

"Not even close, blondie. I gave those up for Lent."

"Lent doesn't begin until Valentine's Day." Sparkle set about extracting the cork with panache. It made a dramatic pop when she withdrew it.

"It figures you'd know something like that," Lilah observed.

"I'm Catholic. It's in the contract."

"Interesting. I had you pegged as something less steeped in liturgy and more rooted in . . . disapproval."

"Such as?"

Lilah shrugged. "Presbyterian?"

"Dear god." Sparkle poured them each a glass of the fragrant wine. "I'd never be able to pull off all those Pendleton plaids."

Lilah accepted the glass from her and inhaled the wine's fruity bouquet of strawberries and red currant. Sparkle had been right: the wine should pair perfectly with Hambone's humble stew.

"Do you want to go sit down and enjoy the wine? We can maybe do a bit of prep before we eat?"

"Sure." Lilah was intrigued to find out what kind of prep

Sparkle thought she needed.

They returned to the living room and took seats opposite each other in armchairs that were upholstered in distressed-looking gray leather.

"Okay," Lilah began. "Where do we start?"

"I thought maybe we could role play. I'll ask you what I expect might be among her interview questions and we can see how comfortable you are with your answers."

"How do you know what she'll ask?"

"I don't know exactly—but I've watched dozens of these interviews, and they seem to follow a similar pattern. She'll do a quick introduction to you and summarize your notable accomplishments. Then she'll drill down on one or two areas of distinction—the things that put you on her radar."

"You mean like me threatening to disembowel the ingrate who started this madness? Or me acting like a circus monkey on the stage at Planet Hollywood? Or possibly, me test-driving a human composting chamber?"

"Although those are among your pick hits, I was thinking more about your keynote address at the conference."

"That wasn't a keynote. It was just a collection of remarks."

"Trust me, Lilah. That *was* the keynote of the conference. And you delivered it superbly."

"If you say so."

"For starters," Sparkle set her wine glass down on an end table, "these profiles are called 'Know Your Value' for a reason. Your fondness for self-deprecation will not serve you well in this forum."

"So, you're saying I should show up wearing aviator shades and have swag to pass out to her crew?"

"Can you manage to be serious for ten seconds?"

"I don't know. I've never tried."

"We don't have to do this if you find it so irksome." Sparkle's tone held more than a hint of annoyance.

Lilah realized that acting like an ass wasn't doing her any favors. "If we don't practice, does that mean I won't get any stew?"

Sparkle drummed her fingers on the overstuffed arm of her chair.

"What kind of heartless bitch do you take me for?" she asked.

Lilah was relieved that Sparkle had recovered her sense of humor, and fought an impulse to say, *I'll take you even if you are heartless . . .* especially *if you are.* But she managed to compose herself.

"I . . . apologize. It's kind of you to offer to help me and I'm . . . grateful So, please . . . let's do this."

"Are you sure?"

Lilah nodded. "Did I mention that I really love Brunswick stew?"

"All right, then. Let's try this again."

"I'm all ears."

"So, Lilah. Tell us a bit about the Good Death movement and why you've become one of its leading proponents."

Lilah did her best to summarize the relationship between emerging, eco-friendly burial solutions and the ongoing need to demythologize death as the best way to move a new generation forward with a healthier and unfettered understanding of our place in the natural, organic cycle of life.

She thought she'd done pretty well, actually . . .

But Sparkle sat watching her with some kind of *something* etched on her face—and it didn't feel to Lilah like it was satisfaction with her answer.

"Was it not good?" she asked.

"No. It was perfect."

"Then why do you look like you just caught me cheating on a math quiz?"

"Sorry. It wasn't your answer. It's your body language."

"My *body* language?" Lilah looked down at herself. "What's wrong with it?"

"Look at how you're sitting. Arms and legs crossed—like you're shutting everything out."

"I'm not shutting anything out. This is how I sit. It's natural."

"Natural?" Sparkle repeated. "Lilah, it looks like you're waiting to have a root canal."

"Okay, okay. So, what do you want me to do?"

"For starters, relax."

Lilah tried to figure out how to comply. She uncrossed her arms, but then had no idea what to do with them. Grasp the arms of the chair? Drop them loosely at her sides? Throw them over her head and wave them around like a Pentecostal at a Wednesday night prayer meeting?

She looked at Sparkle. "I have no idea how to do that."

"Okay. Let's try something." Sparkle got up and stood in front of her chair. "Stand up and do what I do."

Lilah was suspicious but followed suit.

"Now," Sparkle continued, "roll your shoulders and your neck around to loosen them. Like this."

Sparkle demonstrated the maneuvers. Truthfully, Lilah was a lot more interested in watching Sparkle go through her gyrations than actually trying to repeat them.

"Are you going to quit gawking at me and try to loosen up?" Sparkle asked.

"Okay. Fine." Lilah tried her best to imitate Sparkle's

movements, but she knew she probably looked more like a psychotic marionette with a crack addiction.

Sparkle stopped her demonstration. "What is that supposed to be?"

"Me relaxing?"

"No. That's not relaxing. That's more like involuntary muscle spasms."

"So, sue me if I can't replicate your Zumba moves."

"Zumba? Seriously? How much daytime TV do you watch while you're downstairs hiding?"

"In the first place, I do not *hide* downstairs—or anywhere else. Which should explain why my regrettable visage is nightly visible on about a zillion cell phones. And in the second place, the only Stohler I know of who has ever watched daytime TV is my father, who routinely gets locked inside his garden shed after sneaking out there to do so."

"Fine. But instead of flailing around like you're drowning, try to make more fluid motions—like a windmill. More like this . . ." Sparkle demonstrated the maneuvers again.

Against her will, Lilah tried again, but with the same unhappy result. She dropped her arms to her sides in frustration.

"Give it up, Sink. I guess I'm just not cut out for this whole Gumby schtick."

"That's ridiculous. Let me show you."

Sparkle crossed the space that separated them and took hold of Lilah's arms. She began to rotate them in gentle circles.

"See?" she said at very close range. "Like this."

Like this? Lilah thought. *Yeah . . . this isn't going to help me relax . . .*

"Don't you feel looser?" Sparkle asked as their arms continued to move around in circles.

"Not exactly."

"No?" Sparkle dropped her hands and took hold of Lilah's face. "Then let's try your head."

Lilah narrowed her eyes. "Let's try what with my head?"

"Circles," Sparkle explained as she began to rotate Lilah's head. "Tiny circles."

"You do realize that this exercise is having the opposite effect of what you intended, right?"

"Is it?" Sparkle's voice sounded like it was coming from far away. "You don't feel relaxed?"

"Do you?"

"Maybe I'm not doing it right." Sparkle slipped her hands around to the back of Lilah's head and drew it closer to her own. "Is this better?"

Lilah could feel Sparkle's breath against her mouth. "This," Sparkle kissed her gently. Then again. Then with more energy. "This is definitely better."

Their relaxation exercise gained in intensity until Lilah felt her knees grow weak. She would've stumbled if Sparkle hadn't retained such a tight grip on her.

"I think . . ." Lilah breathed between kisses, "I need . . ."

"What?" Sparkle whispered against her mouth. "What do you need?"

"I need to . . . oh, god." Sparkle was now kissing her neck. "I need to skip dinner."

"You're not hungry?" Sparkle was now trailing kisses along her clavicle.

"Not for stew . . ." Lilah drew back and held Sparkle by the shoulders. "Could we go and . . ."

"Lie down?"

Lilah nodded. "I can think of a few more exercises that will be sure to relax me."

Sparkle took hold of her hand and led her toward the bedroom.

"I just bet you can, Black Bird."

They did eventually finish the wine—and heat up the Brunswick stew. It was just as good as Hambone had promised it would be—smoky and savory with just the right notes of autumn. You could almost taste the fresh air and camaraderie of the men who stirred it while they swapped stories and stood by it for the thirty-six hours it gently rolled and reduced inside an old cast-iron cauldron. And it tasted good, too—like the hot bowls of hope and redemption that were cooked up and sold at every small county church during the run-up to Christmas.

And Sparkle's Beaujolais was the perfect accompaniment for it.

So was the Côtes du Rhône they drank after that.

"I suppose we should talk about this," Lilah said after they'd finished their stew and were well into the second bottle of wine. They had gotten dressed. Mostly. And were sitting at Sparkle's small dining table.

"I kind of figured you'd want to."

"I had promised myself this wouldn't happen again."

"I know. I hope I didn't coerce you. It wasn't my plan, believe me."

"Coerce me?" Lilah laughed. "You *were* present, weren't you?" She sighed. "I have an appalling lack of self-control."

"Apparently, so do I."

"This just cannot continue to happen."

Sparkle nodded in agreement. "Because it's so bad? Because you don't enjoy it?"

"No. Not because it's *bad*. It's *not* bad. It's terrific. And I more than enjoy it—which should be obvious to you."

"Then . . . what am I missing here?"

"The forest? That thing beyond all these trees our libidos keep slamming us into."

"I think I'm going to need you to say a bit more about that one, Lilah."

"Sparkle . . . I'm leaving. I'm not staying here. Nothing about this," she wagged a finger back and forth between them, "makes sense. It can't . . ."

"Go anyplace?" Sparkle tried to finish her sentence.

Lilah shrugged.

"I know you keep saying that." Sparkle didn't continue.

"But you're not convinced?"

"Why does it matter what I think? Maybe I don't need more than this."

"I don't believe that. Not for one minute."

"Should I be offended by that?" Sparkle refilled her wine glass and passed the bottle to Lilah.

"I'm saying that because I know it wouldn't be enough for me. You don't seem like a 'friend with benefits' kind of person."

"I don't?"

"No. You're more of a 'let's go and pick out a breakfast china pattern' kind of person."

"So, you have some kind of problem with breakfast china? Is that what this is about?"

Lilah dropped her head into her hands.

"Lilah. Listen to me."

Lilah looked up at her.

"You worry too much. You aren't responsible for me—and you certainly haven't taken advantage of me—even though I almost wish you would. I am capable of making my own decisions—even if they end up being the wrong ones. Please don't keep trying to manage me or make determinations about what is or isn't in my best interest. I'm thirty-five years old. I've been married—and divorced. And furthermore, I have an IQ in the triple digits. Believe me. I can take care of myself."

"You sound pissed."

"No. At least, not yet."

Lilah sat back and folded her arms. "Okay, then. These are *my* issues. And they're familiar ones—now complicated by my uncertain future. Maybe it isn't you I'm worried about hurting."

"Maybe it's yourself?"

Lilah decided it was time to change the subject. Feeling morose was one thing. Feeling pathetic was another.

"So, do you think I'm sufficiently relaxed for my close-up tomorrow?"

"If you aren't, then I must've done something wrong."

Lilah thought about the myriad responses she could make to Sparkle's suggestion. Not one of them would keep her out of harm's way. And she needed to keep herself safe. Especially now that she knew Sparkle was a willing participant in their Devil's dance.

"I think everything worked just fine," she drawled. "So, to recap," Lilah ticked the items off on her fingers, "I don't cross my arms, I don't scowl, I don't drop any f-bombs, I don't refer to dead bodies as corpsicles, I don't offer her a chilled glass of the effluent left over after aquamation, and I say that I *love* being a pop culture icon if it advances the cause of Good

Death. Leave anything out?"

Sparkle nodded. "Just one thing—the most important one."

Lilah thought it over. "Oh! I know. I absolutely do *not* ask her about face lifts."

"Correct. A-plus, Ms. Stohler. I think you're ready."

"Honey," Lilah picked up her wine glass and held it aloft in a salute, "I was born ready."

Lilah left Sparkle's house a little before 8 p.m. Even though she knew she could've stayed the night, she wanted to make good on her internal pledge to clean up her act.

She didn't feel quite ready to go home, so she decided to head back to the funeral home to catch up on some paperwork. Kay Stover's car was still in the parking lot when she arrived— which was unusual enough—but she was doubly surprised to see that the Freeman brothers appeared still to be working, too. Odd since they didn't have any pickups that she'd been aware of. The lights were on in the crematory, so after she parked her car, she headed there to see what they were up to.

When she stepped inside, she was met with a familiar sound: laughter—once again, coming from the conference room. She didn't have to guess what was going on.

There they were—Rita Kitty, Kay, Hambone, and Gee String. Playing cards. The table was littered with Bojangles's boxes and drink cups.

"Let me guess," she said from the doorway. "Uno with three decks?"

"Well, hey howdy, boss," Hambone called out. "Come on in and join us. You had supper? We got some extra chicken legs here and Gee String has a biscuit—don't you Gee String?"

"Sure do." Gee String held up a bright yellow box covered with impressive grease stains. "Got me a meal deal. An this'un's got tea, too."

Lilah held up a hand. "I already ate, but thanks." She pulled out a vacant chair and sat down. "Why do you all persist in playing cards out here? Aren't the rooms in the big house a lot more comfortable?"

"Well, it's true them plushy chairs in the parlor are a lot kinder on the tooshie than these here slabs of wood," Rita Kitty agreed. "But all them rose-colored lights just make everything look too dern pink."

"That's true for sure, Miss Rita," Hambone agreed. "Them lights block out all the blue light—which is great for makin' all them dear dead souls look natural—but it makes seein' the colors on these here cards real hard."

"Plus, Gee String doesn't like feeling like being re traumatized by drunk tank pink." Kay Stover smiled fondly at him. "Do you, Gee String?"

"No ma'am, I sure don't. I been clean and sober for nigh on twenty years now, and them dern pink lights take me right back to all those nights I spent down at Stony Lonesome's, drunker'n Cooter Brown."

Rita Kitty tossed a yellow draw two card on the discard pile. "Sorry, Kay."

"Sure you are," Kay grumbled as she drew two cards. "Your go, Hambone."

"Ain't you got no yeller cards?" he asked.

"Nope."

"What are you doing flitting about at this time of night, Lilah?" Kay eyed her with suspicion. "Did your coaching session end early?"

Lilah chose effrontery. "I wouldn't call 8:20 p.m. early."

"Neither would I." Kay winked at her.

Lilah cleared her throat. "Hey, Gee String? I think I will take you up on that biscuit."

"Feeling peckish?" Kay asked. "Interesting."

"You need another hobby, Kay." Lilah bit into the biscuit. It tasted like it had been soaked in butter for about a year.

"I keep tellin' her that same thing." Rita Kitty slurped on her drink. "She works too dern much. We had to all but hog-tie her to get her to come out here and join us tonight. She only did it 'cause James is off at one of his Demon Deacon ball games."

"Yeah, Kay," Lilah chimed in. "What about taking up some *other* hobby besides . . . oh, I don't know—keeping tabs on *my* comings and goings?"

"Don't flatter yourself, Lilah." Kay drew and immediately discarded a red card. "I'd die of boredom if I relied upon your palace intrigues to keep me entertained."

"We got everything set up for that TV crew tomorrow, Miss Lilah." Gee String nudged his brother. "Don't we, Hambone? Just exactly like they said they needed."

"Sure do. Wardell said he'd have ever'thing spit-shined downstairs, too."

"Downstairs?" Lilah was confused. "They want to film the embalming suite, too?"

"Yes, ma'am. That Brezhnev woman said she wanted a personal tour—there an' the selection room, too. But don't you worry none, Miss Lilah," Hambone assured her. "Me 'n Gee String got all them empties outta there."

Empties? Lilah looked at Kay for clarification.

"Remember your idea about the vodka bar? It's apparently

been adopted by the rest of the staff."

"Oh, dear god."

"Them Teeter Rowan folks thought it was real neighborly of us to be offer'n them refreshment, Miss Lilah. Especially since they ain't havin' nothin' but a remembrance get-together here at our place. But me'n Gee String thought as how they might enjoy a sip or two of that Baileys you and Miss Kay left there earlier."

"Teeter Rowan?" Lilah asked Kay.

"The green burial."

"Oh. Right." Lilah cleared her throat. "Um. Guys? I think it's best if we don't continue offering our clients alcoholic refreshment, okay? Cookies are one thing. Chicken pie gravy nearly landed us in court with a dozen liability lawsuits. But serving alcohol to people without a permit would shut us down for good. So, can we keep those bottles of hooch tucked away where they belong when we have visitors? Please?"

"Yes, ma'am," the Freeman brothers agreed in unison. It was a pleasing sound—almost like they were harmonizing in the church choir.

"And Rita Kitty?" Lilah faced their hairdresser and makeup artist. "Nice work on the Batesville Economy dye job. Maybe we can talk about a more organized approach to these *alterations* in advance—just so we can better tailor them to our clientele."

Rita Kitty nodded with enthusiasm. "I been workin' up an idea that will work real nice for holiday funerals. I tried out some of them store-bought stencils on old satin scraps at home and made some pretty nice holly leaves with big red berries. Kinda arty lookin'—but I think folks would like it."

Lilah looked at Kay for help.

"How about you bring those samples in, Rita Kitty, and

we'll look them over?" Kay played a two of green card and Gee String looked at her with surprise.

"Well, I swanny," he declared. "If that don't beat all. Second time tonight."

Lilah felt an uncharacteristic rush of affection as she watched her crew of crazies play the twisted card game. It would be hard to leave them. They'd been her family for as long as she could remember. She hadn't allowed herself to dwell too much on that aspect of the sale. It was easier to keep those realities at arm's length. But there was one reality she couldn't continue to ignore: she needed to tell them all about her decision. And soon. Their attorney, Kirk, had said that with her sign-off, the sale could be finalized as early as January 15. Then the transition to the new management team could begin.

She looked around the table. Here they all were: the people who had made Stohler's the unique house of aftercare it had become.

More like Fawlty Towers, she told herself.

But that was part of what made their enterprise so unique. So personal. That's what had put them on the radar of people like Mika Brzezinski. And Salem Baking Company. And now, Funeral Services, Incorporated.

She'd already spent most of the evening facing up to her personal demons. Maybe it was time to look this one in the eye, too.

"So, I have something to share with all of you," she began. Kay shot her a quizzical look, and Lilah gave her a nod. When Kay smiled, she felt safe continuing with her news. "You all may have heard that FSI has made an offer to acquire us. Everyone here deserves the credit for that. It's really a tribute to the good work you've all done to make this such a special place."

"Well, I reckon them cookies Miss Sparkle has been bakin' up had a lot do with it, too," Hambone declared. "I can't go no place without folks askin' me for that recipe."

"Those *are* pretty . . . special," Lilah agreed. "But since we're all together here tonight, I wanted to tell you that I've thought long and hard about FSI's offer—about what it will mean for Stohler's and for each of us. And I know that transitions like this one can be difficult. But I think, in the long run, it's the right time for us to make this move. The marketplace for us is shrinking and there are more and more funeral homes opening in our area that can give people different, and sometimes better, options than we're now able to provide."

"Does this mean you're sellin' out?" Rita Kitty cut to the chase.

"I wouldn't call it selling out, exactly. I'm going to work very hard with FSI to be sure each of you can remain on staff—if that's what you decide you want. But yes—I've decided to accept their offer to acquire us."

"Well, I swanny," Gee String said. "It's the end of a era."

"I hope it won't be, Gee String. Dad and I both want the legacy of Stohler's to live on—and it can, through the work you each can continue to provide if you choose to stay here."

"No disrespect, Miss Lilah . . . but them new folks ain't gonna want to keep old-timers like me'n Gee String around."

"They'd be crazy not to, Hambone." Kay Stover took up the charge. "You and Gee String know more about this community and this business than the whole lot of them could ever learn. And the same goes for you, Rita Kitty."

"Well, what about you, then, Kay?" Rita Kitty still sounded dubious. "Are you gonna stay on, too?"

"I don't think so, Rita Kitty. Having time to sit at home with my feet up sounds mighty appealing after thirty years of cooking the books at this place." She looked at Lilah. "It's time for my torch to be passed to a new generation."

"Welllll . . . me'n Hambone been talkin' about retirement for a while now. Mebbe it's time for us to think about lettin' some new blood in here to keep these ol' ovens hot. Ain't that right, Hambone?"

Lilah wasn't sure Hambone shared Gee String's perspective. He looked more confused than anything.

"I reckon that's right, Gee. It's true the men's group is talkin' about takin' on more'n more activities since that stew sale done so great." He looked at Lilah with his clear blue eyes. "We done sold outta stew in *two* hours. Who knew this here would be such a great spot to reach folks. We had cars backed up all along the road out front."

"That's true," Gee String added. "An' we run outta brochures, too." He looked over at Kay. "You might should order some more of them, Miss Kay. We run through most of a box."

Brochures?

"Wait a minute," Lilah said. "You passed out funeral home brochures during your Brunswick stew sale?"

"Yes, ma'am," Hambone explained. "Me an' Gee thought as how folks might like learnin' more about Stohler's since they was here, so we put one of them brochures in ever bag. Most folks was real grateful, too. That Covid's been hard on families since the winter's been comin' on—specially on the old 'uns. But most of 'em wanted to know if there was an order form for them cookies."

Lilah thought about replying but chose to let that one slide.

Only Rita Kitty seemed despondent about Lilah's news. Lilah noted her lack of enthusiasm for the idea.

"What about you, Rita Kitty?" she asked. "You and Wardell would both be able to continue right on with your same contract arrangement. FSI would be lucky to have you—and I'll make sure they know it."

"What about Sparkle?" Rita Kitty asked.

Lilah was surprised by her question. She knew Rita Kitty had developed a good working relationship with their marketing guru but didn't realize her affinity for Sparkle went deeper.

"Sparkle will stay right on in her present role—if she chooses to. FSI is very invested in the special initiatives she's brought to the local market. They may even wish to expand her role to include some of their other franchises in the state."

That seemed to satisfy the makeup artist's concern.

"I hope you all know this wasn't an easy decision for me," Lilah shared. "It won't be easy for me to leave all of you."

"Leave?" Gee String looked like someone had just discharged a firearm beside his head. "Where would you be goin', Miss Lilah? You been at this place near as long as all a us."

"I haven't figured all that out yet, Gee String. But don't worry—any of you. I'll stay on as long as you need me to make a smooth transition. I promise you all that."

Rita Kitty dropped her hand of cards. "I don't feel much like playin' cards no more."

Lilah felt like a schmuck. Maybe this hadn't been the best time to share her news. The last thing she'd wanted was to ruin their evening.

Kay Stover stepped into the void—as Kay always did.

"I have a better idea than cards," she said. "Hambone, why don't you run over to the big house and grab us a bottle of the good stuff from my filing cabinet—and don't pretend you don't know what I'm talking about."

"Yes ma'am." Hambone got to his feet. "You don't have to be askin' me twice to run that kindly errand."

"We'll all toast to a brighter future for Stohler's—and each other. Together, we've done great things—and there's no reason to think that'll stop anytime soon."

"Amen to that," Rita Kitty exclaimed. "I suppose doing hair-n-makeup on dead folks ain't gonna change much, no matter who's buyin' the wax. Besides," she smiled, "it ain't every day we get a drink of the good stuff with permission."

Lilah looked them all over—her self-styled band of Merry Men. For once, she allowed herself to give into an uncharacteristic impulse.

"You know ... I ... love ... all of you." She swallowed and cleared her throat. "So, do me a favor, okay? Don't fuck this up."

There was a chorus of "No way!" as Hambone left the crematory to fetch the good stuff.

Lilah's interview went off without a hitch. By the time Brzezinski's film crew had arrived and collected all its B roll footage, the staff had started referring to the entire enterprise as Lilah's "Leave it to Brezhnev" interview. As Sparkle had predicted, Mika was engaging and well prepped for their conversation. Lilah felt she'd done a credible job appearing relaxed—or the best facsimile of relaxed she could manage—and she didn't sound aloof or sarcastic when she answered questions about Good Death initiatives and eco-friendly solutions for the aftercare of deceased loved ones.

Well. Not too sarcastic, anyway ...

The only rough spot occurred when Brzezinski wanted to

talk about Lilah's skyrocketing Instagram celebrity—including sharing some of the more creative and, to Lilah's mind, embarrassing posts from recent weeks. Most notable were the images of Lilah on the stage with illusionist Nathan Burton—and shots of her emerging from the human composting vessel at the funeral show like a ghost on All Hallows Eve.

She was grateful that none of the images of her draped all over Sparkle outside her hotel room made Brzezinski's cut.

The crew was fast and efficient. Before she knew it, the interview was over, and Brzezinski was on her way to Charlotte for an appearance at a Charlotte Reproduction Action Network dinner. But before she left, she spent a few minutes talking with Lilah and Sparkle—who she was very glad to reconnect with—about steps she thought Lilah should consider making to carry her support for Caitlin Doughty's crusade for Good Death forward to a larger audience—especially in the American South, where people clung to their predispositions about what constituted proper death and burial with the same fervor they expressed defending their God-given Second Amendment rights and declaring their staunch opposition to most methods of legalized abortion.

Brzezinski advised Lilah to consider taking control of her social media persona, and to begin to use it as a platform to talk about issues that mattered to her. She wasn't shy about suggesting that once her Know Your Value segment aired, Lilah would likely be besieged with requests for interviews from other media outlets, and that she should be prepared to embrace those opportunities and leverage them to bring more focused attention to the causes she championed.

Lilah's interview with Brzezinski was scheduled to air shortly after the first of the year. That gave her sufficient time to get her professional ducks in a row. If Kirk's predictions were accurate, the deal with FSI should be done and dusted shortly after New Year's.

Now it just remained for her to make sense of the other parts of her life—the ones that weren't connected to where she worked or how successful she was or wasn't in her Rumpelstiltskin-like attempts to weave her Internet celebrity into gold. It was how to get a start on doing this that confounded her and kept her awake most nights.

During the days leading up to Christmas, Lilah did her best to steer clear of Sparkle—unless it was some supervised interaction where she could be confident she'd be able to manage her . . . *baser* instincts. She was mostly successful in these endeavors. *Mostly.*

The day of the Teeter Rowan remembrance service had been her one near miss. She had offered to help Sparkle carry some trays of ginger chews from the kitchen to the front visitation room where Rowan's friends and family had returned to gather for refreshments after the short interment service in the woods behind his small farm. Lilah had offered to remove a sheet of cookies from the small oven for Sparkle, who was busy transferring the previous batch to a basket. In typical fashion— because she was not anything approximating accomplished in the kitchen, Lilah bumped the side of her hand against the wall of the oven as she attempted to extract the tray of cookies.

"Damn it!" she exclaimed. She jerked backward and bumped into Sparkle, who immediately jerked upright and turned around to see what had happened. That caused Lilah to lose her hold on the hot baking sheet, and both it and the cookies went flying.

"Fuck me!" Lilah immediately bent over to try and retrieve the hot cookies. Unfortunately, Sparkle had exactly the same idea and they banged heads—which nearly sent Sparkle sprawling. Lilah grabbed hold of her by the arms and held onto her to keep her from toppling over. That brought their faces dangerously close together, and they froze in that position for several moments. Lilah wasn't sure if it was the still-open oven that was causing her to feel overheated, or Sparkle's sudden close proximity. It didn't matter. She had just started to move in to kiss her when they both recognized Rita Kitty's heavy footsteps pounding down the hallway toward them. They jerked apart guiltily and proceeded to pick up the scattered cookies.

Yeah, Lilah thought. *That was a close call.*

What the hell was the matter with her? She'd never behaved like this before—like some kind of hormone-addled teenager. And Sparkle Lee Sink had been the last person on the planet Lilah ever expected to feel any sort of inclination toward, much less have to fight off the impulse to pant after like a dog in heat.

Her head was filled with these mortifications when she returned home that evening. Her mood did not improve when she picked up her phone to scroll through the latest Instagram postings about her dark and dastardly avian escapades.

It was ridiculous. How could so many people keep this insanity going?

"Does wisdom perhaps appear on the earth as a raven which is inspired by the smell of carrion?" –Friedrich Nietzsche. #BlackBirdOfChernobyl, #DeathBecomesHer, #deathquotes

Black Bird demonstrates that sleeping is a lot like death without the commitment.

225

#BlackBirdOfChernobyl, #humancomposting, #Recompose, #BoneyardBabes

#BlackBirdOfChernobyl proves that death as a terminal inconvenience can grow on you— literally. #Recompose, #humancomposting, #restinpieces, #DivaOfDeath, #BoneyardBabes

Black Bird's bloody cauldron spills its chunky guts in crematory parking lot. Pickings for all! #BlackBirdOfChernobyl, #DeathBecomesHer, #DivaOfDeath, #StohlersMortuary, #WalburgBaptist

Fire burn and cauldron bubble at Black Bird's epic Brunswick stew meltdown. This soupçon spelled one hell of a hot mess for mourners. #BlackBirdOfChernobyl, #StohlersMortuary, #WalburgBaptist

The posts just weren't slacking off. And what was even worse: they were becoming more *erudite*. That meant her "followers" had transitioned from the realm of more provincial teenaged fringe users to encompass a more mainstream audience. *Great.* Just what she needed . . . *not.*

How the hell was she supposed to take control of something that had already left the building and taken on a life of its own? For her money, the whole "Leave It to Brezhnev" theory about controlling the messaging was a bunch of hooey. Even if she'd wanted to take over the ownership of her online image, she was beyond clueless about how to manage, much less leverage, it. It was like the people on these platforms spoke a different language—one Lilah understood about as well as Klingon.

She'd always been a misfit. A Luddite. A troglodyte. A proudly profane anchorite. And a baker's dozen of other states of being that ended in "ite."

And she'd always been happy about her lot in life—and her choices. Until now.

Now she wasn't sure what she wanted—except to be left alone. That was the real dynamic that led her to the decision to sell the business to FSI. It wasn't about altruism or her burning desire to blaze a trail as another pioneer of the Good Death movement. True. She cared about those initiatives. Cared deeply, in fact. But it was the freedom selling Stohler's would afford her that had the greatest appeal. What better and more expeditious a way to be released from her current life than fleeing it?

If she left, she could reinvent herself—as *herself*. Her true self. Not some faux social media creation that had about as much basis in reality as the terrifying, mythological black bird that supposedly foretold disaster for the superstitious residents of a small Ukrainian city in the Kyiv oblast, called Chernobyl. *What the serious fuck had that been all about?*

For once, the Greek chorus in her head wasn't weighing in on the side of flight.

You cannot outrun this, they chanted. *Wherever you go, there you are.*

She still wasn't sure what they meant by that last refrain . . .

The truth was there were no platitudes or aphorisms that could help her sort through all of this. She was going to have to sit in it—like Job in his bed of ashes—and wait for either enlightenment or some kind of reprieve. Frankly, she didn't expect either to be forthcoming. That just wasn't the way life worked—at least, not for her.

Kay Stover had said her job was to live her own life—not to fulfill the expectations or honor the legacies of anyone else. Not her father's, nor any of the other grizzled Stohlers who preceded him. Not her mother's, who never asked her for more than she could give—except for granting occasional permission to style her hair. Not Frankie, who always seemed to accept her big sister's eccentricities without question—even when they involved questionable experiments with her home chemistry set and an assortment of household cleaners.

Not even Sparkle, who'd made it clear that she wasn't asking Lilah for anything she couldn't give. And that one was a harder pill for Lilah to swallow. Why did that assertion on Sparkle's part bother her so much? She'd felt almost irked by it—as if she'd been cheated by Sparkle's blithe assurance that Lilah wasn't that much of a threat to her well-being.

And why the hell not?

Didn't she feel exactly the opposite way about Sparkle?

She did. Sort of.

What the serious fuck was that about?

And it was clear her strategy to avoid close contact with her personal enigma was failing miserably. She'd nearly pushed her down and ravished her right there on the kitchen floor, atop a bed of those hot damn ginger chews that were becoming her personal harbinger of disaster.

The company Christmas party was tomorrow night, too. They'd be stuck together at her parents' house for the entire evening—with every facial tic being scrutinized by their resident Sybil, Kay Stover. Kay was determined to out Lilah—to bust her for being so damn weak. For allowing herself to become a drooling hostage to a perky blonde with smarts, chutzpah, and a great set of . . .

Enough, she chided herself. It was time to get off this ridiculous, pastel-colored Hallmark merry-go-round that was giving her emotional vertigo. She had to.

Even if she had to lie to herself and everyone else to do it.

The Stohlers' annual Christmas party was typically a grand affair with more than a score of guests. Lilah's mother was in her element when she entertained, and to be fair, she did it superbly. It always amazed Lilah that she staunchly refused to bow to the pressures of her busiest season at the salon and have the damn event catered. Nope. Not good enough for Janet Stohler. She prepared every last canapé, amuse bouche, profiterole, vol-au-vent, mini quiche, crudité, and heavy hors d'oeuvre known to man. The only exceptions were the iconic mainstays of any Winston-Salem holiday party: pit-cooked barbecue from Hambone's church—and macaroni and cheese soufflé and Miss Ora's fried chicken wings from Sweet Potatoes restaurant. This year, however, Frankie and Nick, who volunteered to pick up the only catered items, dared to bring along a little something extra from the James Beard-nominated hand of Chef Stephanie Tyson—two big bags of her signature, light as a feather, fired pork rinds. Nick confessed that Frankie made her stash those in the trunk to prevent her from cracking into them on the short drive to the Stohlers' West End home.

For the Stohlers, no holiday table was complete without these mainstays of food that was good for the soul.

Lilah's father was in charge of the bar—and he prided himself in leaving no stone unturned when it came to providing a cornucopia of spirits. The only thing Abel Stohler was as scrupulous about as making sure everyone had a glass filled with holiday cheer was that they also had designated drivers on hand to see them safely home. If not, he'd made prior arrangements with a couple of off-duty Uber drivers to be on high alert for the evening.

"Well, dern, Miss Lilah," Hambone declared when he looked over the bar set up on a table on the enclosed porch. "You got more bottles here'n Miss Kay has in that ol' filin' cabinet."

"Just pace yourself, Hambone," Lilah told him. "The night is young."

Kay's husband, James, laughed. "At least something out here is young. Have you noticed it's all us old-timers huddling around the liquor?"

"Well, them young folks is all inside drinkin' up beer from that keg Mr. Abel set up in the kitchen."

"Beer?" James asked with interest. "What kind is it?"

"I think I heard tell of somebody sayin' it was that Carolina Blonde—you know . . . one of them Foothills beers."

"Really?" James looked longingly toward the kitchen.

"Not so fast, Big Jim." Kay took hold of his arm. "Beer then liquor, never sicker," she quoted.

His face fell.

"It's okay, honey." She patted his hand. "As a consolation prize, I promise not to complain if you eat the garlic hummus."

"I'd take the deal, James," Lilah suggested. "It's especially garlicky this year."

"Really?" It was clear James wasn't persuaded.

"Oh, yeah. I think it could be used to ward off werewolves."

They all heard laughter coming from the living room. It appeared that Rita Kitty had arrived with her *date du soir* in tow.

"Oh, dear god . . ." Kay muttered. "Where does she find them?"

"Do you think he's an Elvis impersonator?" James asked. "Those muttonchops cannot be real."

"Mutton?" Hambone asked. "Ain't that like lamb? I can't eat that gamey mess. It cramps me."

"No, Hambone," Kay explained. She pointed at Rita Kitty's escort. "James is talking about those sideburns."

"Oh." Hambone nodded. "Gee tried growin' them things one year, but he looked like he was walkin' around with Brillo pads stuck to his face. And Mr. Abel said he didn't want any of that mess fallin' into the cremulator, so Gee had to wear a beard mask. He got tired of that real quick." He chuckled. "It was pretty comical, though. He kindly looked like a squirrel with his cheeks stuffed full a nuts."

Lilah excused herself. "I need to go greet Rita Kitty and her date. My mother pressed me into hostess duties."

"Oh?" Kay asked. "Is that why you're wearing such festive attire?"

Lilah looked down at her ensemble. It was as somber and unvarying as ever. "Festive?"

"*Irony*, Lilah. Look it up." Kay pushed her toward the crush of people milling about and chatting in the living room. "Go. Be wondrous."

Christmas music was playing at a low volume. She saw Frankie and Nick, huddled together beneath some mistletoe— making good on the requirement of their location.

God, those two make me want to drown kittens . . .

She returned her attention to the music. It was an eclectic mix this year. Eartha Kitt's "Santa Baby" had just morphed into Yo-Yo Ma playing "Dona Nobis Pacem." *Strangely appropriate for this crowd,* Lilah thought as she crossed the living room to welcome Rita Kitty and her beau.

Rita Kitty saw her approach.

"Here she is." Rita Kitty elbowed her companion. "Earl, meet Lilah Stohler, the genuine Black Bird of Chernobyl herself."

Earl's gaze swept up and down Lilah's long frame. "Pleased to meet you, Miss Black Bird," he all but crooned. "Lemme tell you, those Insta photos don't do you justice."

"Thank you. I think. Nice to meet you, too . . . Earl." Lilah looked at Rita Kitty, who was decked out in some kind of red satin regalia that looked like it had been ripped off a drapery rod. "How long have you two been seeing each other?"

"Me and Earl ain't 'seeing' each other." Rita Kitty laughed heartily. "Earl just offered to be my Mr. Right Now for the evening. Didn't you, Earl honey?"

Earl was still giving Lilah the once-over. It was starting to make her feel itchy beneath her clothes.

What the fuck, dude? It was ironic that she hadn't had to confront the creepier aspect of her celebrity up close until tonight—when she was standing in the middle of her parents' living room.

"Earl works as a daytime manager over at Sally Beauty Supply," Rita Kitty prattled on, oblivious to Earl's preoccupation with the plunging neckline on Lilah's blouse.

I never should've let Frankie twist my arm into wearing this damn outfit. I look like Irma la Douce working a funeral.

"How lovely," she dropped her voice to its lowest octave. "Why don't you two make your way to the porch for some refreshment?" She turned to indicate the bar area. Hambone was still standing there, staring back at them, and he waved energetically.

232

"I think we just might do that." Rita Kitty grabbed Earl's meaty forearm and nudged him to move. "Come on, Earl. Let's go get us some of Stohler's finest." She leaned toward Lilah to whisper, "I told him y'all served top-shelf booze at these parties. Earl is real particular about what he puts in his mouth."

Yeah. Lilah gave Earl a surreptitious glance. *I kind of doubt that . . .*

Before the pair made their way to the porch, Earl made a point of stopping to meet Lilah's eyes.

"I hope our paths cross again, Black Bird."

It was worth noting that Earl's eyes held all the allure of a map of the Interstate highway system.

"Where would we be without our fantasies . . . *Earl?*"

Lilah beat a hasty retreat before Earl could elaborate any further on his passion for exotic birds.

Why didn't I get myself a damn drink? This night is going to be a hundred hours long.

Someone touched her on the sleeve. She turned around to see Sparkle, resplendent in a ruched, green velvet midi dress. She looked . . . well . . . hot as fuck.

Lilah hadn't seen her until now. Sparkle must've arrived while she'd been on the porch with Kay and James.

"You look . . ." She didn't trust herself to finish.

Sparkle raised an eyebrow while she waited for Lilah to complete her statement.

"Green?" Lilah offered lamely.

"*Green.* Good. That's exactly the look I was going for. You look . . . *nice,* too."

"Impossible," Lilah countered. "Besides, this isn't my outfit—it's Frankie's. Mom made me wear it."

Sparkle laughed. "Mom knows some things. Sexy but

aloof suits you."

"Sexy?"

"Oh, yeah. I'd say so."

"I feel like a painted circus pony." She looked down at her ensemble. "Except those don't usually come in black."

"True. But you're wrong, Lilah. The outfit works."

"You're nuts."

"No, I'm not. It works because it screams your signature, 'I'd rather be flattening wrinkles with a tissue reducer than wearing this' vibe—but it's still chic as hell and drips sexiness with the neckline on that sheer blouse."

Lilah couldn't ever recall a time she'd gotten a thrill from discussing wardrobe choices.

To say it was unsettling was an understatement.

Sparkle must've sensed her discomfort. "Here." She held out a pewter cup.

"What's that?" Lilah sniffed it.

"Eggnog."

"I hate eggnog." Lilah tried to hand the cup back to her.

"Too bad." Sparkle pushed it back. "Drink it anyway. I put two shots of cognac in it."

"On the other hand," Lilah took a generous sip, "desperate times call for desperate measures."

"So, how do you think the party is going?"

"Well, since no one has fallen into the rock pond yet, I'd say it's a smashing success."

"Don't get cocky. The night is young."

"True," Lilah agreed. "The smart money is on Earl."

"Earl?"

"Rita Kitty's boy toy." Lilah tossed her head in the direction of the bar. "He's hard to miss—looks like a cross between lounge lizard Elvis and James Dickey."

Sparkle casually stole a peek at the bar. Her eyes grew wide.

"Now they look like a set of strange bedfellows—*Deliverance* meets 'Don't Be Cruel.'"

"Yeah, I'd say it's more like 'Return to Sender.'"

"Well, nobody ever said Rita Kitty was all that picky when it comes to male companionship."

"True. I guess when you spend your days backcombing hair on dead people it does tend to dull your sensibilities about the finer things in life."

"I'd have to agree with that."

"Well, well," a familiar voice declared. "Don't you two look good enough to eat."

Lilah was surprised to see Dash approaching them. He wasn't wearing any glad rags but was attired in his usual delivery attire.

"What are you doing out on the loose?" she asked. "Did somebody here order an extra tray of cold cuts?"

"Very funny, Stohler. You crack me up with your searing wit." He smiled at Sparkle. "You must be the redoubtable brand identity expert. I'm Dash—otherwise known as death's delivery man."

Sparkle extended a hand. "It's a pleasure to finally meet you, Dash. Please call me Sparkle."

"And in that outfit, it won't be hard." Dash all but leered at her.

"Just how many of those have you had?" Lilah pointed at Dash's red Solo cup.

"None of your business, warden." Dash returned his attention to Sparkle. "I have to say that, in this respect," his eyes took their time roaming over her . . . *everything*, "your reputation has not preceded you."

"Seriously, Dash? Did you leave your manners in your other suit—along with your sobriety?"

"Will you take a chill pill, Stohler? I just finished a double shift and I'm trying to spread a little holiday cheer here."

"Yeah. You're spreading something, Dash—but it doesn't smell like holiday cheer."

Sparkle laughed and took hold of Dash's arm. "How about we go and peruse the buffet, Dash? I think a bite to eat might do us all some good. Join us, Lilah?"

Lilah drained her eggnog. "Why the hell not?"

The three of them made their way to the dining room, where Sparkle proceeded to fix a plate of food for Dash. Then she led him to a vacant chair beside a sideboard loaded with dessert confections.

"You tuck into this, Dash," she instructed him. "And I'll be back to check on you. Okay?"

He nodded his assent and picked up a chicken wing. "Damn, I love Miss Ora's," he said. "Really takes the sting outta ferrying dead people around all night, you know?"

Sparkle nodded and patted his hand. "I am sure that's exactly what they intended, Dash."

She rejoined Lilah. "Think somebody should get his keys?"

Lilah held up a nondescript fob with several keys dangling from it. "Way ahead of you."

Sparkle's jaw dropped. "How'd you pull that off?"

Lilah leaned closer to her and whispered, "Magic."

"Amazing."

"You think so? I got a million of 'em."

"Tricks?"

"Sleights of hand. It's one of the first things they teach us in mortician school. Right after an intensive session about best practices in up-selling burial vaults."

Lilah's mother entered the dining room bearing a fresh platter of curried crab and corn vol-au-vents.

"Pick up that empty plate for me, won't you, Lilah?"

"Sure, Mom." Lilah did as directed, and her mother replaced it with the piping hot platter of hors d'oeuvres.

"I can't keep these coming fast enough."

"That's your own fault, Mom." Lilah quipped. "I told you to go with those Geno's Pizza Rolls."

"You'd have gotten no argument from your father on that one."

"The food is amazing, Janet."

"Thank you, Sparkle. We're so glad you're here with us this year. Aren't we, Lilah?"

"Uh . . . sure. Yes. Of course. Righto."

Janet shook her head. "My daughter. A real wordsmith."

"Hey. Elocution is overrated in my line of work."

"Yeah, well, thinking about other duties as assigned, your father is looking for you."

Lilah cast about. "Where is he?"

"The porch. I think he needs help restocking the bar."

Behind them, Dash held up his Solo cup. "I'll take a refill!"

"Oh, god," Sparkle said. "I'll help, too."

Five minutes later, the two of them were headed out back to the garden shed, where Abel had stashed all the backup stores for the party. Sparkle had jotted down a list of what he'd said he needed to replenish the dwindling stores of liquor and mixers.

Once they'd left the house, the music and laughter all quickly receded. The moon was nearly full, but it was mostly occluded by the clouds rolling in from the northwest. The light that did escape cast dramatic shadows across the beautifully hardscaped back yard. It had grown a lot colder since Lilah had arrived. It was breezy, too—all from the storm front moving in overnight. She hoped the holiday soirée would wrap up before the serious rain arrived. A gust of wind slammed into them. Lilah was glad her outfit included a jacket. She wondered if she should offer it to Sparkle—but thought better of it when she remembered that her damn organza blouse was all but transparent.

Hopefully, their errand wouldn't take long, and they'd soon be back inside.

"This is a gorgeous spot," Sparkle commented.

"It's my mother's passion—right after canapés, balayage hair painting, and reminding me that introducing a hint of color to my wardrobe will add a bit of needed flair to my life of abject solitude."

"I think she's wonderful."

"Of course you do."

"What's that supposed to mean?"

"Just that you two seem like birds of a feather."

"I think that might be the nicest thing you've ever said to me."

"Watch your step, here." Lilah took hold of her arm as they descended some stone steps.

Abel's garden shed was mostly concealed behind a trellis covered with English ivy. Lilah used the key her father had given her to unlock the door.

"Be careful not to let this close behind you," she warned Sparkle. "It sometimes locks and it's impossible to open if you're stuck inside."

"Roger."

They entered and Lilah flipped the switch for the overhead light, but nothing happened. She tried it again. No dice.

"Oh, *great*. The bulb must be burned out. Thanks, Dad." She felt around through the clutter on a nearby workbench until she located a small flashlight. "Here we go." Its narrow beam illuminated the interior of the space.

The shed was pretty typical of most backyard storage buildings except in one respect: there was an overstuffed armchair and a wall-mounted, flat panel TV tucked away in the back corner.

"That looks cozy." Sparkle observed.

"Yeah. This is his self-styled man cave. He comes out here to watch NASCAR races and reruns of old movies on TCM."

"I think that's sweet. Well. The movies, not the races."

"I was wondering . . ."

"Okay, let's get these bags loaded and head back to the heat." Sparkle did her best to read off the list in the dim light. "Tom Collins mix."

"God, do people still drink that?" Lilah shifted some boxes around until she found it. "How many bottles?"

"Two."

"Got 'em. Next?"

"Four bottles of tonic."

'Check. Next?"

"Um." Sparkle squinted to read the list. "Celery bitters?"

Lilah stood upright. "What the fuck are celery bitters?"

"Hey," Sparkle showed her the list, "don't shoot the messenger."

Lilah rolled her eyes and proceeded to dig around inside one of the boxes. She held up a minuscule bottle.

"This must be it."

"Can you read the label?"

"Not really, but nothing else in there is this small." She tossed it into one of their bags. "Next?"

"It looks like that's it for the mixers. We're down to the liquor now."

"Good. That's all over here in these cases."

A sudden wind gust rattled the windowpanes in the shed. Lilah was beginning to feel cold, and she was sure Sparkle had to be, too.

"Let's hurry this shit up. I'm afraid the rain is moving in sooner than they predicted."

Sparkle read the next item on the list. "Limoncello."

"Seriously? Who is *at* this damn party—the Gay Men's Glee Club of the Triad?"

"He also wants another bottle of Chambord."

"Now you're just fucking with me."

"Sad to say I'm not. Do you want to venture a guess about what's next?"

"I'm going with something in the nut group. Frangelico?"

"Not even close. St-Germain Elderflower Liqueur."

"Elderflower?"

"Afraid so."

"If that's what Dash was swilling out of that Solo cup, I'm totally going to resign my membership in the Crepe Hangers Guild."

"Is that a thing?" Sparkle sounded dubious.

"Not anymore." Lilah had to move a crate. "Okay. Here it is. I sure hope all this candy-ass swill is tax deductible."

Another wind gust shook the shed and, this time, it blew the door shut. Lilah heard the pronounced click as it latched.

Oh, God . . .

She made her way to the door and tried to open it. It wouldn't budge. She turned toward Sparkle in frustration. "You were supposed to keep this door open."

"*Me?* How was I supposed to prevent the wind from blowing it shut?"

"I don't know. Force of will?"

"Is it locked?"

"Of course, it's locked." Lilah jiggled the doorknob to prove her point. "Take out your cell phone and call Dad."

"I don't *have* my phone."

"What do you mean you don't have your phone. You *always* have your phone."

"Not tonight. You may have noticed that there are no pockets on this dress."

Lilah thought about Sparkle's dress. She must've missed that detail during her examination of the garment's other attributes—like how it clung to every sculpted curve of her body.

"I don't suppose you brought yours?"

Lilah gave her a withering look. "And ruin the drape of my jacket? What do you think?"

"I think we're screwed. You got any ideas?"

"Apart from praying for a Christmas miracle, not one." She looked around. "Unless . . ."

"Unless what?"

"Here." Lilah handed her the flashlight. "Hold this." Lilah dragged a wooden crate over toward the side wall.

"What are you doing?"

"I'm going to try to open this window and climb out."

Another wind gust hit with ferocity. They could hear raindrops beginning to pelt the roof and windowpanes.

Lilah climbed up onto the workbench and crawled across it to reach the window. She felt something snag the fabric of her pants. When she stopped and tried to jerk it free, she felt the fabric resist, then tear.

Great. Fucking great. Now I ruined Frankie's damn suit.

"Sonofabitch!"

"What happened?" Sparkle asked anxiously.

"I just tore these fucking pants."

'Oh, no. Did you cut yourself?"

"Probably." Lilah tried in vain to open the window. It was hopeless. The thing had probably been painted shut for decades.

Dejectedly, she sat down on the workbench. "You were right. We're screwed."

"Sooner or later, someone will wonder where we are."

"Don't count on it. Our best hope is that someone with a terribly esoteric palate will have a hankering for another designer cocktail that includes celery bitters as a key component."

"And if that doesn't happen?"

"Ever seen *The Donner Party*?"

Sparkle shivered.

Lilah wasn't sure if it was from the cold or the scope of their plight. She climbed down from the workbench and walked over to join her.

"Let's look around for something to wrap up with until someone finally comes looking for us."

In the end, they found an old cardigan of Abel's, which Lilah insisted Sparkle take. And a couple of recycled burlap coffee sacks her mother used to aid with weed control in her raised beds. Lilah wrapped those around her neck and shoulders.

The minutes ticked by, and the rain increased in intensity.

"Wanna watch TV?" Lilah asked hopefully.

"Are you nuts?" Sparkle was really shivering now.

"Come on." Lilah grabbed a random bottle out of one of the boxes and led Sparkle toward the overstuffed armchair. "Let's at least sit down."

"You're crazy. We can't both fit on that thing."

"I realize that. You'll have to sit on my lap."

"Seriously?"

"You got a better idea?" Lilah sat down and patted her leg.

"Are you sure you didn't plan this?" Sparkle obeyed Lilah's order and gingerly perched on her lap.

Lilah took pains to use one of her coffee sacks to cover Sparkle's legs. "This isn't so bad, is it?"

Sparkle started to relax and sink deeper into Lilah's arms. "If you say so."

"Here." Lilah handed her the bottle. "Let's tuck into this. It should help to keep us warm."

"What is it?"

"I have no fucking clue."

Sparkle peered at the label. "It's . . . Calvados."

Apple brandy? It could've been worse. As eclectic as her father's stash was, she could just as easily have grabbed Aperol— or Cinzano.

"That'll work. Crack it open."

"Are you sure?"

"Do you not hear my teeth chattering? Yes, I'm beyond sure."

Sparkle complied and passed her the bottle.

"Bottoms up." Lilah took a healthy swig. The Calvados burned deliciously. *Oh, yeah.* This was gonna work just fine. She passed the bottle back to Sparkle. "Your turn."

Sparkle took it from her reluctantly. "Something about this feels . . . degenerate."

"Don't think of it that way. Think of it as yet another thrilling story you'll never be able to share with your grandchildren."

Sparkle took a tentative sip of the brandy and immediately choked.

"Smooth, isn't it?" Lilah asked. "Try it again. Only let it slide down the back of your throat. Don't guzzle it."

"I did *not* guzzle it. It's just strong." Sparkle tried it again. This time, it seemed to go down much more easily.

"See? Told you."

Sparkle turned to look at her. That was all it took. With the wind rattling around them and the brandy snaking through her system like liquid fire, Lilah realized she no longer cared about the party, the shed door, the sale of the business, the fate of the planet, or what-ever-in-the-hell else might get posted about her on Instagram. Her world filled up with one thing only—and that one thing was staring back at her with eyes that glowed like green embers.

They met each other halfway. What began tentatively quickly escalated to a full-scale, full-contact entanglement that Lilah knew was certain to land them in the middle of an even deeper well of confusion—or at the very least, the floor of the shed.

Sparkle tried heroically to stop it. She laid a palm against Lilah's chest and pushed back as much as the confined space would allow.

They were both breathing heavily.

"You don't want this."

Lilah had to strain to hear Sparkle's voice over the intensity of the rain and the roar inside her head.

"What?" she asked.

"You said you don't want this. We need to stop."

Stop? Was Sparkle asking her to stop? She wasn't sure. The roaring grew louder. The noise was making it impossible for her to think. She couldn't tell if it was coming from the ferocious drumming of rain against the metal roof of the shed, or the hammer blows of her own heartbeat.

"Stop?" she whispered against Sparkle's mouth. "I don't want to stop."

"Lilah . . ."

The sound of someone banging on the outside of the shed door caused them to lurch apart.

"Are you two in there?" More banging. It was Kay Stover— and she sounded . . . *pissed*.

Lilah saw the beam of a flashlight sweep the interior from outside the window.

"Fuck," she whispered. "It's Kay."

"I kind of gathered that."

Sparkle disentangled herself from Lilah and struggled to her feet.

"Yes!" Lilah called out. "The door locked behind us. Do you have a key?"

"I do." Kay began to fumble with the lock. "Why are the lights off in there?"

"Ask Dad," Lilah replied. "The switch wouldn't work."

The door swung open, and Kay Stover stood there, her silhouette framed in backlight from the house, dripping wet and suffused with equal parts annoyance and curiosity.

"What the hell were you two doing all this time? Or do I even need to ask?"

Her flashlight blazed across their rumpled figures.

Lilah raised a hand to shield her face. "Do you mind not blinding us with that thing? It's like a damn car headlight."

"You should welcome it." Kay stepped inside and reached for the door handle.

"Don't close it!" Sparkle and Lilah cried in unison.

"Good God." Kay dropped her hand. "All right, all right." She flipped the wall switch on and off several times.

"I already told you," Lilah said impatiently. "It's burned out."

"Is it?" Kay took several steps forward and reached up to

245

yank on the pull chain that hung down from the overhead light fixture. The space was suddenly flooded with light. She glared at Lilah, who stood before her, rapidly blinking and trying to shield her eyes. "Not the sharpest scalpel in the embalmer's kit, are you?"

"Give me a break, Kay." Lilah was slowly starting to adjust to the light. "You know I do my best work in the dark."

"As would be indicated by your present appearance."

Lilah was still wearing one of the burlap coffee bags and the gaping rip in her trousers was much larger than she'd thought.

"It's . . . complicated."

"Isn't it always?" Kay demanded. She shifted her gaze to Sparkle. "And I don't know what to think about you."

"It's not what it looks like, Kay."

"It isn't? Then do, please, enlighten me." She looked them both over. "You two have been missing for more than an hour. Abel was having a fit of the vapors because he was running out of everything."

"Oh, really?" Lilah began to brush off her jacket. "Did someone have a Chambord emergency?"

"Why didn't you call someone to come and let you out?"

"We didn't have our cell phones with us, Kay." Sparkle managed to sound a lot calmer than Lilah was sure she was feeling.

Kay seemed to accept that explanation—for once.

"Why were you the one dispatched to come and check on us?" Lilah wanted to know. "Why not one of the Freeman brothers?"

Kay's explanation was simple. "I volunteered."

"Volunteered?" Lilah looked down at Kay's feet. "In those tasteful little shoe-ettes?"

"I had a feeling you might be otherwise . . . *engaged.*"

Kay explained. "I didn't want to expose your gross breach of employment ethics to anyone else."

"Right." Lilah grabbed their bags of liquor and handed one to Sparkle. "Shall we rejoin the party?"

Sparkle took the bag from her and made her way to the door.

"Hold on," Lilah stopped her. "Take one of these to cover your head." She tossed Sparkle one of the burlap bags.

"Good thinking." Sparkle draped the sack over her already disheveled hair and sheepishly pushed past Kay. "See you both inside."

She disappeared into the rain and darkness.

When Lilah attempted to follow suit, Kay reached out a hand to grab her coattail and yanked her to a standstill.

"Not so fast, Drusilla."

Lilah turned to face her with resignation. "Look, Kay— there's nothing you can say to me that I haven't already said to myself a thousand times. So, save your breath."

"Oh, really? You think you know what I'm going to say to you?"

"Of course, I do. You don't exactly hide things in your heart."

"Well brace yourself, Sybil. I'm about to shatter your illusion."

That declaration got Lilah's attention. "What does that mean?"

"It means that where *she* is concerned," Kay pointed outside in the direction Sparkle had gone, "I think it's past time for you to shit or get off the pot."

"Meaning?"

"Meaning, quit yanking her around like a yo-yo. If you're unwilling or unable to make any kind of commitment to her, then leave her alone. What you're doing is selfish and borderline abusive."

Abusive? *Okay . . . that seemed a bit strong.*

"I am not abusing anyone, Kay. Sparkle knows what she's doing. Believe me . . . she told me she does in very direct language."

"I wasn't talking about her. I was talking about you. You're abusing yourself, Lilah. Just like you always do. It's time to change that—while you still can."

"And you think that means leaving Sparkle alone?"

"Oh, my *God*. Earth to Stohler. Have you not heard a word I've said?"

Lilah was confused. "What do you want from me, Kay?"

"I want you to get your dark head out of your ass and for once in your life, do something that has a shot at adding a dose of happiness to that simmering pot of morbidities you call a lifestyle. And if you cannot figure out what that means, then by all means, keep right on doing what you're doing. I am sure you and that iron maiden you call a companion will continue to find comfort in a life of solitude and regret."

"Are you pissed at me?"

Kay rolled her blue eyes. "What tipped you off?"

"I heard you, okay? I really did. I'll . . . think about it. All right?"

Kay nodded. "One other thing."

Lilah was afraid to ask.

"What the hell happened to your pants?"

Lilah looked down at the jagged tear that had ruined he sister's suit.

"Well . . ." she began.

"Never mind." Kay held up a hand to stop her. "I don't think I want to know. Let's get inside before Dash stumbles out here in search of more chicken wings."

"Okay." Lilah started to exit the shed but remembered

248

something. "One second." She walked back to where she and Sparkle had been seated and grabbed the open bottle of Calvados. "Waste not, want not," she told Kay with a rakish smile.

"What-ever." Kay pushed her toward the door. "It's time for you to face the music. For once."

The only thing Lilah felt sure about in that moment was that Kay had spoken the truth.

The rest would have to wait.

Fortunately for both Lilah and Sparkle, the partygoers were too far gone on rich food and fussy drinks to notice or care about their pointed absence. Although more than one person did notice Lilah's pants, only Frankie bothered to ask her what the hell had happened. Lilah managed to assuage her sister's ire about the ruination of one of her best suits by promising her that she would volunteer to take care of Carol Jenkins during the Christmas skiing trip to Jay Peak Resort she and Nick had planned with Sebastian.

Talk about cheating death, Lilah thought. It had been an inspired peace offering—one she knew she'd live to regret. She steeled herself to be ready to watch seventy-two consecutive hours of *Locked Up Abroad*. It really was the only way to appease the corpulent cat—that and ordering lots of takeout from the Jin Jin China Buffet in Mocksville.

Carol Jenkins was enamored with their sweet and sour pork.

The majority of their party guests had departed well before 9 p.m. The plummeting temperatures and early arrival of the rain, along with some late predictions for the possibility of mixed precipitation, led most of their guests to cut their revelry short. By 9:30 everyone but Dash, who was in no condition to drive, had left, and Lilah was able to make her departure from her parents' house a little before ten.

She took one for the team and offered to drive Dash to his apartment on Queen Street, versus pouring him into an Uber—and she made sure to see him safely inside, leaving the keys to his van atop the bookcase beside his front door.

"You can take an Uber to pick it up in the morning," she told him as she removed his shoes.

He nodded at her. "Thanks, Stohler."

"No problem. You give me a call if you need anything, okay?"

He fell across his sofa in an ungainly heap. Lilah knew he'd be snored off before she got back to her car.

"Stohler?" he murmured.

Lilah stopped. "What?"

"That hot little cookie of yours is a keeper."

"Go to sleep, Dash."

"Okay," he slurred. "Don't fuck it up."

"Goodnight, Dash. I'll check in on you tomorrow."

"Yeah. I'll call you if I wake up . . ." His voice trailed off.

"Good plan."

Lilah let herself out.

What the hell was with everyone trying to manage her damn life?

None of it made any sense to her. Why couldn't people just stay in their own goddamn lanes? She wasn't used to this—all this prurient interest in her private life. Even though she had to admit that a few of those Instagram posts from Vegas didn't help matters . . .

Unlike most of the partygoers, she hadn't had much to

drink. She wished she'd had—it might have helped her avoid another mostly sleepless night. Driving from Dash's place to her house took longer with the intensity of the rain. In the beams of her headlights, she thought she could make out some kind of chunkier-looking precipitation.

Probably ice. It figured. They never got snow anymore. She reached for her cell phone to take a quick peek at the weather forecast.

Shit. No phone. She'd accidentally left it on the desk at her parents' house. She hoped Dash would have the sense to try her landline if he needed her and couldn't reach her by cell.

I don't need to worry about him, she thought. *He'll probably sleep until Tuesday.*

She was surprised to see a car in her driveway when she pulled in. It was a smart-looking Volvo XC40.

Sparkle? What the fuck was she doing at Lilah's at this hour? She felt a surge of embarrassment because she'd intentionally avoided her after they'd made their walk of shame back to the house after the shed . . . *incident.* Maybe Sparkle wanted to have it out about that? Or about something else equally mortifying.

Frankly, the reasons for ripping her a new butthole were becoming too numerous to keep track of.

She had to fight an irrational impulse to back out of the driveway and floor it for parts unknown. But she didn't. She stayed on to face the music.

Sparkle got out of her car and entered the garage before Lilah could turn her engine off.

Lilah climbed out of her Mini and approached her with trepidation and a hefty dose of contrition.

"I think I can guess why you're here," she began.

"Lilah . . ." Sparkle stopped her by laying a hand on her arm.

"I have something . . . *awful* and . . . heartbreaking to tell you. No one could reach you by phone, so I came over."

The look on Sparkle's face was so distraught that Lilah forgot about her attempt at a lame apology.

"What is it? What's happened?"

"There's been a . . . a death . . . in our . . ." She stopped to try and compose herself. "One of our dear friends has passed, Lilah. Tonight."

"Passed?" Lilah was trying to make sense of what Sparkle was telling her. "Died?"

Sparkle nodded. "I am so very deeply sorry, Lilah."

"Who?" Her mind raced. "Mom? Dad?"

"No, Lilah."

"Frankie? Dear god . . . just tell me."

"It wasn't Frankie, Lilah. It was . . . it was Kay. A massive heart attack. She . . . never regained consciousness."

Lilah felt the ground seize up beneath her feet. *Kay?*

"Kay?" she repeated with disbelief.

Sparkle nodded. Her eyes were glistening. She stepped forward and wrapped her arms around Lilah.

Lilah stood rigidly, without speaking, watching the rain mix with snow in the murky yellow light that fell across her driveway.

Kay Eileen Stover
February 1, 1951–December 20, 2023

Kay Eileen Stover, 72, of Winston-Salem, NC, passed away suddenly on the evening of December 20, 2023. She was born in Culpepper, Virginia to the late Martin R. and Suzanne D. Hamilton on February 1, 1951. In 1986, she met and married James Allan Stover, a financial adviser from Traverse City, Michigan. Kay and James loved to spend their summer holidays at their cottage on the shore of the clear blue water of northern Lake Michigan. Kay loved boating, fishing, and walking the beaches looking for Petoskey fossils. She was a longtime member of St. Timothy's Episcopal Church in Winston-Salem, worked tirelessly as a volunteer for the Maya Angelou Women's Health Center, and served as a board member for Hospice of the Piedmont.

Kay spent the last thirty years of her work life as director of business operations at Stohler's Funeral Home in Winston-Salem, where she presided over the expansion of the business from a small, family-owned concern to a thriving, client-centered enterprise. Kay's steady leadership, keen insights, and razor-sharp instincts will be missed by her devoted colleagues. Prior to joining the management team at Stohler's, Kay worked for twelve years as assistant controller for Flow Automotive Group in Winston-Salem.

Kay was known and loved by her family and friends as an honest, engaged, straight-talking realist whose business instincts were always informed by her huge heart and self-deprecating humor. She will be eternally missed by her family, her community, and her beloved colleagues.

A private memorial service to honor Kay's too-short life will be held at Stohler's Funeral Home in Winston-Salem. Memorial contributions to advance the important work of The Order of the Good Death may be made at www.orderofthegooddeath.com/donate.

Posted by Stohler's Funeral Home, Winston-Salem, NC

Stop All the Clocks

Lilah insisted upon accompanying Hambone and Gee String to pick up Kay's body and return it to Stohler's. It was, after all, a kind of homecoming—one Lilah had no choice but to be present for. Hambone insisted that they take the best hearse they owned instead of the innocuous van they normally used for such nighttime errands.

They were all somber and quiet during the drive to Kay's house in Old Town. When James met them at the door, he looked as shellshocked as they all felt. Lilah didn't speak when he looked at her with vacant eyes, but stepped forward and wrapped him up in her long arms. She held him tightly as he quietly sobbed into her shoulder.

Hambone and Gee String carefully retrieved Kay's body from their bedroom and wrapped it in a dark blue velvet first-call pouch before transferring it to their gurney.

Lilah's parents arrived while they were loading Kay's body into the hearse. Janet Stohler hugged her daughter tightly and told her to be strong before going to stand beside James. Abel stood with Hambone and Gee String for a few moments before they closed the bay door on the hearse. When he turned around to join Janet and James, Lilah could see the tears streaming down his cheeks.

Lilah took her leave of James before they departed with Kay's body.

"She'd been talking about looking into aquamation," James said. "But we never did. We both thought we had plenty of time."

"That's okay, James," Abel Stohler said gently. "We can do that for you if you want us to. We could take care of all those arrangements." He looked at Lilah, and she silently nodded her assent.

"No." James shook his head. "It mattered more to her to be cared for by all of you—by Stohler's. That's what she would've wanted." He wiped at his eyes. "That's what I want, too. So, I'll bring back her ashes and keep them here so we can be together when my time comes."

"Okay, James." Abel looked solemnly at his daughter.

"I'll take care of her, James." The words caught in Lilah's throat. "She won't be alone."

James nodded to her gratefully.

Lilah squeezed his hand before joining the Freeman brothers in the hearse for the twenty-minute drive back to the mortuary.

It was snowing steadily as they made their way across town. There was little traffic. The winter weather had already driven most people in for the night. The streets seemed deserted. Quiet. Like they'd gotten the shocking news about Kay, too.

When they reached the mortuary, Hambone asked Lilah where they should take Miss Kay.

"To the prep room in the big house," Lilah told them. "I will take care of her myself."

"Don't you want to do that in the morning, Miss Lilah?" Gee String asked gently. "Hambone and I can tend to her before then."

256

"No. It's okay, guys. I'll see to her tonight. I want to do it. By myself . . . you know?"

"Okay, Miss Lilah." Hambone backed the hearse into the big bay at the back of the main building, and he and Gee String unloaded the gurney containing Kay's body.

"You want we should wait on you, Miss Lilah? Me and Gee can sit in the conference room until you're finished up. Can't we, Gee?"

"Yes, ma'am. Miss Kay meant the world to us, too, Miss Lilah." He slowly shook his head. "This don't seem right. Not at all."

"It's okay, guys. You go on home. And be careful driving in that snow. I promise I'll call you if I need anything. Okay?"

"Yes, ma'am." Hambone and his brother left the bay and paused to close the overhead door behind them.

Lilah stood alone with Kay's body thinking about . . . *nothing*—before pulling herself out of her stupor and pushing the gurney through the set of double doors that led to their prep room.

The message light was blinking on the wall telephone and, since she still didn't have her cell, Lilah walked over to it to listen to the message. It was from her father, telling her that James had decided to go ahead and do the cremation right away— and just have a small gathering beforehand in the crematory to say goodbye—just himself, their closest friends, and the funeral home staff. Abel said he'd checked the schedule with Sparkle, and they could hold the service at 2 p.m. tomorrow afternoon.

Lilah set about doing her job. Kay would expect that.

She removed Kay from the first-call bag and proceeded to wash and massage the muscles in her body. Then she carefully wrapped her in a soft cotton sheet. The last thing she did was

257

remove Kay's wedding rings so they could be returned to James. When she lifted the sheet to tuck Kay's hand back inside, she found she had difficulty letting go of it.

So, she didn't.

She sat down on a stool beside the prep table and held Kay's hand. She didn't know for how long. It didn't matter. Finally, shock and exhaustion got the better of her and she knew she'd either have to go home to get some sleep or lie down beside Kay on the other table.

Once she had carefully shifted Kay's body from the prep table onto the gurney, it was time to leave her for the night.

For the night, she kept telling herself. *Not forever.*

Forever inhabited a different realm—light-years away from the one she occupied right now in the small, antiseptic world that contained just the two of them. Forever was a place she had no plan or desire to visit.

Not now. Not tonight.

And not ever with Kay.

Before leaving the prep room, Lilah stood with her head pressed against the door of the mortuary cabinet, waiting for . . . what?

For Kay to tell her what to do next?

For some other message. For something—*anything*—to make sense out of where they both were now.

Tell me what to do. Tell me like you've always told me . . . whether I wanted to hear it or not.

But there was nothing beneath her ear but the silent hum of the cooler. Kay's voice had gone as silent as the snow falling around them.

Lilah turned off the lights and went out to greet the gathering darkness.

The snow continued to fall all night, and by morning the city was blanketed with a glistening carpet of white. They were holding the small service to honor Kay in the afternoon on December 21—the winter solstice. The shortest day of the year.

The symmetry in that was hard to miss—almost as if Kay had scripted the event herself. After all, it was the one day in the year when the sun stood still. The solstice was the official start of winter, and the day the warmth of the sun was the farthest away from Earth.

It was simple, really.

No fuss. No muss. Do your business and move along. Time was wasted when you tarried. And the one thing Kay could never abide was wasting time.

Especially on the shortest day of the year.

Lilah hadn't slept much the night before. In fact, she hadn't really slept at all. She drifted in and out of consciousness like the ebb and flow of a tide: barely touching the border of sleep before her tired mind hastily pulled itself back to the inky depths of despondency.

Sleep? Sleep was like another country—a foreign place with mysterious customs and a language she no longer understood.

The words of W.H. Auden ricocheted around her tired mind.

Stop all the clocks, cut off the telephone . . .

Death's earworm. No matter how hard she tried to drown them out, the words kept coming back—louder and more

259

insistent with each revolution.

> The stars are not wanted now: put out every
> one . . .

She felt helpless—like a steel pinball, stuck bouncing against hell's bumper in a world on tilt.

> For nothing now can ever come to any good.

Enough. It was enough. It needed to stop. She'd lose her mind at this rate.

She got up and walked to the window of her bedroom. The snow was coming down steadily now. If it continued at this rate, the city would be on lockdown by morning.

They'd hold the small gathering for Kay inside the crematory. That was James's wish. It would be just James, Kay's lifetime best friend, Joan, and the Stohler's family: her parents, Frankie, the Freeman brothers, Rita Kitty, and Sparkle. James had asked for Lilah to say a few words. She honestly had no idea if she'd be able to.

Come on, Morticia, she imagined Kay saying. *Put on your big girl panties and deal with it.*

So, she'd try. Otherwise, Kay would never let her rest.

She finally gave up on returning to bed. She heated some water and made herself a steaming mug of peppermint tea.

Then she sat in front of a big blank window and watched the snow continue to fall. She stayed there until a skinny ray of sunlight heralded the end of the snow, and the beginning of the shortest day of the year.

Hambone and Gee String made sure that everything was in place for Kay's send-off. That was what James preferred to call it. They weren't saying goodbye to her, they were just seeing her off on the next leg of her journey—the same passage they'd all make when their times came.

The Freemans had placed Kay's body inside a simple, wooden casket. James had spent a few minutes alone with her before they all gathered in the crematory. He still looked shell-shocked and hollow—but that was to be expected. It had not even been twenty-four hours since Kay had collapsed in their bedroom, shortly after arriving home from the Christmas party. She did not suffer. The attending physician said death had been instantaneous.

It was just like Kay to perform even that last act with economy and dispatch.

As they stood together in a close group surrounding the casket, James cleared his throat and addressed them with a shaking voice.

"I think you all know how much Kay loved this place and how dear each of you always were to her. She spent some of the happiest days of her life working here with you—and being a part of what you all did together to make this very experience a better one for grieving families. And I know it would've been her wish to have you all here to see her off. Kay was a big believer in knowing when a job was finished, and it was time to leave. And even though nothing about the timing of this makes sense for any of us, we have to trust her to know better—just like we always did." He bent down and kissed the top of the simple pine box. "Sleep well, my Katydid. Wait for me."

He wiped at his eyes before nodding to Lilah.

She steeled herself before beginning to speak.

"I've made death my calling," she said. "It's always been the one constant in my life. I never questioned its place in the ordering of our lives. It is, and has always been, understood by me as the natural period at the end of our mortal sentence. But now . . . now I think I was wrong. Death isn't a period at all. Death is more like an ellipsis—the thing that tells us a sentence or a story is *not* over. There is yet more to experience. There is yet more to understand. That we don't die in the sense that we once were and aren't anymore. It shows us that death is not an ageless mystery to keep shrouded behind dark curtains and masked with incense. Death is a revelation. A grand passage that carries us along the next leg of our journey. And that's because death is the natural end of life—a joyous culmination of this phase of our existence—one that allows us to return to the earth in our purest form.

"We hurt. We mourn." She looked down at the plain box. "We grieve the loss of you that for each of us, came too soon. But for you, it came exactly on time—just like everything else you did. We will always miss you terribly—more than any pathetic words can say. But we will *never* really be without you because you have become one with the thing that surrounds us all. You are now, and will forever be, reunited with the earth that made you." Lilah's voice broke as she added, "Godspeed, my dear friend. I will always love you."

She closed her eyes and recited a poem she had learned in childhood.

Emily Dickinson—who understood more about death than any student could ever learn.

Exultation is the going
Of an inland soul to sea,
Past the houses past the headlands
Into deep Eternity

Bred as we, among the mountains,
Can the sailor understand
The divine intoxication
Of the first league out from land?

Hambone gently slid the pine box into the cremation chamber and closed its exterior door.

As James had requested, each of them placed their hands atop his over the button that would ignite the cleansing fire inside.

"Are we ready?" James whispered.

There were silent nods of acquiescence all around as James slowly pushed the button.

Without being asked, Sparkle and Lilah's mother had prepared a respite for the small group of mourners inside the big house. They'd set up a simple buffet containing some of the items from last night's party. And they had prepared hot tea and fresh coffee, too, although they were fairly confident that most of their group would opt for some of Kay's special hooch—which Gee String insisted Miss Kay would want to serve at such an occasion. They found it hard to argue with his logic. Rita Kitty had tuned the sound system to a playlist of instrumental Christmas music. Lilah feared at first that the music might be too upbeat—but, instead, the selections were just right: timeless and familiar motifs, imbued with all the hope and optimism of the season. Even James seemed to briefly rally as he stood with them, sipping on Irish whiskey and saying he'd be back by in a week or so to clear Kay's personal belongings out of her office. Kay's friend, Joan, was going to stay at the house with James for a few days, until his brother and sister-in-law from Michigan could arrive to spend the holidays with him.

Hambone and Gee String had agreed to take turns staying in the crematory with Kay. Neither of them was willing to leave her there alone. It was after their first shift change that James took Lilah by the arm and led her aside to a quiet corner of the room.

"I have something to give you," he began. "I went to her office to get it." He reached inside his pocket and withdrew a small stone. "She was never without this from the day she found it, on the beach just outside of Traverse City one year when we were vacationing there." He took hold of Lilah's hand and pressed the shiny, smooth stone into her palm. "Do you recognize it?"

Lilah nodded stupidly. "It's . . . her worry stone."

"That's right. But it's much more than that, Lilah. It's a Petoskey stone—a fossil from an ancient coral reef that was originally created more than 350 million years ago. When you find them, they don't look like this at all. They're just . . . gray. But if you're smart enough to recognize them, and you fuss over them—clean and polish them—they reveal their hidden beauty. So, you keep this, and know that this is the message Kay wanted you to have."

Lilah found it difficult to speak. She gripped the stone tightly. It felt hot and heavy in her hand.

"What message?" She had difficulty getting the words out.

"The thing that gives this stone its magic. The myth of the Petoskey states that when the Chief of the Ottawa nation was born, rays of the sun illuminated his face—indicating that an era of great promise lay ahead."

She nodded at James.

"She loved you like a daughter, Lilah. Embrace your promise." He smiled at her sadly, and squeezed her arm before leaving her to rejoin her parents.

Lilah stayed rooted in place for several minutes. She knew she needed to circulate—maybe offer to spell the Freeman brothers and take a stint sitting with Kay. But she was finding it difficult to do anything other than stand there, feeling the stone in her hand and imagining its connection to ancient history . . . and to her history—with Kay.

"Here." Sparkle had joined her so quietly, Lilah hadn't heard her approach. "I brought you some hot tea," she said. "I know you prefer it to coffee."

Lilah took the cup from her gratefully. "Thank you for pulling all of this together."

"Don't thank me. Your mother deserves most of the credit."

"I owe you thanks for something else, too."

Sparkle looked puzzled. "What's that?"

"Coming by my house last night to tell me about Kay. That can't have been a pleasant errand."

Sparkle dropped her eyes. "I didn't think about it that way. I didn't want you to find out in a phone message."

"No," Lilah agreed. "That wouldn't have been . . . good."

"How are you?"

Lilah shrugged. "As you see."

"Not great?"

Lilah met her eyes. "No. Not great."

"For what it's worth, I thought your remarks about Kay were . . ." She didn't finish.

"Were?" Lilah prompted. "Too canned? Stiff? Smarmy?"

"Not any of those things. They were . . . *right*. Just right."

Lilah was unaware that she'd been involuntarily clenching and unclenching the hand that held the Petoskey stone. Sparkle must've noticed it because she commented on it.

"What's that in your hand?"

"It's," Lilah held it up so Sparkle could see it, "something James gave me. It's—"

"Kay's worry stone," Sparkle completed her sentence. "I recognized it right away."

"James said it's actually a fossil—an ancient one Kay found decades ago on a beach in Michigan."

"I know." Sparkle traced a finger over the tiny honeycomb pattern visible in the stone. "I asked her about it once, and she told me its history." Her eyes sought Lilah's. "It's wonderful that he gave this to you. It's difficult to imagine anything of Kay's that would have been more personal."

Lilah smiled. "Except maybe her big rubber PAID stamp."

"That's true," Sparkle agreed. "She was inordinately attached to that."

"It's hard to think about how this place will go on without her."

"I know. I was even struggling with that when she said she was planning to retire once the sale went through."

"That would've been equally impossible to imagine."

They lapsed into companionable silence. "Do You See What I See?" morphed into "Angels We Have Heard on High."

"I think I know the answer to this," Sparkle asked, "but were you able to get any rest last night?"

266

"The truth?"

Sparkle nodded.

"No. Not a wink. After I left here, I sat up and watched it snow."

"I wish . . ." She didn't finish her sentence.

"What do you wish?" Lilah asked.

"I wish you had called me, so you wouldn't have been alone."

"Thanks. But I would've been alone if I'd been standing in the middle of Times Square on New Year's Eve."

"I guess I understand that."

"Do you?"

"In my own way. Believe me when I tell you that you can miss what you've never had almost as much as something that's always been in your life."

"Yeah. I suppose that's true."

Lilah saw Hambone enter the parlor. She decided the time was right for her to take a shift, too.

She looked down at Sparkle. "Would you mind if I left to go spell the Freemans in the crematory?"

"Not at all. Would you mind if I came with you?"

Lilah was surprised at how little trouble she had deciding how to answer.

"Not at all."

After checking in with Hambone, they left together to keep watch over Kay.

After the remembrance service ended and most people had left, Lilah went to her office to try and do a bit of work, but it was pointless. She was unable to concentrate on anything for more than two seconds. She spent more time staring out her narrow window than anything else, killing time until her appointment to go meet Kirk to discuss the particulars of the sale to FSI.

Pretty rotten timing for that, she thought. But if she wanted the sale to be finalized early in the year, she needed to keep the process moving forward.

The snow had mostly melted throughout the day, but the nighttime temperatures were forecast to dip back close to the freezing mark, and since sunset was coming so early that day, she told everyone to close up and head home at four to get a jump on traffic and avoid any potential for frozen patches on overpasses and secondary roads.

After expressing shock and genuine sadness over the news about Kay Stover, Kirk set about reviewing all the final paperwork with her. The details spelled out just about what Lilah expected. FSI planned to release the Freeman brothers and Rita Kitty. Wardell would be given the opportunity to join their corps of contract embalmers, working across several of their franchises in the state. Kay Stover's former job would be handled by a regional business manager. The conglomerate was only interested in retaining the Stohler family name—and keeping Sparkle and Lilah on staff. They understood that Lilah preferred for her role to be transitional only, and that she would rotate out between twelve and twenty-four weeks, depending upon how smoothly the newly minted operation adapted to the FSI model.

Their model, Lilah thought. *It was a winning formula, all right.* FSI focused its business operations on so-called "traditional" funeral home models—meaning a primary emphasis on selling grief-addled consumers total packages that included open-casket funerals, necessitating embalming services and high-dollar purchases in their retail sales rooms. The vast market for caskets, urns, burial vaults, cemetery plots, and other memorial *objets* was the cash cow that formed the nexus of their lucrative strategy.

It was a bitter pill for Lilah to swallow, but she knew it was a necessary one if she ever hoped to pursue her goal to increase awareness of natural and environmentally friendly alternatives to the $28 billion-a-year death industry that fed on the cognitive impairment of consumers who were too distracted to question whether service packages and price tags were rational, appropriate, or even necessary. Lilah understood in her viscera that the culture's morbid reliance on cosmeticized and plasticized corpses being displayed in polished caskets that cost more than most people earned in a month was changing. People were becoming more responsive to cost-effective solutions that offered greater respect for the emotional well-being—and the pocketbooks—of grieving consumers. And were kinder to the seriously endangered environment.

And the most expeditious way for Lilah to effect these changes was by moving into an arena that was more favorably disposed to nurturing emerging alternatives to the FSI model.

She told Kirk she'd take the papers home with her and review them all with her father. With luck, she could return them all to him signed no later than the day after Christmas.

She left Kirk's office and headed back to the funeral home to make a last check on Kay. Hambone had said he and Gee String would complete the process and have her remains ready for James to take home tomorrow. She didn't have any difficulty locating the vessel containing Kay's ashes. It was a hand-crafted, wooden urn made to look like a river stone. Kay herself had been the one to add this unique, one of a kind urn to their inventory.

Lilah recalled how she had exclaimed over it when it arrived—and how she rejected Lilah's insistence that the thing was too goddamn expensive and esoteric to have broad appeal.

"If it doesn't sell," Kay told her, "I'll buy it myself and keep paperclips in it."

"Pretty damn expensive caddy for a box of paperclips that cost five bucks," Lilah had replied.

"You're just a cretin." Kay sat holding the urn, rubbing her hands over its smooth surface. "I'm the one who will depreciate it as a tangible asset."

"My fear, Kay, is that one day you'll do that with me, too."

Kay had given her a good dose of her vintage side-eye. "What leads you to believe I'm not doing that already?"

Lilah placed the wooden stone back into its box and left the small storage area intending to head home for the night. On impulse, she diverted before reaching the back exit, and headed down the back hallway toward Kay's office. She stood in the open doorway for a minute before entering the space where Kay had worked and bossed them all around for more than thirty years.

Lilah stood behind her desk and looked down at all the tidy notes and files Kay had neatly stacked before leaving the day before. It was nearly dark, so she turned on Kay's desk lamp and sat down on her creaking chair. Every place she looked, she saw evidence of a life interrupted. Kay's Wake Forest coffee mug—washed and ready for its first morning cup. The old blue cardigan she kept on a hook behind her door. A pair of comfy shoes she'd slip on when her feet ached—which was always. A couple of Sparkle's ubiquitous ginger chews on a small plate covered with plastic wrap. And the beloved fossils she'd spent a lifetime collecting along the northern beaches of Lake Michigan.

Lilah pulled the worry stone James had given her out of her pocket. It was worn so smooth it almost felt like skin—like the second skin it had become during all the decades Kay had used it to siphon off her nervous energy. Its shiny surface was marked by its faint honeycomb pattern of fossil coral. Lilah sat letting it warm the palm of her hand and felt its tangible connection to the woman who had sat in exactly the spot where she now sat, absently worrying the small stone while she solved their problems and ordered their affairs for three decades. Lilah couldn't remember a time without Kay Stover in her life. She had grown up with Kay as her business mentor.

Who was she kidding? Kay was *more* than that. Kay had been her confessor. Her confidant. Her moral compass. Her most ardent critic—but also her unwavering and tireless supporter.

She loved you like a daughter, James had said to her.

"What am I going to do without you?" Lilah said to the void. "I don't know how to do this. I don't know how to *be* without you."

"I think you take one step at a time."

Lilah jerked her head toward the doorway. Sparkle stood there.

"I'm sorry, Lilah. I shouldn't have intruded on you like this. But I couldn't . . ."

Lilah was still trying to compose herself. "Couldn't . . . what?"

"Leave. You." She made an oblique gesture. "Leave you *alone*. I can come back later."

"No. It's fine. Sit down."

Sparkle looked dubious.

"I mean it. Please," Lilah added, "sit with me for a while."

When Sparkle complied and sat on a chair opposite Kay's desk,

Lilah continued. "Why are you still here? I thought everyone left early."

"I had a few things to take care of. And . . . I wanted to see you before I left."

"Well. You found me."

Sparkle nodded. "When you weren't in your office or downstairs, it wasn't hard to figure out where you'd be."

Lilah nodded. "Creature of habit, I guess. This is where I always ended up when I was in a state."

"What kind of state?"

"Take your pick." Lilah waved a hand. "Pique. Umbrage. Ennui. Psychotic episode. You know. The usual."

"I gather she always knew what to do?"

Lilah nodded. "She'd make us each a mug of tea, listen very carefully to me. Then enumerate all the ways my logic and perceptions were terminally flawed."

Sparkle laughed. "That sounds about right." She got up and walked over to a lateral filing cabinet, where Kay had set up a mini-beverage station with an electric kettle and some extra mugs. She checked the water level in the kettle before switching it on.

"What are you doing?" Lilah asked.

"Making us some tea."

Lilah sat with that idea for a few moments. "Good night for it," she finally replied.

"I thought so," Sparkle agreed.

"Don't expect me to spill my guts, however."

"Oh, I don't. You'll be quite safe. Besides," she added, "you're on the wrong side of the desk for that."

"Good point." The kettle began to hiss and roll. "Damn. That thing works fast."

"It's Kay's." Sparkle was readying their mugs. "What did you expect?"

"Nothing less, I suppose."

Sparkle poured boiling water over their tea bags and carried the two mugs to the desk.

"Which one do you want?" She held them up so Lilah could read their respective advertisements. "Old North State Bank or Rusty Wallace?"

"I'll go with Rusty." Lilah took the mug from her. "Life in the fast lane suits me."

"I suppose it will soon."

"Meaning?"

"Once you leave here. Isn't that your plan? To finally kick your aspirations into high gear?"

"I suppose. Although I don't know that I'd characterize my future as any kind of fast lane."

"No?" Sparkle was busily dipping her tea bag in and out of the mug. "Why not?"

"Because becoming a good death advocate is hardly going to be like flooring it on the autobahn of the funeral industry."

"No?"

"No. It's going to be the milk route. Slow. With a zillion stops along the way."

On impulse, Lilah reached over and picked up the plate of cookies. She removed the plastic wrap covering them.

"What are you doing?" Sparkle asked.

"Isn't it obvious? I think it's finally time I tried one of these." She picked one up and sniffed it. "Maybe Kay left these here for a reason."

"Maybe."

"They aren't, like, laced with hemlock or anything, are they?"

"Not this batch, as I recall."

"Okay. I'm going in." Lilah took a cautious bite. Her eyes grew wide. She looked at Sparkle with an expression of amazement before taking another bite. "What the fuck is in these?" she said around her mouthful of ginger chew. "Prednisone?"

"What do you mean? Don't you like it?"

Lilah was too busy stuffing the rest of the cookie into her mouth to answer.

Sparkle watched her with surprise. "I'll take that as a yes."

"Jesus God . . ." Lilah finished the cookie and took a healthy sip of her tea. "Are there more of these in the kitchen?"

"Why?"

Lilah snapped up the remaining cookie. "Because I think I'll have need of them later tonight when I can't sleep."

"Seriously?"

Lilah nodded. "Unless you have a party-sized bag of Nacho Cheese Doritos in your bag."

"Not tonight. Sorry. And there aren't any more of these right now—but I'll bake you some."

"Fuck me . . ." Lilah sat chewing and looking at the remaining half cookie she held. "Why didn't you tell me about these things sooner?"

"You're joking, right? Tell me which one of your tirades about the blasphemy they represented I was supposed to interrupt to shove one into your mouth?"

Lilah thought about her comment. "Good point."

"Well, I'm glad I got to witness this before . . ."

"Before what?"

Sparkle reached into her purse and withdrew an envelope. "Before giving you this."

"What's that?" Lilah was immediately suspicious.

274

"This is the reason I was looking for you." Sparkle handed the envelope to Lilah. "It's my letter of resignation."

Sparkle's words dropped like a brick between them.

"You're *what?*"

"My resignation. I'm leaving, Lilah."

Leaving? Lilah felt the cookies she'd just eaten turn over in her stomach.

"But, why?" she asked with bewilderment. "Have you been unhappy here?"

"Of course not. I've been happier here than I've ever been working anyplace else." She considered her remark. "It figures, right? Of all places to finally feel like I belong."

"If that's the case, then why leave?" Lilah held out her arms to encompass everything in Kay's office. "Especially now."

"*Especially now* is exactly the reason, Lilah. Kay is gone. Soon, the Freeman brothers and Rita Kitty will be gone. And then . . ." She didn't finish.

"And then—what?" Lilah asked.

Sparkle met her eyes. "You'll be gone, too."

"Oh." Lilah didn't fully trust herself to say much else.

"So—the magic that made this place what it is. The heart that it had. That will soon be replaced by another model. One that holds no appeal for me. I thought long and hard about what James said today about Kay—that she always knew when it was time to go. So, I had to face my own music. This is my time to go, too."

"I don't know what to say."

"I know you don't. And if I'm going to be bitterly honest, that's part of this, too."

It seemed like Lilah had a universe of looming insights to search with only a nanosecond of time to do so.

"Don't worry, though. I'll stay on until the transition to FSI is complete."

"But they specifically stated that they wanted you to stay."

"I won't blow up this deal for you, Lilah."

"No . . . that isn't what I meant . . ." Lilah tried to explain.

"It's not me they want. It's those cookies. Once the deal with Salem Baking is signed, they won't care whether I stay or go." Sparkle got to her feet. "So, I've decided to go and try to find my own road to someplace . . . better."

"Wait . . ."

"For what, Lilah?" Sparkle picked up her bag and walked to the door. "Don't stay too late. This mess outside is starting to freeze."

She disappeared down the hallway.

Lilah dropped back against Kay's chair and listened to Sparkle's retreating footsteps.

Goddamnitalltohell.

She withdrew Kay's worry stone from her pocket and began to work it, hoping against hope it held some of the same magic for her.

Sparkle had been right. By the time Lilah left the funeral home, the puddles that had been left by the melting snow had begun to freeze over. The sky was inky black, and the stars were shining so brightly they looked like tiny tea lights in the sky.

She was running on empty, and she knew it. It was all too much. Not even twenty-four hours had passed since Kay died. She had hardly begun her journey from being here to joining that other realm—the one of grief and remembrance.

But Lilah hadn't begun to grieve yet. The naked truth was that she didn't know how. Sure, she'd lost people before. Grandparents. Casual acquaintances. Even a close college friend who'd died of uterine cancer after a long illness. But their deaths were expected. Their deaths were timely. She'd never lost anyone like this. Never anyone . . . *essential.*

Never anyone like Kay.

She didn't know what to do with the emotion. It was foreign to her. If she so much as dared to crack open the door to look at it, she could see it roiling and looming like a tidal wave heading straight for her. So, she resolved *not* to look at it.

She'd even pile furniture against the damn door if she had to.

She was nearly home when she took a curve too fast and hit an icy patch in the shadows. The back end of her car swerved crazily. She instinctively overcorrected and sent her car spinning toward the shoulder, where she ended up stopped on the snowy grass, pointed in the opposite direction.

Jesus H. Christ. What the serious fuck?

She'd been lucky there'd been no other cars around her because she surely would've taken somebody else out with her on her insane ride.

She sat there for at least three full minutes, waiting for her heart rate to return to normal. Her car was still running. That was the good news. And she had managed not to hit anything. That was the other good news. Apart from that? She could see little good in her situation. In any of her life situations.

What had Kay said to her that time she'd been thinking about cashing in her chips at mortuary school and going into pathology instead? Lilah had come home for the holidays and was helping her father out in the funeral home because the week leading up to Christmas was always a busy one in the death trade. Whether it was a metaphor or the simple luck of the draw, lots of people conspired to die during the holidays. Her father always said it was because families tended to be gathered together, and that gave people the permission they needed to leave. At any rate, Lilah had been working late, cleaning up the prep room after a busy day and Kay found her there on her way out for the night.

"Why are you still here?" she'd asked.

"I told Dad I would tidy up so he could go home."

"It's Friday night, Lilah. Isn't there someplace you'd rather be?"

"No," Lilah told her. "I actually like being here. It . . . works for me."

"Are you still thinking about changing your major when you go back to school after New Year's?"

"Of course," Lilah nodded. "Why?"

She recalled how Kay watched her continue to wipe down one of the prep tables before speaking.

"Let me ask you something, Lilah. What's the first thing you do when someone comes up behind you and taps you on the shoulder?"

"I don't know," Lilah remembered saying. "Turn around?"

"Exactly." Kay nodded. "You turn around."

In the end, Kay had made her point, and Lilah stayed on in mortuary school.

Now here she was, again—sitting alone in the dark on the side of the road—facing the wrong goddamn direction.

There was no Kay to tell her which way to go this time.

Something caught in her throat. Before she could rethink it, she pulled back out onto the road.

It only took her ten minutes to reach her destination. It took every ounce of restraint she possessed not to stop herself from ringing the doorbell. She knew she'd given in to an insane impulse—one she was sure she'd live to regret. Already, her emotions were hanging by a frayed thread.

The door swung open, and Sparkle stood there looking back at her with a mixture of surprise and something else—a look Lilah had trouble deciphering because she'd started crying. The tears were coming so fast and furious she couldn't stop them— nor could she make out much of anything else. Sparkle and the warm room behind her became lost in a liquid blur. The tsunami of grief and raw emotion she'd been trying to hold back since last night had finally breached the door and engulfed her.

Sparkle reached out and pulled Lilah into her arms before leading her inside and closing the door against the cold.

Dash had agreed to meet Lilah for a cocktail the next night after work. He was elated to be doing his final stint on the day shift. His colleague, Benson, had recovered sufficiently from his fall to return to work, so Dash was set to resume his regular night shift hours beginning tomorrow night. Lilah had offered to meet him downtown at one of the popular watering holes, but Dash had said he'd rather come to Stohler's and toast Kay's memory in the selection room. He even offered to bring the booze—but Lilah assured him that Kay would want them to share some of hers.

Dash did not disagree.

So, just like before, the two of them sat with their feet propped up against a Titan XL, drinking Kay's last bottle of single malt scotch.

It was a good one, too. Dalwhinnie. A superb highland malt famous for being distilled in an area of Scotland's rugged terrain that boasted its most extreme conditions. Perfect for Lilah's mood.

"There are a lot of things I'll miss about Kay Stover," Dash opined. "But her taste in good hooch is one of the biggest."

"I think you're right about that, Dash. Kay told me that all of the liquor in her hideaway was what my mother had confiscated from Dad's ill-fated attempt at setting up a bar in this joint. But I think she was blowing smoke. That event happened back in the '80s, so there's no way she was telling the full truth."

"What makes you say that?"

Lilah handed Dash the bottle of Dalwhinnie. "Look at the bottom of the bottle and tell me what you see."

Dash raised the bottle and examined it in the beam of light shining above the Batesville Economy Rita Kitty had generously . . . *upfitted.*

"I don't see anything but a bunch of numbers and letters."

"Right. Those are the codes for the distillery and batch number. The last two digits in that sequence are the year the scotch was bottled."

Dash examined the bottle again. "Twenty-two." He looked at her. "So, this Dalwhinnie was bottled in 2022?"

"Correct."

Dash laughed heartily. "That little toper. She always acted pissed off and staged those bouts of righteous indignation that everybody was drinking up her secret stash—like her greatest fear was that it was going to run out. And all along, she was secretly replenishing it just to be sure we never *did* run out."

"Exactly."

"Damn." Dash poured himself another finger of scotch. "That was one fine woman."

"You'll get no argument from me on that." Lilah clinked rims with him.

"So, what are you gonna do, Stohler?"

"What do you mean? Do about what?"

"About this." He made a sweeping motion with his glass to take in the space surrounding them. "This place. This business." He stared at her. "The rest of your life."

"Whoever knows the answer to that one?"

"Fair enough. Let's take the other items in the queue." Lilah recrossed her long legs. "What do you think about the liner color on that Batesville you've got your feet propped up on?"

"I think it looks like shit."

"I do, too."

"But if there's one thing we've learned in this business, it's that people make all kinds of irrational choices when they're in the throes of trying to expunge their guilt over how badly they probably treated Mamma or Daddy during their last days. Mark my words: some grief-ridden schmoe out there will see this and be reminded of how much their now-sainted and freshly dead Mama just *loved* Hawaiian Punch—then you'll be off to the races."

Lilah thought about his comments.

"It actually does remind me of Hawaiian Punch."

"Either that or the hickey your collar isn't quite concealing."

Lilah impulsively raised her hand to her neck. "What are you talking about?"

Dash chuckled. "It's okay, Stohler. I'm not here to judge you."

"I still don't know what you think you're referring to."

"Forget about it. Tell me about your plans—starting with

the business. What'd you decide?"

"I thought you already knew that."

"The last time we talked, you were leaning toward taking the offer from FSI. But it seemed like you still had some lingering doubts—like if you'd be able to stomach what you know they'd do to the nature of the business and the people."

"That's true," Lilah agreed. "But I talked it over with everyone—and with Kay—at length."

"And?"

"And they all convinced me that they'd be fine—and in the case of Kay and the Freeman brothers, they'd been thinking about retiring, anyway."

"So. You're going through with it?"

"It looks that way. I picked up all the paperwork from the attorney yesterday."

"Why don't you seem happier about the decision?"

Lilah looked at him sadly. "I'm not able to summon much happiness about anything right now, Dash."

"Yeah. I suppose not." He finished his drink. "This has sure been one helluva holiday season, hasn't it?"

Lilah nodded. "And it ain't over yet."

"Gotta say, Stohler. You surprised me."

"What about?"

"I never thought you'd walk away. I really believed that when push came to shove, you'd be smart enough to stick it out for the long haul."

"Wait a minute . . ." Lilah was fighting her irritation with Dash. "Didn't you tell me I'd be an idiot not to take the offer from FSI? Didn't you say it would untie my hands so I could decide what to do with my one precious life, or some bullshit like that?"

"Maybe." Dash replied. "But that's not what I was talking about walking away from."

"Then what the hell were you talking about?"

"Boy, you really don't get it, do you?" Dash chuckled. "I'm talking about your sweet little hometown girl scout ... you know, the one with the cookie franchise?"

Lilah felt heat suffusing her face. She hoped Dash would blame it on the rose-tinted light above them.

"She's not my *anything*, Dash."

"Really? Could've fooled me. You two looked pretty damn cozy at that Christmas party."

"I fail to see how you can remember anything from that night. As I recall, you were too preoccupied with the contents of your Solo cup and that platter of Miss Ora's chicken wings."

"Don't be a hater, Stohler. And don't lie to yourself either. At your age, it's pathetic."

"I am *not* lying to myself."

"Oh, yeah? So, you're gonna sit there with your feet propped up on that monument to the grim reaper's value chain and tell me you have no feelings for the hot little sparkler you've been dipping your doodle with ever since photos of you doing precisely that went viral on the damn internet?"

"Fuck you, Dash."

"'The lady doth protest too much, methinks,'" Dash quoted.

'Again, I say—fuck you."

"Listen, Stohler. It's not often the *Bible* can trump Shakespeare. But occasionally, there are some tidbits of wisdom in it that are worth the price of admission."

"Do I want to hear this?"

"Probably not. But I'm going to tell you anyway. 'For what shall it profit a man, if he shall gain the whole world, and lose his own soul?'"

"What does my soul have to do with a platter of ginger cookies?"

Dash finished his drink and got to his feet. "That's a question only you can answer, my dark friend. Me? I'm outta here. I've got the graveyard shift the next two nights, so I need to get some sleep."

"You're working Christmas?" Lilah asked.

"Nope. Just Christmas Eve. Let's hope that this year, death takes a holiday."

"I wouldn't count on it."

"Me either." He gave a bitter laugh. "See you around the boneyard, Stohler."

"Goodnight, Dash. And, hey?" He was nearly out the door, but she waited for him to turn and face her. "Thanks for the TED Talk on truth and meaning. For real."

"No bullshit?" he asked.

"No bullshit."

"You've got a good head on those dark shoulders, Stohler. We all expect you to use it."

"I know. I'm trying."

"Then that's the best you can do. Nobody can ask you for more than that." He gave her a final salute and disappeared around the corner.

Lilah thought back over their conversation. *Was she losing her soul by selling out?*

She recalled what Kay had said to her when she'd discovered her with Sparkle in her father's garden shed . . .

> *I want you to get your dark head out*
> *of your ass and for once in your life, do*
> *something that has a shot at adding a*

dose of happiness to that simmering pot of morbidities you call a lifestyle.

Last night, as her car was spinning out of control on the ice, she had had an inkling—for the first time—that she understood what Kay, in her inimitable way, was telling her to do. The question was whether or not she was brave enough to try it.

What did she have to lose? She'd already lost one of the most precious things she'd ever had. And here she still was—sitting with her feet propped up on a ridiculously overpriced casket, drinking some of the booze Kay had kept right on buying just because she wanted to.

She owed Kay. She owed her a debt she could only begin to repay by being less ascetic about her life choices. After all, there were worse things than settling for happiness, weren't there?

Like dying alone with only your regrets to keep you company.

She set down her tumbler of scotch and picked up her cell phone.

Why not see how the other half lives? she thought.

She held up the phone and took a selfie against the backdrop of their artfully lighted display of caskets. Then she navigated to Instagram and created an account.

Here goes nothing.

She uploaded the photo beneath the new header:

Lilah Stohler, posting as The Black Bird
of Chernobyl.

Then she called Kirk.

Part III
Ghosts of the Future

Christmas Eve, an hour before midnight

Back to the Future

Look around.

It doesn't take a rocket scientist to see that today's world is a simmering hellscape of equal parts disappointment, rage, and grievance—or what the locals, with practiced economy, would call a big ol' hot mess. Lilah'd never had a problem with this perspective. The macabre geography she inhabited was one she'd always been temperamentally suited to. It *worked* for her—and not just because she had all the outfits . . .

She'd never questioned her life or any of her choices because she'd never had reason to.

But she'd become aware that everything about the temple of her familiar had changed the night Dash dropped off a yellow blanket he'd just retrieved from the county morgue. It was an hour before midnight on Christmas Eve, and she'd drawn the short straw because their mortuary was the only one still open—as usual—and she'd made the colossal blunder of answering the phone. It was one of those rare Christmases when it snowed—the first time in more than a decade. Of course, that threw everything in Winston-Salem into panic mode. The entire city had been on lockdown since midday. Everything had ground to a halt. Public transportation, frenetic last-minute shopping trips, holiday parties—all shut down.

Well . . . every kind of activity but *this* one.

Death tended not to be bothered much by the weather.

Fifteen minutes later, she stood just inside the big bay doors at the back of the building, trying to dodge the swirling snow while Dash backed the county's nondescript black van into their receiving area. She thought about Dash as she waited for him to get out of the van. He was a wiry little guy of uncertain age who'd been ferrying bodies around for the county since the Dead Sea was just . . . sick. Standing there in the cold, Lilah thought back over how strange it was that in all the years she'd known him, they'd rarely had conversations in the daylight. That was largely because Dash delivered his dark passengers during the night shift.

Lilah's father always called him *DoorDash*—death's delivery man.

That was about right. But this modern-day Charon piloted a beat-to-shit Ford Transit Van that burned oil and belched black smoke like a steam shovel.

"What's the story with this one?" Lilah asked, idly—more to kill time, than for any other reason, while Dash transferred the body bag to one of their gurneys.

"Beats the hell outta me. Some urban camper who froze to death under the Miller Street overpass—poor bastard arrived dead, and stayed that way. No ID. Merry fucking Christmas." Dash handed her a clipboard. A chewed-up ballpoint pen attached by a frayed string swung crazily in the cold wind. "Gimme your Santa Hancock on this so I can get the hell outta here. This is my last drop-off."

Lilah signed the chain of custody ticket and handed the clipboard back to him.

"Kind of sad."

Dash looked at her with his colorless eyes. "Holiday spirit gettin' to you, Stohler?"

"Of course not." Dash's suggestion irked her. "But even you have to admit there's an epic sadness attached to dying alone in the cold at Christmas."

"Yeah. Just like a goddamn Tolstoy novel." He tore off a copy of the receipt and handed it to her with a shrug. "Seems to me like we die alone no matter what damn day of the year it is." He shrugged. "Oh, well. Whoever the hell he *was*—now he *ain't*. That's it."

"That's it," she agreed.

Dash continued to stare at her with narrowed eyes. The snow had gained in intensity while they'd been standing there. The baggy cardigan she'd pulled on wasn't doing much to keep the wind out.

"You okay, Stohler?" he asked.

"Oh, yeah." Lilah nodded and waved him off. She wanted to get back inside. And she figured their latest John Doe had already spent enough time outside in the elements, too. "You get on out of here. You've got places to be."

"What about you?"

"What do you mean, what about me?"

"Don't you have someplace to be?" Dash asked. "I mean besides this damn cold-cut pantry?"

"I didn't," Lilah laid a hand on the black bag atop the gurney, "but it seems I just acquired a date for the evening."

Dash laughed. "You're a freak, Stohler. Anybody ever tell you that?"

"All. The. Time."

He gave her a little salute and climbed into the van. She stepped back to avoid the explosion of black smoke she knew was coming. She watched his taillights recede until they disappeared behind the snowy curtain of night.

Lilah punched the button to close the bay doors and stood there a moment, shivering and alone with her new companion.

Mom always said I went for the silent type . . .

"Come on, Mr. Doe." She kicked off the foot brake and pushed the gurney toward the freight entrance. "Let's get this party started."

When Lilah pushed the gurney through the double doors into the prep room she was surprised to hear Christmas music playing.

What the fuck? Did Wardell leave the damn radio on again?

But that wasn't possible. Wardell hated Christmas music with a passion. He'd rather listen to rebroadcasts of Rush Limbaugh than sit through a smarmy rendition of "Silent Night."

There was something else, too. *Lights.* Tiny white lights hanging beneath all the cabinets. They were twinkling like a thousand stars.

Then she saw her.

Sparkle.

She was sitting on the steps leading to the upstairs. Lilah was stunned.

"What on earth are you *doing* here? It has to be near midnight. And it's snowing like hell out there."

"I kind of figured you'd still be working, so I thought I'd

drop by and try to lighten your mood. I think I can guess how cheerless this night must be for you."

Lilah laid a hand on John Doe. "Not as cheerless for me as it is for this poor fellow."

"Who is he?" Sparkle asked.

"No clue. An indigent. Froze to death beneath the Miller Street overpass."

"My god." Sparkle got to her feet and walked over to join Lilah. "That's terrible."

"Yeah. No Christmas miracles for Mr. Doe, I'm afraid."

"Were you planning to . . ."

"Prep him?" Lilah finished Sparkle's question.

"Yes."

"I had thought I might. But since you were kind enough to stop by, maybe I won't. He'll be just fine waiting for me until tomorrow."

"I brought you something."

"Oh? Does Santa have you on retainer?" Lilah tensed.

"That's privileged information." Sparkle handed her an oversized bag.

"It's heavy." Lilah hefted the bag up and down. "What's in here?"

"Open it and find out."

"Okay." Lilah carried the bag over to her small desk. She pulled out a paper-wrapped box. "Intriguing. Too heavy to be cigars."

"Unless they're lead-lined."

"That is true." Lilah tore off the paper and laughed like hell. The box contained 250 rounds of .410 shotgun shells. "How *sweet*. And just what every girl dreams of for Christmas."

"They arrived today. I thought you'd appreciate the gesture."

293

Lilah was still laughing. "You have *no* idea."

"There's more," Sparkle prompted.

"This one will be hard to top." Lilah pulled out a bright orange box. "*Veuve Clicquot?* Are we celebrating?"

"You are."

"What am I celebrating?"

"Seriously? Isn't it obvious? New beginnings. Finally getting the life you want. Coming into a butt-ton of money. Any of these things jog your memory?"

"Oh. Right. *That.*" Lilah reached into the bag again to remove the last item. It was a square metal tin. "What have we here?"

"Oh, that's just something I promised I'd do for you."

"Oh, really? If memory serves, I seem to recall quite a few promises you made."

"It's not any of *those.*"

"Bummer."

Lilah opened the tin and was immediately assailed by the scent of ginger and a heavenly host of other warming spices.

"Oh, my god . . . Christmas crack."

"Ho, ho, ho," Sparkle chanted.

"Hey, wait a minute." Lilah held up one of the cookies. "These look . . . *different.*"

"I customized them for you. I know how uncomfortable you are around anything sweet."

"Black sprinkles. How very funereal of you."

"I do eventually pick up the clue phone."

Lilah laughed and returned the cookie to its tin. "I have something for you, too. I was going to give it to you tomorrow— but look," she pointed at the wall clock, "it's already tomorrow. So . . ." she opened her desk drawer and withdrew an envelope.

"Here you go. Merry Christmas."

Sparkle took the envelope from her and looked at it with confusion.

"Isn't this my resignation letter?"

Lilah nodded.

"I don't understand."

"Then let me simplify it for you. I don't need this, because you aren't going anyplace."

"I'm not?"

"Nope. And here's the other half of what I hope will be a welcome Christmas present: neither am I."

Sparkle was looking at her like she'd suddenly donned an evening gown and burst into a spirited rendition of "Don't Cry for Me, Argentina."

"You're not . . . leaving?" she asked.

Lilah shook her head. "I decided not to take FSI's offer."

"I'm . . . I don't know what to say." She searched Lilah's face. "Why did you change your mind?"

"There's still too much to do here. I can't leave this twisted, innovative, and oddly inspiring business plan we've got going in the hands of those money-grubbing turkey buzzards. And I for sure can't leave the Freeman brothers, Wardell, and Rita Kitty behind. Not when there is more and better work we can do. And Kay? Kay will always be here. *Right here.*" She took hold of Sparkle's hands. "I figured something else out, too."

"What's that?"

"I can't leave you, either. I don't even want to try. Losing Kay was the only thing that could make me wake up and realize that finding happiness in my own life was the most important thing I could ever do—more important than where I went or what I did. Once I made that realization, it was easy for me to see that

295

my happiness had been standing right in front of me. Losing Kay . . . well . . . losing Kay has been the hardest thing I've ever had to deal with. Finding you? Finding you has been the best. And now I'm smart enough to know it."

"Lilah . . ."

"No." Lilah squeezed her hands. "I *mean* it. Stay with me. I have no fucking clue where we'll end up. But I know if we're together, and we're half as lucky as James and Kay, it'll be one hell of a grand and glorious journey."

Sparkle's green eyes were shining. She slowly nodded.

Lilah kissed her, and they held on to each other for a while.

Sparkle finally spoke. "I suppose we should, maybe, stow our friend for the night?"

Lilah drew back from her. "Good idea. Then we can go home and drink this fabulous French swill."

Sparkle kissed her. "I guess we do have something to celebrate now."

Once John Doe was settled in for the night, Lilah took Sparkle's hand and walked her to the bay doors that led to the garage. She flipped off the lights in the prep room, before changing her mind and turning one switch back on.

"I think we should leave the Christmas lights on. How about you?"

"What do I think? I think it's a perfect way to bring death out of the shadows and back into the light where it belongs."

"Please don't put that on my business cards . . ."

"Shut up and take me home, Black Bird."

They exited the garage and walked together into the bright and snowy night.

Acknowledgments

I have many people to thank for helping to make this book a reality. Practical thanks go to Mike at Benchmark RV Services in South Hero, VT, for keeping my furnace running during the five weeks I was in Vermont hammering it out. Susan and Mike Tranby saved me by insisting I borrow their behemoth space heater to use during the days my furnace was off line because of a regrettable mouse incident. Don't. Ask. They also fed me several fantastic, home-cooked meals.

Special thanks go to my erstwhile companion in our small camper conveniently situated between Lake Champlain and an obliging hay field. Hambone (I named him after his counterpart in this book) kept me company each morning and evening when he was most active. After our first few, fraught encounters, we reached an uneasy peace. He grew less afraid of me once I stopped screaming at him and trying to catch him with a striped dish towel. By the end of the third week, we spent our evenings together sharing pizza and watching *Beat Bobby Flay*.

My patient and long-suffering wife, Salem West, kept all the home fires burning—and prevented our dogs, Dave and Ella, from racking up the world's first six-figure Uber Eats bill. Thank you, Buddha, for always being the still point of this turning world. And thanks, too, for your longstanding habit of reading the local obituaries *every single day*. Your familiarity with their quirks and eccentricities paid off a hundred-fold when you sat down and expertly crafted the first six of them that form the structure of this narrative—even though you *refused* to help me when I begged you to explain what in the hell "extreme ironing" was . . .

Eternal thanks go to my Bywater Books family and the unending support and inspiration they provide every day. My stalwart editors, Fay Jacobs and Nancy Squires, consistently make me sound smarter (and funnier) than I am. And huge thanks to Elizabeth Andersen (Radar), for finding some elusive bugaboos that saved me from a decade of mortification. Carleen Spry was a godsend ferreting out a few holdover bugaboos in the final typeset.

To that end, Bywater's very own *petit marteau*, Christel Cogneau, regularly checked in on me during my retreat and offered dulcet words of encouragement. "You *only* wrote thirty-five hundred words today? That's fifteen hundred words below target! You're now more than *two days* behind schedule. I'm calling you at 4 a.m. tomorrow to help you get back on track."

The manufacturers of No-Doz thank you, Christel, for the record profits they enjoyed during the last quarter of 2023.

Sandy Lowe gave me insightful and invaluable feedback on the story. (It's amazing what wisdom pours forth when you ply her with fresh-baked cookies . . .)

My greatest debt of gratitude goes to the remarkable Caitlin Doughty, founder of The Order of the Good Death and author of *Smoke Gets in Your Eyes: And Other Lessons from the Crematory* and *From Here to Eternity: Traveling the World to Find the Good*

Death. Doughty also produces the hugely popular YouTube series, *Ask a Mortician.* I won't deny that Doughty's pioneering work demystifying our arcane predilections about death had a profound influence on my desire to write a romantic comedy about a mortician.

One last note. I left Vermont on November 3 with this finished manuscript tucked into my backpack. Mother Nature clearly smiled upon me because November 2 was the *only* night during my long weeks of isolation that my pipes froze . . .

Dulce et decorum est.

About the Author

Ann McMan is the author of thirteen novels and two collections of short stories. She is a two-time Lambda Literary Award winner, an eleven-time winner of Golden Crown Literary Society Awards, a five-time IPPY medalist, a Foreword Reviews INDIES medalist, and a recipient of the Alice B. Medal for her body of work. She divides her time between Winston-Salem, NC, and Grand Isle, Vermont.

She can be found at:

www.annmcman.com

www.bywaterbooks.com/ann-mcman/

https://www.facebook.com/ann.mcman/

A Note on the Type

The body of this book is set in Adobe Caslon Pro. William Caslon was an English gunsmith and designer of typefaces. In 1722 he created an extended set of serif typefaces that were based on seventeenth-century Dutch old style designs. Because of their remarkable practicality, Caslon's typefaces met with instant success. These, as well as all of their consecutive revivals, are referred to as Caslon. Among those revivals are two Adobe versions, called Adobe Caslon (1990) and Adobe Caslon Pro, which includes an extended character set.

Bywater Books believes that all people have the right to read or not read what they want—and that we are all entitled to make those choices ourselves. But to ensure these freedoms, books and information must remain accessible. Any effort to eliminate or restrict these rights stands in opposition to freedom of choice.

Please join with us by opposing book bans and censorship of the LGBTQ+ and BIPOC communities.

At Bywater Books, we are all stories.

We are committed to bringing the best of contemporary literature to an expanding community of readers. Our editorial team is dedicated to finding and developing outstanding writers who create books you won't want to put down.

For more information about Bywater Books, our authors, and our titles, please visit our website.

https.bywaterbooks.com

Printed in the USA
CPSIA information can be obtained
at www.ICGtesting.com
JSHW082251190624
65057JS00002B/11

9 781612 942872